SHADOWEYES

KATHRYN PTACEK

TOR

A TOM DOHERTY ASSOCIATES BOOK

SHADOWEYES

Copyright © 1984 by Kathryn Ptacek

All rights reserved, including the right to reproduce this book or portions thereof in any form.

A TOR Book

Published by:

Tom Doherty Associates, Inc.
8-10 West 36th Street
New York, New York 10018

First printing, March 1984

ISBN: 0-812-51858-6
Can. Ed.: 0-812-51859-4

Printed in the United States of America

There was never any other choice.

For Charlie, co-conspirator in life

PROLOGUE

Junior Montoya tossed another piñon branch onto the fire and watched as sparks danced beyond the ring of stones. The flames, yellow as the autumn moon hanging above the ridge, crept closer to the new wood and for a moment smouldered. Resin oozed like amber blood, then crackled as the fire touched it. He rubbed his hands together over the heat, willing his old veins to warm up.

"Cold night, old man?"

It was one of the *gringos*. Junior glanced in the man's direction. Large with a belly just beginning to hang over his turquoise-studded belt. Pink face, grown pinker by the bottle of Jim Beam in his hand. Grizzled sideburns. Trying to make himself look younger, Junior thought, and grinned.

"Cold, yes. But it gets colder. Way colder in the winter. When the snows come," Junior said. He accepted the bottle the *gringo* held out to him and, putting it to his lips, leaned back. The whiskey splashed down his throat, trickled out of his mouth. He wiped his damp lips and chin on the sleeve of his red-checked flannel shirt and handed the bottle back.

He looked at the other *gringos*. Two men and two women. The men older, probably in their mid-forties; the women not out of their twenties yet. They didn't think he knew what was going on, but he did. They weren't married, although they claimed to be. He shook his head. Texans. Texans always thought they could fool you, especially when you were a no-account half-breed. Indian and Mexican. Lower than vermin—if you were a Texan. But still they used him, came to him and asked for his services. He was the best guide, after all, the best in Albuquerque. And they all knew it.

"Tell us about this here place," one of the women asked.

She was a white blonde, with hair all curly and fake-looking. She would have been pretty, but her face was completely pockmarked. In an attempt to hide her ragged skin, she wore a heavy layer of makeup that ended in an orange line under her chin. She must be one hell of a lay; Junior ran his tongue over a broken tooth as he stared at her too-tight pink Angora sweater. Her nipples were hard in the night's coolness, and Junior looked away and licked his lips.

The other girl, with long blonde hair, hadn't spoken a word all night. She was dressed in jeans and a man's shirt and wore cowboy boots. The second man was just as flamboyantly dressed as his male companion. Silver bolo tie with a thumb-sized turquoise nugget set in it, silver and turquoise belt, expensive designer jeans, snakeskin cowboy boots, a satin-looking western shirt and a Stetson that'd never had a sweat stain around its rim. The rings on his fingers flashed as he massaged the back of the woman who'd spoken.

Tell the *gringos* about this place, eh? Junior peered around, past the firelight at the surrounding forest. Beyond the piñons and juniper trees he could see faintly the gash in the scarred face of the mountain. Slip in there and you would find . . . the place.

He grinned to himself, took a long swallow of coffee from the tin cup by the fire ring and stared at them, his face now quite serious.

"No one ever goes back there," he said, indicating the break in the cliff with a jerk of thumb.

"Why not?" the man named Tyler asked.

"It is haunted."

"Haunted," the talkative blonde girl echoed. She smiled at him, as though she didn't believe him. "By *what*?"

"Ghosts, you silly thing," Hannet, the second man, said. He slapped playfully at her shoulder and she giggled and arched her back so that her breasts thrust forward. The other girl looked at Junior, her brown eyes regarding him seriously.

"No ghosts," Junior said in a whisper. "Worse than that."

"What's worse than a silly ol' ghost?" the girl, DeeDee, demanded. She jerked her purse, white leather with a gold clasp, over to herself and reached in for a compact. He had noticed her doing that several times that night. She patted her nose with a pink powder puff, returned the enamel compact to the purse's interior.

"What are they, boy?" Tyler asked.

The wind moaned down through the canyon, and overhead the needles on the trees clicked. Junior cocked his

9

head and listened. There were the small rustlings of the night creatures. Crickets sang in the darkness, and off in the distance sounded the husky call of an owl. But there were other sounds as well. Sounds that did not belong to the desert.

"What's worse, old man?" Hannet asked, his voice rising slightly with fear.

Junior edged closer to the fire and smiled across at the *gringos.* The light stained his face yellow, hollowed his eyes, and with the gaps in his mouth he looked like a skull, bits of flesh still clinging to it. He pushed back a strand of greasy grey-black hair and chewed on a ragged fingernail.

"The Indian spirits," he said at last, as he watched the Anglos fidget. All four of them kept glancing over their shoulders; the women edged closer to their men. They were nervous. Good.

"Kachinas?" the second girl asked. Her voice was low and pleasant. She didn't sound Texan at all. Maybe she had been picked up someplace else.

"More than kachinas," Junior said. He fished out a flattened package, moved the cellophane aside and searched with stained fingers for a cigarette. He found a butt two inches long. He pulled it out and put a twig in the fire. It caught and he lit his cigarette with it, then flicked the wood into the campfire. He inhaled and coughed. He scratched his nose and stared at the young woman. He couldn't remember her name. Candy? Sandy? He shrugged to himself.

"What do y'all mean—more than kachinas?" Tyler asked. "Ah thought they were about as horrible as y'all can get out here."

"No. Not horrible. Kachinas are representations. That is

10

all. They are not real. But here—'' His eyes shifted toward the cliff beyond them—''there is a place of great evil. A dead pueblo of a dead people is there. Indians who have not known this world since before Coronado came.''

"Why hasn't it been excavated?'' Tyler frowned at him and thoughtfully tapped a large front tooth.

"They have tried.'' His cigarette had burned out and he flipped it into the campfire. No one spoke as he stared into the flames. They shot up without warning and one of the girls squeaked, then giggled nervously.

"Y'all say people from the University have tried to, uh, excavate this pueblo?''

"That's right, Meester Tyler. But they all had accidents. Some fall down the cliff. One of them guys got knifed. Another found with a bullet hole in 'im. They're all dead now. All dead.'' Junior grinned at them, the light glistening on his broken teeth.

"Shouldn't we go back to the city now?'' DeeDee twisted a curl around her finger in an attempt to appear casual. She tittered again, nervously. "Ah mean, are we real sure we want to stay up here on this awful ol' mountain tonight after all?''

"They won't bother you—if you leave them alone.'' Junior stared across at her. He had seen plenty of her type in his day. They drifted from wealthy man to wealthy man and left when the money went or they got bored, and generally both did pretty fast. Sometimes, when the women like her had been around for a long time, they looked tired and were tired, and weren't particularly choosy about their men. He had seen some of the big Chicano studs with women like this. Castoffs from the Anglos. Always the castoffs, man, the very dregs. He licked his lips. He wouldn't mind a dreg like this.

Seemingly aware of Junior's musings, DeeDee demurely crossed her legs at the ankle and tucked her feet closer to her body, as if by doing so she would protect what little virtue still remained to her.

"But what killed them, Mr. Montoya?"

It was the quiet woman again. He liked her well enough. For an Anglo. "They say that when the wind rises, you can hear voices." He paused as they all listened. Strained. Heard . . . the wind. The rustle of branches. The . . . what? Voices? Of what? "You can walk into the canyon and out of the walls, in the shadows, you see them. Watching you."

"What?" Tyler's voice carried a slight waver. He swallowed another mouthful of whiskey, started to put the bottle down and changed his mind.

Texan comfort, Junior thought. His mouth was dry; he wanted another drink, but knew he shouldn't. He had still too much to do this night. Too much to do. He needed a clear head.

"What do you see, Meester Tyler? You see their eyes. Bright eyes that stare at you. Evil eyes that don't look away. Eyes that hate, eyes that—"

"Ah think that's enough," a rough voice cut in.

"If you say so, Meester Hannet." Junior spread his hands in a conciliatory manner. He would play the dumb mixed-breed, go along with the man and then— No, that would come later.

He shrugged and got up, moved away from the fire. He lay down in his bedroll and stared upward. It was black now that they were so far from Albuquerque. No housing developments were close by and you could see the sky as God—or the gods—had intended man to. If he craned his head back a little, he saw the darker shadow against the sky—the cliff, waiting. The stars were bright and cold, and so very distant. A leaf flew by his cheek and for a moment he started, then chuckled to himself. He was as bad as the Anglo girl.

He heard the others as they talked. Texans never spoke in low tones; their voices were loud, piercing, and they did not know the meaning of whisper.

"When y'all said we were comin' on a vacation, Ah *thought* y'all meant—"

"Hey, baby, don't be upset. Y'all know Ah'd never—"

"I don't like it."

"Now, don't fret yo' little ol' head, Sunny—"

"Ah'm leavin'."

"DeeDee, come on. Just stay tonight and then Ah promise y'all the biggest ol' dinner yo' daddy can buy."

"Well, all right."

"I still don't like it."

"Don't worry, Deedee," the man's voice said. "Just don't worry."

Junior closed his eyes and stretched his lips back into a smile, more a grimace than anything. These *gringos* were the same, all of them. They came to town and knew no one and wanted someone to guide them. One way or the other, word got back to him and he would appear, offering his services. Usually they were reluctant to trust him. But he convinced them. And he would show them—for a price. A stiff one. And when it was the last night, he would take their wallets and steal the cash. He would be gone, and by the time they discovered their loss in the morning, it would be too late. He looked like any other wino down on Central Avenue. There were too many of them to run in, so the cops would do nothing. Besides, the cops always thought it funny when the Texans got ripped off. Didn't they do that to the state, eh?

He waited until he heard them settle down. He waited even longer for their breathing to become regular. When it was at last, he crawled out of his bedroll. The fire had died down until it was little more than red embers. He moved to Tyler and hunted around on the ground until he found the thick black wallet. Inside were ten one hundred dollar bills. Junior grinned at his good luck and pocketed the money. The other man had almost as much. The girl DeeDee had only fifty dollars. The second one, Sunny, had a few tens and a five.

He grinned at the sleeping quartet, made a mocking bow and softly said, ''Adios,'' as he slipped into the welcome darkness.

Sunny awoke sometime later, her cheek sore from the blanket, and blinked. What had wakened her? She stared around in the darkness. The fire was almost out. Maybe she should put some more wood on it. But wasn't that Mr. Montoya's job? He was, after all, the guide.

She yawned and rubbed her eyes with a fist. It wasn't her idea of a luxury vacation, but it beat walking the streets in Lubbock. Everything was free, and few demands were made of her. Hannet was impotent. He just liked to keep a girl on his arm. That she didn't mind.

The stars overhead were cold, little lights that didn't cheer her. The moon was no longer in the sky, so there was little light. The wind had risen more and as she raised her head, a strand of hair blew across her shoulders. Tyler and DeeDee were side by side in the sleeping bag. Hannet had rolled over onto his other side, well away from her, and was snoring in rippling sounds.

She propped herself on one hand and stared around.

Junior Montoya was nowhere to be seen. Maybe he'd gone off into the bushes. But as the minutes passed and he didn't return, she got more and more nervous. Maybe he had gotten lost. Maybe something had happened to him. Should she wake the others?

The wind rose and she heard it. The voices. High voices. Alien voices, sibilant. And soft whispers caressed her mind. She thought of Montoya's story earlier. But that was nonsense. Just superstition. He told us that tale to make us nervous. He'd succeeded.

A twig snapped. Her head moved and her eyes strained to look through the blackness. But she could see nothing. There were lots of creatures, harmless creatures, that roamed at night. Mice and such. There isn't any such thing as a ghost pueblo and evil spirits that stare—

They called to her. Leaves stirred; there was a pattering and—

Eyes stared out of the darkness at her. Round yellow eyes. Unblinking. A scream rose out of her throat as the shadoweyes crept forward.

CHAPTER ONE

He paced the north perimeter of the wall. Thirty paces. And fourteen back here. Around the stone bench. Now look toward the holy cross on the roof, down at your toes again, Father, and—

You're a failure, he told himself. His eyes filled with tears. "A failure," he said aloud in the loneliness of the garden. A yellow leaf drifted slowly from the branch of an elm and fluttered past him. He reached out to grab it, but the leaf shot away from him, almost as though it had its own life.

"You can't hold on to anything," he said. "Nothing. Pray; dear Mother of God—hold onto yourself, Father." The tears now ran freely down his cheeks, his flushed skin, flushed because of his desire, flushed because he couldn't let himself do it, he couldn't, he couldn't—

Christ, he wanted a drink.

He clasped his hands in front of him; they shook as though he held a divining rod. Leaves crept across the brick patio in the walled garden and the branches of the trees hanging over the wall rustled.

The sun had been shining since early morning and it was hot, too damned hot for the decent autumn he was accustomed to. But just as he looked toward the sun, long, thin clouds, almost black, slid across the sun, and everything around him became grey. A wind whispered through the tops of the pines and he thought he heard soft voices calling to him. He shivered from the sudden coolness and headed toward the building. Stopped. He had come out here to be alone, and alone he would remain. With only himself and his thoughts . . . and his desires.

A sudden gust of wind sent the leaves on the patio skittering past him. One caught on his pants cuff and he bent to remove it. It felt almost leathery between his fingers and he stared at its thin veins. Another gust of wind tore it from his fingers. He grimaced. The wind always blew. He didn't think there was a day since he'd come that the wind hadn't been blowing. It was the way of the mountains, so he'd been told by some insufferable wind-blown native, and he laughed soundlessly, bitterly.

He hated it here. Didn't want to be here. But he hadn't had a choice in the matter. He had been pulled—ignobly, without warning—jerked from his wonderful, loving, safe parish, brought up before the unforgiving hard-assed Bishop, accused unjustly and sent packing to this Godforsaken place.

Where the wind blew day and night and everything was covered with the goddamn dust that went with the goddamn wind.

Christ, he wanted a drink.

These were the Sandia Mountains. Just east of Albuquerque, New Mexico. And where precisely was *that*? Father Kevin Michael O'Dell demanded.

Where? The middle of the desert. Not a decent city around for hundreds of miles. He couldn't have been sent to some civilized place. No. He'd been booted off to the San Carlos Mountain Retreat. Mountain retreat—what a laugh! Father O'Dell's lips stretched back tautly. Read for retreat the Roman Catholic home for troubled priests. New Mexico was the dumping ground of the nation, the cesspool of unwanted clerics, those flushed away from their parishes. Everyone in the Church knew that. Everyone.

Christ, he wanted a drink.

A branch scraped along the wall. One of those ugly little sparrows no doubt. They didn't even have colorful birds here, not like back East. Nothing had color here. It was all muted shades of browns and greys and beiges, and how was he supposed to appreciate anything when he was locked day and night behind these walls?

"That's not true," he whispered. He wasn't locked in. Not physically. Just mentally. A prison of his own making, for he wouldn't allow himself to leave the walls of the retreat, to go down into the city, to see the temptations along Central Avenue at every good and not-so-good hotel, in every grocery market, that—

Bright eyes stared at him from the shadows.

Fourteen paces, miss one, hurry up with the left foot, and continue.

Christ, he wanted a drink.

"The Mother Church doesn't approve of alcoholic priests," he remembered Bishop Sullivan saying on that terrible day. "That's why we're giving you a chance, Father. We're sending you to—"

Hell. It might as well have been hell. It *was* hell.

Already he'd been here two weeks, two weeks without a drink, two weeks in which his skin had stretched and dried, and his mouth had cotton in it, and he didn't feel well, didn't have any energy, couldn't do what he used to do. It was hell. All he wanted was a little sip. Nothing more. He'd be satisfied with that.

Christ, he wanted a drink.

Something dark flowed across the stone patio to the statue.

His eyes filled with tears as he recalled his lovely parish in rural northwestern New Jersey. The lovely old Church. The lovely old congregation. The lovely old communion wine.

That had been the beginning. A sip here and there. On the sly. Nothing much at first. But then a sip hadn't been enough. He'd needed more. Demanded more. And he'd found more. Occasionally—and he was big enough to admit it—he had been a little late for the mass. But not often. Not really. Not at first. A few minutes, what did they matter? He could still say it. It wasn't like he had to chant in Latin. That had all been swept out years before. He could still speak fairly well, without the faintest trace of a slur in his words.

It had been that Mrs. Franklin Wells. She had been the one who had denounced him, the one who had gone to the bishop, the one who had led the committee to remove him from his position. He was sure of it, even though the Bishop had never said.

He wasn't a drunk, he thought indignantly.

Christ, he wanted a drink.

"A small nip now and then," he whispered. The leaves rattled on the limbs, mocked his words. Fourteen paces and two more, and he half-stumbled across a raised brick, and then—

"I'll be blunt with you, Father," Bishop Sullivan had said as he leaned forward in his chair. He had steepled his fingertips and gotten the most pious expression on his thin face that Father O'Dell had ever seen on anyone. Probably practiced it before a mirror. "If you don't dry out, you'll be kicked out of the Church. It's that simple. You have no other choice. Give up the liquor—or give up the Church."

He loved the Mother Church. He had served her faithfully ever since he'd found his vocation when he was sixteen. For fifteen years now he had been a good priest, a well-loved priest. Everyone had praised him, had said he was the ideal priest. But then he had stumbled, just as surely as he had stumbled across that brick. Just that once—and they were animals, his parishioners, waiting for the smallest flaw, the tiniest weakness, waiting for him to fall to the ground and when he was down they were ready to rush at him and tear his throat out. Animals, each and every one of them. Hypocrites. They had baked pies for him and asked after his mother when she was still alive, had sent him birthday cards, and what did it matter after all? They had just been waiting.

Animals. He pulled his lips back. And tasted the salt of his tears.

Christ, he wanted a drink.

"Mother of God, please," he said aloud, talking to himself, "help me." His hands twisted together. He heard the voices calling to him, the voices of temptation, seeking to lure him, to take him away from the Church. "I want to serve you," he said. "I want to. But it's so hard. So very hard. Because of the demon."

21

Demon rum? He almost laughed. A cliché.

You're all washed up, Father O'Dell, one part of him asserted. Washed up on the shore in a sea of booze. Alcoholic flotsam.

Christ, he—

No more drinking, the Bishop had said. No more. he couldn't go without it. He couldn't take it. He had gone years without notice, years that had slipped by. Why had he started drinking?

It was school. He hadn't liked the seminary, and the boys had been boys, for all their priestly devotions, and they'd tasted whiskey and wine and beer. After his investiture his drinking had steadied. But he was lonely and unsure of himself, and so young, he'd thought, when he looked at the other priests. And his mother got sick, and inch by inch she died, protesting all the way, railing against man and God—what sort of God allowed this? he had wondered as he stared down at her cancer-ridden body, and he drank more in his sorrow. Her heart was strong, and she lived, even though her mind was fading and her body was racked with pain. Through months, years, she lived. Then finally she died. With a curse on her lips. She cursed God, cursed the doctors and nurses who had slipped the tubes into her and kept the oiled machines humming, cursed the Catholic faith in which she had been born and which believed that rational suicide was a mortal sin for one's soul. And she cursed him. Because he had been a priest. Because he had prayed over her. Because he had prayed for her release, prayed for her recovery. Because he had served the God she now despised. Because he hadn't stayed with her day and night, minute by minute in her last agony.

Christ, he wanted a drink.

What sort of God had he been serving all these years? What sort of God allowed the misery that the world faced each day? Allowed people to live like animals in inner cities, allowed them to starve till their eyes were big and bulging, their ribs sticking out, their bellies distended?

"God?" His voice was a hoarse whisper.

No one answered.

Except the low whispering voices that mocked him, that laughed at his disbelief, that cajoled him, that lured him. Their sibilance filled his head, forced him to look at himself, to see the absurdity, the futility.

Animals. All humans were animals. God was an animal. No one was human. No one. He laughed again—loudly, the sound echoing. He was getting silly. If he had a drink, he'd be okay. He'd be steady enough. Yeah, that would do it. Just one drink.

He wiped his hands on his jeans. His fingers plucked at the grey sweatshirt.

"God," he asked quietly, "where are you? Why did you leave me? Why did you leave my mother? Why did you desert us?" The tears fell freely, soaking his shirt.

Why wouldn't God answer? Why was He so reticent? He thought, in the past, that he had heard God answer him. But perhaps that had been delusion. A religious delusion. Part of his vocation.

Vocation? A joke. He had no vocation. He'd chosen the Church because he was scared of life, scared of the prospect of having to look for a job in the real world, scared of sex. Unlike many of his brethren, he was still a virgin. He had touched neither man nor woman, nor did he intend to. But he had touched the bottle. That had been his downfall.

Intemperance.

He remembered reading about Carry Nation and her

axe-wielding forays into the saloons of a century before, and smiled.

He heard a bird trilling somewhere in the trees; it was a pleasant sound. A small chipmunk hopped along the top of the wall, stared at him with bright eyes, and he stopped to watch it. He glanced back at the cross, breathed deeply of the fresh crisp air, and a tightness swelled in his chest.

How could he doubt? How? There *was* a God. But He couldn't be explained. Not rationally. Not by him anyway. He wasn't a Jesuit. He knew, he *felt*, there was a God. It wasn't God who did this to man. It was man himself.

And he had a second chance—an opportunity to renew his belief, to sort out his problems, to work them out and to return a new man.

He could still hear the coaxing voices, but he pushed them away; he wouldn't listen to them. He strode to the statue and stared at her. Mary. She stood, peaceful and serene, in a brick niche. Her blue robe had been freshly painted and her lovely face bore the slightest of smiles. A smile for him. And her eyes, brown and compassionate, seemed to meet his. She knew of his problem, of his struggle, of its resolution.

He smiled broadly and fell on his knees in front of the statue.

Claws clicked on the patio.

"Dear Mother of God," he began, but got no further when something sharp seized him from behind. He whirled on his knees and screamed.

They eased out of the shadows of the bushes, flowed down the trunks of the trees, and covered his head, his chest, his arms. Father O'Dell threw himself around the patio in agony as the razor-like teeth tore into his clothes and skin. Blood streamed down his face, into his eyes, and he screamed as part of his scalp was lifted from his skull.

"Jesus, Jesus!" He plucked at the demons with his hands, and teeth bit down, severing his right forefinger. He stared at the white bone protruding, the blood pumping, and pain assaulted him. He groaned and writhed on the brick patio. Nothing he did would remove *them* . . . the demons.

He hadn't been faithful enough. He was being punished for his disbelief.

God had sent them. Satan had sent them. Someone had sent them. Someone . . . something. . . .

He was so numb now. Could barely move. He lay in a pool of blood and realized, without caring, that it was his own. His clothes were sticky, and he lifted his hand and stared into the yellow eyes of the creature there. His hand dropped and he stared up. He could see the statue of Mary. She was still smiling, still serene. Still plaster. That smile had been painted on. That was all. She didn't care. God didn't care. He didn't care.

Only the caressing voices cared. He shut his eyes as the teeth and claws reached for his throat.

CHAPTER TWO

Trumpet notes, tinny and sharp like needles, exploded from the tape-decks in the painted vans and low-slung cars. Competing mariachi music battled for the supremacy of the airwaves while raucous laughter beat a counterpoint. Every so often a high squealing giggle punctuated the blurred noise.

But no one listened. Not really.

Timmy Gallegos, just nineteen and much too thin for his age and height and with the scraggly beginnings of a moustache that he carefully cultivated daily, watched Ned Tafoya demonstrate his new car. It was a '78 Seville, painted an electric blue. Inside, blue shag carpeting covered the walls, the dashboard and the shelf in the back window. Huge foam-rubber dice dangled from the rearview mirror, while the steering wheel, chrome and just shined to perfection, gleamed in the autumn sunlight. At the moment the back end of the Seville bounced up and down, and the ring of Chicano men around it whistled appreciatively.

"Hey, man, where you get that?"

Ned grinned and scratched his nose. "You know that place out on North Second, heh?"

"Yeah," said one of the Chicano men. Trini Pacheco, short and wide with a fringe beard, was dressed in all black so that he looked like an oil barrel. He ripped off the pull-tab on the Coors beer can and flipped the ring into the bushes. He swallowed the entire contents in one swig and Timmy watched, fascinated. Trini never came up for air. Man, he wished he could do that. He'd tried once. He'd almost choked, and the girl with him had laughed. So he'd never done it again. He guessed he just wasn't as macho as Trini.

Somewhere a girl squealed and Timmy looked around, saw the flash of tan buttocks on one of the blankets. He licked his lips and kept watching as the couple wrestled back and forth. Then her hips were moving fast. Still, he couldn't take his eyes away. His hand strayed to the zipper of his jeans, but at that moment he saw Ned looking at him. He stuck his fingers in his belt instead and concentrated on the car.

"I got a welded chain steering wheel," Timmy heard himself say.

"No shit? It must have cost the devil," Benny Flores said. He grinned at Timmy. "Where'd you get the money, huh?"

"I got it." Timmy stared defensively at him. "I got it . . . from a job."

"Heh, you got it from your old woman—and I don't mean your girlfriend."

"I didn't get it from my mother," Timmy yelled.

"Heh, heh," Ned said, stepping between the two young

men. "Timmy, you know Benny's just teasin'." He fixed a black eye on Benny. "You—go get another beer."

"I'm gonna go off," Timmy muttered to no one in particular. He scratched his arm and shrugged easily away from Ned's grip.

Pot smoke always gave him a headache, and the picnic clearing was hazy with the stuff. He rubbed a hand across his nose and walked away from the other men. He could hear them whispering none too softly about him.

He shrugged. What did he care about them anyway, man? They were *pendejos*, all of 'em, every last member of the Low Riders Club of Albuquerque. Even the women. Even them. His upper lip curled as he thought of Jovita Roybal. He had tried to put the make on her and, man, she wouldn't have nothing to do with him. Like he was repulsive or had leprosy or somethin'. And, man, he wasn't. Not like Ernie Saavedra. He glanced at the couple who had been rolling around on the blanket, then at a man and woman who sat, their backs propped against the side of a red van, and passed a joint.

Ernie looked up at that moment and grinned. He knew what Timmy was thinking because he looked at Jovita, then slipped a spade-like hand into her blouse. He watched as Ernie tweaked the girl's nipple. Jovita squealed and slapped at Ernie's hand, but not very hard.

Timmy, aware of the growing tightness of his jeans, didn't look away. What did a girl like Jovita see in a guy like Ernie? His beard was long and pointed, his teeth big and white, and he himself was a big man, a giant among the other guys. In a few years Ernie would run to fat. Already was. Timmy tried to see signs of Ernie's disintegrating fitness, but couldn't.

Why'd they have to have the picnic today? He'd wanted

it earlier in the month, but as usual he'd been outvoted. Why did he come to the meetings anyway, man? What did he get out of them? What?

He shrugged again and walked away from the clearing. He glanced up into the October sky. Blue, so blue it didn't look real, and not a single cloud anywhere. Earlier there'd been some thin dark clouds that had threatened rain. But they had gone away. He scuffed the spruce needles under his boot, clearing a patch of the hard earth. All around the leaves were beginning to turn color. Once he'd gone up to visit his cousins in Santa Fe, and they'd driven into the mountains and he'd seen the graceful aspens, with their triangular golden leaves that trembled and the beautiful white trunks. He had been impressed, but he'd joked and laughed and never let on how much he liked the sight. That wasn't macho, man.

Like up here. It was beautiful. But he'd rather be dead than say it. Something rustled in the green bushes beyond the clearing; he grinned.

Chipmunks. But you couldn't even feed the chipmunks no more, because they carried the plague. Jesus, what a place. It had to be the Anglos' fault. Man, the place wasn't half as bad until they got here.

He stretched, feeling his muscles tense, his bones crack, and he grinned. He wasn't feeling so bad now. Maybe it was because he'd gotten away from the smoke or something. Maybe he was just feeling real good. Maybe, after all, he was having a good time. The time of his life. He headed back to the others. There were still some unattached chicks. The day wasn't over yet.

"Chica, chica, chica!" The cry rolled through the forest, disturbing a handful of jays. They flapped out of the trees surrounding the clearing. A high-pitched giggle answered it.

"Eee, don' touch me, Ernie."

"Come back here, Jovita. I got something to show you. And then give you."

She squealed again and jumped up from the blanket. She hadn't bothered to put a bra on that morning, and now that she was running she was regretting it. But when they'd been on the blanket and Ernie had been feeling her, that'd been okay, man. He had said he liked her silver and red blouse and the black pants she'd worn. Just for him, man, just for him had she worn 'em. She didn't dress for herself, just for Ernie. He liked her to wear tight clothing, wear stuff that showed off what he called her cute little ass. Aware of his eyes on her at that moment, she twitched her bottom and was rewarded with a loud laugh.

They'd had too much to smoke, man. She was dizzy. She shouldn't have done it, but Ernie had wanted her to. Whatever Ernie wanted . . . man, he got. He got her, didn't he? Fourteen-year-old Jovita giggled. And her a virgin up to the time she met Ernie. But he got it all. Got it all. She glanced back over her shoulder at the man. He was unbuckling his belt now. She giggled, tripped over a root curling up out of the ground and almost fell. But she recovered her balance and ran off. She began unbuttoning her blouse. She wanted to save time, man. Wanted to help Ernie.

She was running past the trees and the needles under her feet crackled. She didn't care much for the outdoors, but this place was okay. It wasn't too dark, wasn't too spooky. She'd heard lots of little noises while they'd been smoking, but she knew they were chipmunks and squirrels and birds and stuff like that. Harmless things. At least Ernie said they were.

A hand grabbed her from behind, clamping down hard on her shoulder, pinching her shoulder. She squealed and whirled around to face Ernie.

"Eee, you're hurting."

"Not as much as it's gonna," he said, grinning. His hands were shaking as he jerked her zipper open. "Get down, baby." Ernie pushed her back onto the ground.

"Not here, Ernie. It hurts." She wiggled, the pine needles stabbing through her clothes. Yet her arms went around his neck and she opened her mouth to him. He ran a wet tongue over her lips and she shivered. He had ripped her pants off and a breeze touched her bare skin. His jeans were down to his ankles now and he was trying to kick them off. She closed her eyes, sighing as his mouth and tongue caressed her throat, her breasts, her slightly rounded stomach.

"Eee," she breathed and opened her legs wide. His ring was cold against her skin. She stared at the heavy gold ring with the diamond in its center. He was so proud of the ring he'd gotten just yesterday—almost as proud of it as he was of her. She giggled again, and looked at the blue sky above, watched as crows circled overhead. Then her eyes shifted, closed, opened again as his hands kneaded her breasts. Something dark blurred past them; she glanced at it. "Eee."

"C'mon, Jovita," Ernie said from the junction of her thighs. "Don't tighten up so much."

"Ernie, Ernie." She clutched his shoulders and shook him.

He laughed, continued kissing her. She tried to move away from him, but he clamped his arms around her tighter. If she wanted to fight, he'd let the little bitch beat herself senseless.

She was screaming now. Was Jovita coming? That couldn't be. He'd hardly—

Something strong seized Ernie from behind and wrenched him off her.

Goddamn it, it was that Al. He knew they'd get into it one of these days about the girl. Guess this was one of those days. He swung his head around, but it wasn't Al staring at him.

CHAPTER THREE

The old man stood by the side of the highway and waved his arms. Chato glanced in the rearview mirror, then wheeled the battered pickup over to the highway shoulder and leaned across the seat to open the door.

"Thanks man," said the hitchhiker as he climbed up into the truck's cab. He slammed the door and grinned at Chato. Most of the old man's teeth were gone and those left were ragged. His hair was greasy, his eyebrows a dirty grey. An unpleasant old codger, he thought. And a mixed-breed, as well.

He flicked the radio off. He didn't want to listen any longer. It was just the news, and just as depressing as ever. High inflation, fewer jobs, and some poor old priest found dead in the mountains.

"Sure." He threw the truck into gear and eased it back onto the highway. He didn't know why he bothered looking left and right. As usual, there was very little traffic along the interstate. The closest vehicle was more than a mile distant, a huge eighteen-wheeler that shimmered in the heat.

"Where you headed, old man?"

"Albuquerque."

"So am I."

"I know," the old man whispered. Or had he? Maybe he was hearing things. After all, he'd been on the road since dawn and now it was well past noon. All that driving and he was tired, dead-tired.

"What's your name, boy?" The old man was fumbling in a shirt pocket for a cigarette pack. He fished a battered butt out and rolled it between his fingers.

He was amused. No one had called him a boy for more than ten years, not since he'd been in his early twenties. "Del-Klinne. Chato Del-Klinne."

"Apache."

"Yeah." He glanced in the rearview mirror. "What about you?"

"Half Pueblo. Gotta light?"

He took a hand off the wheel and pointed to the dashboard lighter.

"Come up here for a job, eh."

"How do you know that?"

"Only reason a Chiricahua come up here." The old man was staring intently at him now, taking in the details of the strong dark face with high cheekbones, lustrous black eyes, lean frame, shoulder-blade-length black hair neatly gathered at the nape of his neck with a blue cloth, his wrinkled blue jeans tucked into tan Acme cowboy boots, and the blue Levi shirt. He'd gotten warm south of Socorro and had rolled his sleeves up above his forearms.

He smiled, didn't say anything.

"Hey, boy."

"Yeah?"

"You work hard, eh?"

He glanced down at his hands, spare and capable and worn from work, not the hands of a man who'd been a professor, he thought wryly. "I have from time to time, old man."

"You want a job, eh?"

"No. But thanks."

The old man shook his head, puffed on the now dead cigarette butt as though it were still lit. "It might not work out, you know. What you come for."

Chato glanced sideways at his passenger. The man's beady eyes were fixed ahead, but he knew the old man was aware of his gaze.

"It might not. I'll just have to wait and see what happens."

"You got a strong back. Could always use one. You know."

Whatever he was talking about sounded illegal. He didn't mind that as much as he minded the man. There was something about his passenger that made him distinctly uneasy. He knew he should respect age, and this half-breed was certainly elderly, but he couldn't, not this time. All he wanted to do was dump the old man off on Central or wherever he wanted to go.

"Central," the old man said. "You can let me off there."

He started at the seeming reflection of his thoughts. "Sure thing."

They were driving past the exit to South Broadway now, and he spared a glance. Getting back into familiar territory, he thought with a slight pang. The fields and small stucco houses flashed by. Presbyterian Hospital loomed on the right. He flicked on the right hand-signal and pulled over into the far lane, oblivious to the honk of the horns behind him.

"Up by the University all right?"

"If that's where you're going."

He nodded, but didn't say a word. He took the next exit to Central Avenue, then began the few blocks drive, punctuated by stoplights, up to the University of New Mexico. When he was opposite the adobe-style two-story building housing the journalism department, he swung the truck to the curb.

"Is this okay?"

"Sure thing," the old man echoed. He opened the door and slowly got out. When he was on the sidewalk, he closed the door and bent down to look in at Chato.

"Good luck, boy. Remember me if it don't work out. I 'spect I'll see you around, boy."

"What's your name, old man?"

The half-breed grinned, showing his stubs. "Junior. Just Junior."

"Where can I find you?"

He waved a hand with unkempt nails. "Anywhere." He grinned again and waved toward Chato. He returned the gesture and drove off. His last view of Junior was the old man stooping to pick something off the pavement.

He looked across at Yale Park, just north of the journalism building; what the hell, he thought. It had been a couple of years since he'd last toured the University; it was time to go back. He entered through the main gate and headed toward Johnson Gym, then cut down Campus Boulevard, which ran past the park.

He passed Popejoy Hall, where the concerts were held, and stared at the park. They've cut more trees down, he thought, shaking his head sadly. He turned right at the old reservoir and headed toward the biology and geology buildings. He slowed the pickup as he came abreast of the geology building. He'd spent a lot of years there, first as a student, then as a graduate assistant and finally as a professor.

He braked the truck and stared at the stucco building. Northrup, named after an old-time professor. The memories still lingered. The labs off to one side, the office in the front, the lectures day after day, the test papers, the too infrequent field trips, the companionship of his colleagues in the department.

All that had changed two years before.

A dissatisfaction, almost a hunger, had been growing inside him for a long time. His schooling had been interrupted by two years in Vietnam, and since he'd come back to get his master's and go on, something hadn't been quite right. He'd graduated with a doctorate in physical geology and accepted a position at the University, but while he was in the first year of his teaching, he realized that what wasn't quite right was himself.

When he'd been an undergraduate, he'd looked to the future and had wanted to be nothing more than a geology professor. Even before that, though, he'd wanted to be a shaman of his people, and he had even studied with an old shaman. But . . . there had been problems, and he'd ended his training. Had turned his back on that part of his heritage—at least for a while, he kept telling himself—and had set his sights differently, had proved to everyone, most of all to those whites who had sneered and to his family who had quietly not believed, that he could do it. He made it with good grades, got a job; his future was assured. But he wasn't happy, not inside. Something still wasn't quite right.

And so the daydreaming had begun, and he'd remembered growing up in the southern part of the state, in Mescalero, remembered his days with his teacher, and wondered if he'd done the right thing.

He was in the white man's world now, accepted— almost—as a white man. But he wasn't a white man. And he didn't believe, after all the years of thinking that he did, that he really wanted to live like one. He still had that background—the one he couldn't ignore no matter how hard he tried.

In the spring, after the session was out on his second year of teaching, he gave notice to the University administration. Horrified to think they might be losing him, they sent their best people to talk to him, to convince him to stay at UNM. After all, it looked very good with the federal government if they had an Indian Ph.D. instructor. And a lot of time and money had been invested in him. They had reminded him of this often, trying to play on his guilt. That tactic had proved unsuccessful; then his department chairman had argued with him and his fellow lecturers had shaken their heads and asked him why he would want to give up tenure, and he had tried to explain, haltingly, unable to find the proper words, tried to explain the hunger within him, but no one had understood. Maybe least of all himself.

His goals had changed; his life had changed. So he left.

He put the small house he had purchased the summer before up on the market. In a section largely populated by University personnel and their families, it sold quickly. He pocketed the cash, sold off the personal belongings he didn't particularly want, and he left UNM and Albuquerque far behind.

He'd drifted up to Santa Fe, done a few odd jobs until the autumn, had traded in his car and bought an old truck. Then he'd driven down to Las Cruces. There he hired on as a ranch hand at a large cattle ranch owned by a transplanted Texan. The remainder of the two years had been divided between the northern and southern part of the state as he went from job to job. He didn't make a lot of money, but he enjoyed himself. He liked getting out in the fresh air, the elements, out of the office and a suit day after day. Maybe he wouldn't do this for the rest of his life, but for now it was more than okay.

And he still wasn't a blanket Indian. He hadn't gone back to the reservation. Not like his family had expected. His mother had cried when she found out that he quit his job at the University. His father hadn't said a word, but words hadn't been necessary to express his disapproval, and his younger brother had laughed and simply said he'd told him so.

His last steady job out by Grants had ended two months ago and he'd spent the rest of the time taking part-time jobs where he could find them. Finally, he realized he wanted to see Albuquerque again—had to. And, he thought, if he were there, he might as well look for a job. He'd arranged an interview, packed and left for the city.

Was he trying to recapture the past by coming back here? He didn't think so.

A horn honked behind him and broke him out of his reverie. He put the truck in gear, slipped into the parking lot by Mitchell Hall and waited while the white sports coupe swept past him; then he backed out and headed once more down the street.

He glanced at his watch. He wasn't due for the interview for the job until five, and it was only a little after one. He had time to drive around. He left the campus and headed east, past the head shops and record stores and the metaphysical bookstore. He kept driving, not really noticing where he was. Forty minutes later he was on East Central, almost out of the city, driving toward the mountains.

Which seemed like a good idea. After all, it'd been a long time since he'd seen the Sandias, and it was the season of changing leaves.

Still in Tijeras Canyon, he took State Road 14 and drove past Cedar Crest to Sandia Park, where he took a left onto 44. He passed Harm's Ranch, site of a sawmill at the turn of the century, and then a little over a mile later he was entering the Cibola National Forest. He drove slowly by the Tejano Canyon Overlook, past the Sandia Peak Ski Area, then turned up Highway 536 and proceeded past Capulin Picnic Area, past the Crest, to a spot close to the Lookout, which commanded a magnificent view not only of the desert floor below, but of the Sangre de Cristo Mountains forty-four miles to the northeast, the Jemez Mountains to the northwest and Mt. Taylor some sixty-six miles away.

He was far enough away now from the popular tramway and from the restaurant at the top of the mountain and the people who would be there, even at this time of day, that he didn't think he'd see anyone else. He just wanted to get out and walk around by himself, and think. That was part of his problem, he thought. He was a loner. At the University he couldn't be one—not and survive. Out on the ranges, though, it was different. There solitude flourished, was encouraged.

He found a narrow road overgrown with brush, and he

parked there. It would be quiet here. No one around that he could see.

He jumped out of the cab and inhaled deeply. The air was so fresh, crisp and a little on the cool side, and filled, too, with the aroma of spruce. He glanced up at the blue sky. A grey cloud straddled the sun momentarily; the brightness faded. Then the cloud was gone, and once more it was sunny.

He smiled to himself. Typical New Mexico weather. It could be hot as hell one moment, then cold the next as the temperature dropped thirty degrees. But today the predicted high was in the seventies, or so the man on the radio had said. A pleasant day, though a little on the warm side for this time of year. Good for September, but he wasn't so sure about October.

He stepped away from the truck, stopped momentarily as a sandy-colored lizard darted across a flat, broad rock to disappear into a clump of asters. Briefly the tip of the long, thin tail flicked against the purple petals, then was gone.

Lizard . . . the helper of the Child of the Water. He shook his head. That was a long time ago, in a different world with a different Chato—a Chato who still willingly believed in the old ways, a Chato who had believed an old man and thought he was different. Now he wasn't so sure about the Indian way or, for that matter, the white way. But as he watched a trail of red ants march toward a field of dandelions, he knew he wouldn't totally discount the Indian way. Not yet. Because . . . he still dreamed, and he could not ignore that.

He stooped to pick up a resin-coated cone that had fallen from a spruce and, drawing his arm back, pitched it as far as he could. He squinted to see where it landed, but couldn't, and wiped his sticky fingers on his jeans. All he heard was a faint tap as it hit some rock out of sight. He turned and realized, as the wind ruffled the hairs across the back of his neck, that the area was strangely silent. Since the cone had landed, he hadn't heard a single bird. Maybe he'd scared them all away. They never went completely away though. Above him, in the tall firs, he heard the whisper of the wind rustling the needles.

He looked around for the lizard he'd seen earlier, but there was no sign of the reptile . . . nor of the fire ants he'd seen a moment before. Nothing moved except the wind high in the trees. His skin prickled.

Something was wrong. Very wrong.

He whirled. Had he heard something? A voice almost. It was strange, but he hadn't heard any traffic for close to half an hour now. It was almost as if the highway didn't exist, as if he'd stepped into another world or time altogether. He walked forward, past the pebbles and clumps of grass, past the dandelions and faded asters. He peered up into the dark boughs of the trees and thought he saw something up there. Only a wren.

He broke into a trot, nerves overtaking his casualness, and skidded to a stop as he saw something lying half under some leaves by the base of a white fir and grinned. There was wildlife here after all.

He walked toward the chipmunk, but it didn't move. He narrowed his eyes as he got closer. No. It wasn't a chipmunk. No. It was . . . a hand. A human hand, its fingers stiff claws.

He frowned at the hand, bloody above the wrist, and thought it must be some sort of joke. He stepped past it and into a clearing.

Gaudy vans and cars had been parked in no particular pattern. A picnic. But where were the people?

Then he saw it.

The blood. Everywhere. On the cars, the vans, the ground, the flowers, the blankets . . . the corpses. Everywhere he looked he saw the bodies. Bodies leaning against the cars; bodies half under the chassis, as if dragged there by some force. Bodies sprawling in the clearing as though they'd been in flight.

Bodies everywhere.

A black-haired girl, lying not a dozen feet from him, stared without eyes.

Another had only one breast, a ragged wound where the second had been.

A thin Chicano boy smiled, blood on his lips, blood on the raw meat that had been his throat.

Bodies.

And blood.

And silence.

Complete.

He whirled, convinced he'd heard a step behind him. He scanned the trees again.

He was being watched. Watching by something . . . not someone.

Something. Off in a bush he saw something and stared without blinking, his eyes watering from the effort.

Eyes.

From the shadows.

Eyes that stared with malice. Hate. Evil.

He had seen eyes that hated before . . . eyes that watched as his army patrol walked on top of the buried land mine and was blown into disjointed arms and legs and halves of buttocks, eyes that watched as their comrades ambushed

45

the patrols by jumping out of low-hanging trees, eyes that watched, and hated—and all around, gagging them until they could hardly breath, were effluvia of rotting vegetation, of sour, days-old sweat, of gun-metal grease, of dried blood, of fear itself.

The memories were still strong after so long, and they made him afraid.

Not wanting to find out what the eyes belonged to, he ran for the truck.

That was when he heard the sound . . . the sound that he couldn't place, not even from the jungles of Southeast Asia, the sound that now pursued him. He heard the voices—soft, sibilant, seductive—voices bidding to him to stop, calling to him by name to stand where he was, to let them come to him. Voices that made the hair on his arms prickle, voices that made him lick his lips, voices that made him sweat.

NO!

His chest heaving, he flung himself in one final burst of speed into the cab and rolled up the window in spurts. God, don't let it stick on me now, he prayed. God, please, not now. Not daring to look outside, not wanting to see how close his pursuers were, he reached across the seat and rolled up the other window and locked the door just as the first creature flung itself at the glass.

He didn't look. Something dropped onto the roof of the truck and he heard scrambling outside the cab. His breath coming in short gasps, he threw the pickup into gear and roared, jerked backward. The pickup bucked as it ran over something, something that hissed in his mind. His hands trembled as he gripped the wheel.

He glanced back into the truck's bed. Clear. He slammed

into first, the gears grinding their protest, and the truck almost spun completely around with the frantic effort.

He heard the voices again, soft, and knew he wasn't rid of the creatures. He spotted a low branch ahead and gunned the engine; the truck raced for it. The needles and limb scraped across the cab. He glanced in the rearview mirror in time to see darkness drop to the ground.

His mind refused to give the darkness a name, refused to think about it . . . . He had to concentrate on the murders. He had to get to the sheriff, had to tell him about the bodies, had to tell him about the things.

My God. He shuddered, licked his dry lips, felt the sweat running down his face, his spine. He was frying in the pickup. It didn't have air conditioning, but he wasn't about to open one of the windows. Not until he was in the city. Not until he was safe.

Something scrambled across the roof of the cab. Once more he threw the truck into gear, roared backward. Slipped it into first. Hoped that the thing was gone; hoped, but didn't dare to look.

He was on the road leading away from the Crest now, on the road down to the main highway in the canyon, and he swung around a curve, taking it wide, in the outside lane. He flicked a look to his immediate left. Beyond the side of the road was space ending hundreds of feet below in a tumble of sharp boulders and a dried river bed. He looked up to see a gold and white camper barrelling straight toward him in the lane. He caught a slight glimpse of a plump face, its mouth opened in mute terror; then the camper's horn blasted, and he hauled to the right on the wheel—the two vehicles missed colliding with each other by mere inches, and he barely avoided sending the camper spinning off the road and over the edge and himself against the mountain face.

Calm, gotta get calm, he told himself, wiping the palm of his hand across his forehead. Sweat and dirt came away and he brushed his hand on his jean leg. His hand was trembling.

Calm. He breathed deeply. He had seen worse, heard worse. But far away, in another time. When he had expected it. Not here. Not in the mountains. Not to see . . . those . . . things.

He shuddered and heard in his mind, or so he thought, the cackle of the old man he'd given the ride.

CHAPTER FOUR

"Sheriff's Department" read the weathered sign. He wheeled the pickup into the parking lot and, raising a plume of dust behind, skidded to a stop, then looked around as he caught his breath.

This office of the Sheriff's Department was located in Cedar Crest on State Road 14, not many miles from the picnic grounds where he'd found the bodies. It hadn't taken him too long to get there either. Heading toward town, he had whizzed past the office, made a U-turn in a bank's parking lot down the way, and then driven back.

The office was a white mobile trailer set on blocks. Nothing special to look at. And even though he was still in the mountains, it was hot, hotter than it had been on the Crest. Too damned hot for the season, too damned hot for the location. He rolled a window down and breathed deeply, still shaken from his near-miss with the camper.

The aluminum screen door swung open and a man came out to stand on the top cinder-block step.

"Yeah?" the man asked.

Chato shaded his eyes with one hand against the glare of the sun and stared at the white man. He was large, and mirrored sunglasses perched on his sunburned nose. He didn't have to see the man's eyes to know the expression. He could sense the man's prejudice. He would have to carefully walk that thin line. Again, he thought wearily, again. And remembered for a moment how free the academic world had been of that singular prejudice. It had possessed others unique to the university, but this he found he hadn't missed.

"I need to report a crime." That's all he could say about the slaughter. It was a crime. Yeah. But not a crime like any other, no crime of passion. It was a crime of . . . what? Again uneasiness prickled along his spine, and he wished he'd delayed in coming to the city.

"C'mon in."

Boy. The word hung between them, unspoken, and he felt the anger boiling inside, then pushed it away for the moment.

The sheriff had already gone back inside, the door slamming shut. He walked up the five steps, opened the door and stepped into a blast of refrigerated air that made the hairs on his forearms stand up after the blast-oven heat outside. Inside, two Chicanos, one obviously a dispatcher, sat behind scarred, government-surplus metal desks and stared at him without expression. A large map of Bernalillo country, straight pins with colored heads stuck into it in a random design, hung on the wall behind them. The single room was cluttered with papers and coffee cups, a broken-open shotgun, and in the corner, by one of the Chicanos, a radio intermittently cackled to itself. The large man had settled behind a third desk, larger than the other two, and had stuck his legs, crossed at the ankles, up on the desk. He stared at Chato without speaking.

"Do I have to fill out forms?" he asked finally, irritated at the lengthy silence.

"Why don't you just tell us about the crime you're reporting," the white man said.

Boy again.

One of the Chicanos giggled and Chato refused to look at him.

"I took a drive up into the Sandias and stopped at one of the picnic grounds. I got out to walk around and found . . . found some dead people."

"Dead people?" echoed the man. "What kind?"

"They looked like low-riders to me. They had vans, you know, that sort of thing." He made a vague motion with his hands. He wanted them to find out for themselves, to be as horrified as he had been; he wanted to prove to the man that he had seen the bodies.

" 'Bout what time you see these bodies?"

"Not over an hour ago." he frowned. "Don't you believe me?" He hadn't considered that possibility, hadn't thought there would be any problem.

"Sure do." *Boy.* The white man slowly brought his feet down and stood and hitched up his pants. He stuffed a pair of handcuffs into his back pocket, then scratched his stomach where the stained shirt had gaped open. "Manny, you stay here. Look after things. Lennie, you come with me and the—" *Indian.* "With this guy and me. We'll go in my car."

Outside, they piled into the sheriff's white car, and Chato, sitting in the backseat, was painfully aware of the mesh screen separating him from the others.

"My name is Chato Del-Klinne," he said as they pulled

51

out onto the highway. This cop was pretty damned lax. Didn't question him; didn't want him to fill out forms. Didn't really believe him, one part of him said.

"What tribe you from?"

"I'm a Chiricahua Apache. From the Mescalero Reservation by Ruidoso." When the sheriff said nothing, he added, "Down south."

"What're you doing up here in Albuquerque?" The sheriff, who still hadn't introduced himself, glanced briefly into the rearview mirror where he could get a good look at him. Chato met his eyes steadily.

"Looking for a job."

"Looks like you found more than that."

No one spoke as they drove. The window on Lennie's side was down and the wind blasted into the backseat, blowing tendrils of Chato's hair across his face, but the slight coolness of the air felt good. He could feel the sweat staining under his arms, trickling down his back. Not all of it was from the heat. The sheriff drove without great speed, cutting in front of station wagons and semi-trailer rigs, and cursing under his breath from time to time when someone darted in front of him. They were soon at the cutoff to Sandia Crest.

He directed the sheriff to the spot where he'd parked earlier, and as they got out of the car, the back of his neck prickled. They were being watched, as he had been earlier.

"Over here," he said, walking away from the sheriff and deputy when neither man seemed inclined to do anything. He led the way through the low bushes, and then they were standing in the clearing. With the blood. The bodies. The carnage.

"Oh my God," the sheriff said. He slowly took off his sunglasses, as if believing he could see more clearly. The deputy, apparently made of less stern stuff than his superior, bent to vomit in a bush. Chato drew away from the Chicano.

In the short time he'd been gone animals had already been at the bodies, and he licked his dry lips. The sheriff stepped carefully across the picnic area and stared, without saying a word, at the destruction. He bent at one point to examine the remains of a girl by a green car, then stood and turned away for a moment. When he turned back, he walked well around her.

Lennie had recovered and was rubbing his mouth on a red bandana. Sweat stood out on his face and his brown skin held a sickly pallor under it. He glanced at Chato, then away, never once looking back at the bodies.

The sheriff wiped his boots on a flat rock a few feet away. Each stroke of a foot left red traces. Chato waited while the man finished his business.

Finally the white man put his sunglasses back on and stared at him.

"Well, Sheriff?" he demanded impatiently. "What do we do now?"

"I believe, Del-Klinne," the man said, "I believe that what we do next is return to my office. I'm gonna hold you for questioning in the murder of these folks." He took the handcuffs from his hip pocket and reached for Chato's wrists.

"Now, as you know, the Party's rally and annual fund-raising barbecue have been planned for this Friday, right before the International Hot-Air Balloon Fiesta. At that time I will give Senator Kent, who arrives the day before, the Indian statue, which he, in turn, will present to the Smithsonian Institute in Washington, D.C., as a gift from the peoples of New Mexico.'' Mayor Douglas Griffen paused, his hands placed on either side of the podium, and smiled, the plump skin on his face wrinkling with the effort, at his audience, who remained for the most part impassive.

The small room Griffen used for press conferences was filled with wire-service reporters, camera people from television stations, and a sprinkling of radio news directors. The air was heavy with smoke, hot because the air conditioning had once more broken down, and no one much wanted to be there on a glorious autumn day listening to a politician. Griffen, aware that he was dangerously close to losing the attention of his already bored audience, dabbed his white handkerchief across his sweat-streaked forehead, sipped at the glass of tepid water laced with bourbon by his elbow and smiled once more.

''Any questions, ladies and gentlemen?''

Some hands shot up in the front row and Griffen devoted his attention to the two reporters bold enough to be the first.

''Fancy that!'' one of the Associated Press reporters murmured in a mock astonished aside to Laura Rainey, sitting to his right. The man, a reporter she casually talked with on those rare occasions when she attended the monthly meetings of the Society of Professional Journalists and whose name she couldn't remember offhand, winked broadly at her. ''I guess he thinks we don't read or something. I mean, we've only known about this wingding for the last five months.''

Laura smiled, aware that Griffen was frowning in their direction. He always seemed to hear the whispering or snide comments in the back rows. He would have made a wonderful high school teacher, she thought wryly. ''Yes, but you must understand. Politicians never overestimate their foes. And obviously they think we don't read—because they don't read.''

He laughed, and she bent over her note pad, her dark hair fanning to hide her face. Griffen was now looking directly at her and frowning, his expression making him look like a petulant baby. It wouldn't do to get him angry at her . . . again. After all, he still hadn't forgiven her for her article earlier in the month about the city street's numerous potholes. And she didn't need to have this source dry up on her.

''Mister Mayor!'' someone said, vigorously waving from the side of the room.

He flashed a bland politician's smile at the man. ''Yes?''

The man, rangy and dressed in jeans and a western shirt, unfolded his long legs, stood up and faced the reporters. In a booming voice, he said, ''I'd just like to emphasize again to the members of the press that the Balloon Fiesta Committee is not trying to endorse one political party over another or make a particular political stand. In the years since the first Fiesta it has always been our stand to be neutral in these affairs, no matter what was going on at the time. But, of course, now that's different. Well, it's just that . . . .''

''Yes, yes,'' Griffen said, impatient.

''That things seem to work out that way.'' The man sat down without another word. There was a smattering of applause.

''Are there any further questions?'' Griffen smiled again.

Laura had rarely seen him do anything but smile. Of course, that was one of his duties as a politician. Too, his term was up the following year. And there was little doubt that he would run for office again. Campaigning already, it would seem.

"Will Father Lopez, who discovered the Indian statue, be on hand at the ceremony?" one of the women from the all-news radio station asked.

For a moment Laura thought Griffen's smile slipped just a little, but he quickly recovered. "Father Lopez is exceedingly happy that he found the statue in his church, but he disdains publicity, as you know from his reticence to talk to you all this past month, and he plans to retire to a contemplative order up north."

"What's on the agenda for the Senator?" the reporter from AP asked.

"I believe my press assistant, Miss Buddeke, has already handed out a schedule for the Senator's visit," Griffen said.

"Are there any changes?" The AP man asked.

Laura listened with only one ear as Griffen went on to point out laboriously that no changes had been made, that none were expected in the immediate future and that the members of the press would, of course, be notified at once of any changes. He continued to answer the other perfunctory and polite questions.

She rubbed a hand across her nose and thoughtfully stared at her colleagues. Not one of them was asking the questions she would have—would—once she had the courage to speak up. They were scared, she thought, noting the tightened lips, the restrained conversation. Scared, but of what? Her fingers fussed with the top button of her cotton blouse as she considered her next question. Should she ask it? She'd been worried about accessibility to the Mayor's office. If she went ahead, she certainly wouldn't have to worry about getting in to see the Mayor. The doors would be shut tight in her face.

But, on the other hand, if she didn't ask the question, what kind of a reporter would she be? The others hadn't asked because they were all older, more established in the news community than she was. Who was she? Just Laura Rainey, who'd come to the University of New Mexico in her second year from Colorado, obtained a Bachelor's in Journalism from the University, then gone on to get a lowly job at the *Courier*. Only recently she'd been promoted from writing obituaries to covering city hall. Her duties didn't include covering the important events, only those small, day-to-day, mundane meetings and news releases that no one else was interested in.

No one except Laura Rainey, who wanted desperately to get a toehold in reporting and would take anything, anything, just to write, to work on a real newspaper.

No one asked it.

Go ahead, one part of her prodded.

I'm afraid, too. I don't want my career to end before it's started.

There are other papers, other cities. Go ahead. What have you got to lose?

"Mister Mayor!" She had her arm up in the air now and waggled the fingers just enough to catch the man's roving eyes.

"Yes, Miss—" He paused. He knew who she was, but he wanted to embarrass her a little in front of the others. One of his games.

"Ms.," she corrected automatically. "Laura Rainey. With *The Albuquerque Courier*." She smiled sweetly at him, not letting him bother her.

"Go ahead." His hands were now folded in front of

him on the podium and he looked so serious, so intent she could have laughed.

She took a deep breath, then plunged. "I have just one question. How will the murders in the Sandias affect Senator Kent's stay?"

Some of the reporters around her murmured and the AP man stared at her, while Griffen continued to regard her blandly.

"Murders?"

"Yes, you know, Mister Mayor." Her voice was sharper than she would have liked, but she didn't know why he was pretending ignorance. She knew he was aware of the murders, knew because one of the *Courier*'s reporters had talked to a relative in the police department about them. Why couldn't he just answer the question, for God's sake? She went on. "The recent ones in the mountains. Those Texans killed on Sunday. And we have reports of some picnickers killed as well."

"An unfortunate encounter with a wild animal. The police are handling it." He took another drink. "I'm sure the deaths—not murders—will have little effect on the Senator's visit. They were, after all, highly isolated. Next question, please."

"Mister Mayor—about those murders." She couldn't let him wiggle out of giving her an answer.

"Miss Rainey, I believe I've already answered your question." He looked to another upstretched hand. "Mr. McDonald?"

She was suddenly left standing alone in the middle of the room and she knew she looked foolish. The other reporters assiduously avoided looking at her—she'd embarrassed them as well as herself. Anger flooded through her, and the pencil in her fingers snapped in half. She threw it down on the floor, drew up her cloth purse and rummaged through its contents for another.

"Tough break, kid," the man from AP said, leaning over to hand her a tooth-marked pencil. She accepted it gratefully and faintly smiled her thanks. "You'll get used to it—that is, if you stick around long enough. It's all part of the game, all of us believe we can change it when we start." He winked. "But now we know better."

Damnit, she wasn't going to let it stop her. She wasn't going to know better. She *was* going to pursue this matter, pursue it until she could get a straight answer from the man.

A woman from the NBC affiliate stood up. "Are you worried, Mr. Mayor, about the proposed protest by members of the National Coalition of American Indians? I understand they're concerned about the removal of the statue from its rightful home."

"I haven't worried about Indians for the past one hundred years," Griffen said with a smile. "But seriously," he said, after the laughter had died down, "I don't think there'll be much of a protest. There's been a lot of talk and I think that's all it is—a lot of hot air. Which should be quite welcome at the Balloon Fiesta!"

She had had enough. Deliberately she tucked her closed notebook under her arm, hung the strap of her purse over her shoulder and stood and pushed past the knees of the men and women in her aisle. She was aware that most eyes were on her, but she really didn't care. She just hoped they couldn't see her trembling.

She reached the door of the conference room. "All of you," Griffen said, pausing slightly, "are of course invited to the cocktail party and barbecue this Friday." She knew he was watching her closely. She opened the door and left not a little quietly.

War, she thought with a savage smile, had just been declared.

"So you don't know anything, Del-Klinne," Sheriff Roy Daltry, who'd finally introduced himself, said for the third time.

"That's right, Sheriff," he replied for the third time. How many times would he have to repeat his words before the cop would believe him? *No, he hadn't seen anyone. No, he hadn't heard anyone. No, he didn't have any idea how long the Chicanos had been there.*

Hadn't seen anyone . . . The sheriff hadn't asked if he'd seen any*thing*.

Was that obstructing justice, if he didn't say anything about the strange noises? Yet, what could he say? That he'd heard whispers in his head? That something dark had chased him, had tried to hurt him? The sheriff wouldn't believe him. He wasn't sure he even believed it. Even now it seemed remote, unreal.

"Okay, you can go."

"What?" He was startled. He stared at the sheriff. He hadn't expected this so soon.

"Go on. Just give us a call when you find a place to bed down. We want to stay in contact with you."

"Sure."

He stood up, stretched and walked across the scuffed linoleum floor to the window to retrieve his belongings. He had been at the sheriff's main office downtown for over two hours now. He had missed his job interview— lost it, for sure. He was hot, sweaty, tired, and he wanted get something to eat. And he wanted to sit down with his feet propped up.

But at least he wasn't suspected of murdering all those Chicanos. Jesus, he thought, with a shake of his head, he'd have had to have started early in the morning. And how the hell was one solitary guy supposed to have attacked all those people and butchered them? Apparently Sheriff Daltry had seen it that way, too.

Finally.

Maybe.

He had mentioned his hitchhiker, and the cop had put an APB out on the man. But he didn't think the old half-breed would be found. Too many places in town for him to hide; too hard to find a man like that who wanted to stay hidden. He could have collaborated Chato's story, confirmed that he had picked up Junior in the early afternoon, that he was far away from the Sandia Mountains when the picnickers had been murdered.

But he guessed that wasn't necessary now.

He waited a little impatiently as one of the deputies told him to stay in town, gave him the phone number of the sheriff's department, droned on. He knew he'd be followed for at least a day, but he didn't care. He didn't have anything to hide. He got the contents of his pockets, thoughtfully packaged by the police in a manilla folder, then walked out the glass doors.

Outside on Marquette, away from the stale odor of the bureaucratic offices, he inhaled deeply. Couldn't smell much of the autumn here, but it was a hell of a lot better than being inside. There was still a little light left in the sky, and the clouds reflected streaks of brilliant pink and gold. Over the horizon, just above the row of extinct volcanoes, was a solitary star.

He found his pickup in a back lot, claimed it from the suspicious guard at the link-wire gate, then got in and drove away without a backward glance.

The traffic light blinked red and he braked sharply to avoid hitting a low-slung Pontiac. He rolled down his window, stuck his elbow out and waited. It was his luck—the cops let him go just at the height of rush traffic. It was a little after 4:30, so there was no way he could make it to his interview—not the way he looked or felt.

He waited while the cars seeped from the government office parking lots, waited as the city buses, swollen with their loads of Grades 3 and 5 and 7, slid away from the yellow zones, waited until there was some distance between the truck and the next car.

Seeing the Pontiac, its back fender almost scraping the pavement, reminded him of what he had seen earlier in the day.

He wished he hadn't decided to go for a simple drive in the mountains. To see the goddamned pretty leaves.

A simple drive.

And here he was, almost a suspect in a multiple slaying, out of a job, caught in a bunch of traffic in downtown Alburquerque, and. . . . Absurdly, he started laughing.

A cool rush of wind, signalling the advent of evening, swept across his face at that moment, and he felt a little better. He had other things to worry about now. Such as lodgings.

He cut over to Central and cruised along, looking at the gaudy neon signs of the stucco motels. The Sundown, The Sunup, The Sunrise, The Sunset, the Buena Vista, The Sandia Vista, the Manzano Vista. With Air Conditioning, Triple X-Rated Movies, Waterbeds, Privacy. All the extras he really didn't give a damn about. All he wanted was a simple room that didn't cost him much and was convenient in location.

He found what he wanted just a few miles north of the University on Central. The Siesta Motel, with its dingy pink walls and a broken neon sign that showed a palm tree, was set back far enough from the busy street that he thought he wouldn't have headlights shining through his window all night long, and it was cheap as well, just fifteen dollars a night. Around the corner was a dingy mom-and-pop convenience store, and up a few doors was a Mexican restaurant with a faded "B" rating. Not the best, but he didn't think he'd die from anything he ate there.

He located his room, tossed his suitcase on the bed, then walked straight across to the bathroom, a trail of clothing behind him. He turned on the water as hot as he could stand it, lathered himself vigorously, then rinsed off. Slowly the weariness drained from him. After that it was a cold spray, which left him feeling numb and a little more alert than before. Just a little. He yawned and wrapped a white towel around his middle, and leaving wet footprints on the worn beige carpet, he walked across to the phone and called the sheriff's department to let them know where he was.

He fell back on the bed and stared up at the crack radiating along the plaster ceiling. He'd get dressed, then walk up to Niño's and Son and get a heaping plate of cheese enchiladas, rellenos and rice, drink as many cokes as they had, then come back and watch a little television before he went to sleep.

The last thing he remembered, before blackness swept over him, were the sibilant voices he had heard in the forest.

* * *

He awoke to a shrill ringing. A little confused, he slowly sat up and groggily rubbed a hand over his chest, looking around, trying to remember where he was. His skin was cool, a little damp.

And he had been dreaming again, dreaming strange dreams that disturbed him while he slept, but now that he tried to remember them, he couldn't. The ringing continued. Grey light filled the room. He yawned as he glanced at his watch.

8:15 a.m.

A.M.? Christ, he'd slept over twelve hours. He blinked blearily. Groggily he realized where the ringing came from and leaned over to get the phone. He cradled it against his shoulder as he pulled the towel off and began reaching for his clothes.

He cleared his throat. "Yeah?"

"Sheriff Daltry here." The man didn't wait for him to respond. "All charges have been dropped against you, Del-Klinne."

"Good." He paused, buckling his belt. "Why, if I may ask?"

There seemed the slightest hesitation in the Daltry's voice, and then the sheriff was saying: "We called in one of those anthropology profs at the U last night after you left."

"Yeah." There was something odd in the man's voice. The last vestiges of sleep fled and he was now wide awake. "Go on."

"He took casts of the toothmarks. Said he'd get right back to us. He worked all last night, called early this morning to report."

He sensed the man wanted to be prompted, wanted to talk—even to him. "And?"

"And. . . ." The man's voice deepened, lowered, became almost a whisper. "He said the toothmarks weren't human." He cleared his throat explosively. "He said, that professor, that he's never seen a toothmark like what was seen on those Mexes. Said he didn't know what it could be."

CHAPTER FIVE

After he'd finished talking with the sheriff, he left the motel and walked down to the convenience store to buy the early morning edition of the *Courier*. Back in his room, he spread the newspaper on the chocolate-brown bedspread and began scanning the long columns of the help-wanted section. There were plenty of jobs for barmaids, sales clerks and other jobs he was either not interested in or not qualified for.

He'd called his prospective employer right after Daltry had hung up, but as he'd suspected already, the position of hand on the horse farm outside Albuquerque had been filled. Not many outside jobs on farms or ranches were offered, and he figured they generally weren't advertised through a newspaper.

Which left him out of a job and without much money to his name. He could last for another couple of months before worrying, but he didn't want to use it all up.

But what then?

He closed his eyes, and saw again the mangled bodies and the blood. Remembered again the unnatural silence.

Something was happening.

Something was wrong.

He knew it; he . . . sensed . . . it. Sensed. Hunches had no part in the scientific world. They belonged only in the past—in his past.

Sensed. Oh no, he didn't believe in that anymore. He didn't want to . . . but he still sensed.

And he had those dreams, those vague memories that threatened to come to the surface, but floated away whenever he reached out to them.

Wrongness.

It wasn't his business, he reminded himself.

Except those . . . things . . . had come after him. And if they had caught him, would he have ended up like the low-riders? Dead. Dismembered.

He shook his head, trying to push away the unpleasantness. No hunches, please; just the facts. But the fact was, the day before had certainly been strange. First there'd been the curious hitchhiker. And then the gruesome deaths in the mountains.

But it's not my business.

I don't want to get involved. Just as he hadn't wanted to get involved when he was younger.

But . . . But he had to see. Had to see what was left in the mountains after he had reported the deaths.

Agitated, he ran a hand through his hair, then left the room, the keys of the pickup jingling in his pocket. He drove quickly out Central with the yellow sunlight, just edging above the mountains, shining in his eyes. It was a cool morning, and he had brought along a jacket, knowing it would be even cooler in the mountains, but he also knew that long before noon the day would be warm.

Too warm.

Too strange.

He glanced in the rearview mirror and saw, suspended above the Rio Grande Valley, two hot-air balloons. He grinned at the sight. In only a few days the International Hot-Air Balloon Fiesta, held annually in Albuquerque, would commence and the city's skies would be graced with hundreds of the rainbow-hued balloons. For over ten years the Fiesta had been held in the city, but the sight of the immense balloons, their burners firing every few seconds, drifting overhead in the perfect blue sky, never failed to bring traffic in the streets—and on the freeways—to a full stop. The rate of minor traffic accidents rose dramatically at this time, but no one seemed to mind.

Once he'd gone up with a friend who'd crewed for one of the better known balloonists. It had been bitterly cold at that high altitude, and he had been a little wary of the gondola basket, which he'd thought too flimsy, but the magnificent aerial view of Seven Sisters volcanoes to the west, of the green ribbon of trees along the Rio Grande, of the sheer flatness and deep coloring of the desert below for miles, had more than compensated for any physical discomfort he'd suffered.

Maybe he'd go again this year. After all, he was out of work and didn't have anything else planned.

If he managed to get a job in the city, he supposed he should let his parents know. He didn't talk often with them; it was too painful for everyone. "You're a disappointment," his father had said to him one year, "to me, to your family, to your people." He wasn't, though, but he couldn't convince him otherwise.

Occasionally he received a brief letter from his mother, relaying news about his aunts and uncles and his cousins, and always, always there, written not in ink, was her unhappiness. His father never wrote to him. Maybe if he had stayed there, continued his training as a tribal shaman, maybe then things would have been different. Maybe then his father would have been proud of him. Maybe. But he hadn't. And that had been the beginning of the years-long rift.

His shaman training. When Chato had been fourteen, his father had taken him to the old man, who lived at the edge of town, and said, "The boy is a dreamer of dreams." He had left Chato with the grey-haired man, Ryan Josanie, Josanie who was so old he did not count his life in years and whose face was deeply lined like the sun-baked earth. Josanie had studied him in the dimness of the house, and then, at last, had said, even as the boy was beginning to shift about uncomfortably, "The old ways must be taught, must be preserved. And you are gifted with the sense— touched." He had nodded, not knowing what else to do, believing what his father had said when he'd told about the dreams, and that day had begun his training. He had enjoyed it, thought it was exciting, fun, something to boast about to the other kids at school. It was a game to him, but Josanie said it was an honor—and a burden that he must come to accept after a time.

"Spiritual power comes through visions," the old man went on, "and you have many images in your head. I will teach you the symbolism of color, the use of pollen, stones, shells. I will show you the old ways, and they will live in you. They will never die, for when you are old, you will pass then onto another who is young."

They will never die, the old man had said.

70

And he learned, and studied, and each day when he left the school, he would go to Josanie's house, and he would listen to the old man until the light faded from the rooms, and then he would go home to do his school homework and to think about what Josanie had taught him that day. His parents were impressed with his progress. "Josanie says you're one of his best students," his father said gruffly, and slapped him on the shoulders—proud of him, he knew. His mother had smiled proudly, and he, too, had felt proud. His brother Ross, just eleven, had said nothing, although Chato had known the kid was impressed. He worked hard for a year and then entered high school, where he began to play football seriously. And football practice was after school, and that interfered with his sessions with Josanie. "On the weekends come," said Josanie in a voice Chato knew was disapproving. He came on the weekends, and studied, and listened, and Josanie told Chato he would save the Chiricahua people, and Chato had scoffingly said that they no longer exist, that their time was gone. "You were named for the chief," said Josanie, "You can be a great man for our people. You can bring them back to the glory of the past." "As warrior or medicine man?" Chato asked. "As both," Josanie said.

He went home, and dreamed dreams, and saw himself years later as a shaman, and his people came to him, asking for his wisdom, asking for his decision, asking for his help, and always there was Josanie, an amorphous face floating over his shoulder, whispering to him that he had the power to make them great. His father began to talk of the greatness of the Apache, and he listened quietly. "You have been picked," he said, "for Josanie tells me so. Picked to help us become great again," and in that moment Chato learned of the great anger that had gone so long unacknowledged in his father's soul, the anger that was in many of his people's souls—anger at the way they had been treated by the white man, anger at how their tribe had been reduced from its once great numbers, anger at how the old ways were rapidly being lost.

Anger. They were all angry, but he wasn't. He didn't feel the anger inside, the anger they wanted him to feel, and in his sixteenth year he became uneasy, and the dreams he dreamed were of blood, white man's blood and white woman's blood, and he heard the war cries of old, and he knew it was because of him. And he did not speak of it to Josanie, and though he continued to study, his mind was not fully on it now. Then, in his seventeenth year, the day after high school graduation ceremonies, he walked out to the lonely house and told Josanie he wasn't going to study with him any longer. It was a burden he didn't want to assume. It was too great for him, too much; he couldn't handle it. And Josanie had turned away, his face to the wall, and had not even tried to talk him out of his decision. And he had gone home and told them. His father had raised his voice and fists to him, and he had gone to his room, and packed, and left, though his mother, between sobs, begged him to stay.

He hitchhiked up to Albuquerque, where he found jobs to bring in money. He had already been accepted at the University, had a scholarship, and he worked hard at his studies, worked hard at forgetting the visions and the shaman training. But the dreams remained. They came to him in college, in the war, came afterward, when he went to graduate school and became a professor, persisted even when he quit to find outside work.

They haunted him, these dreams, and made him unhappy,

uneasy, never satisfied with what he was doing, and so he drifted.

And that was his real reason for returning to Albuquerque. He had had a dream. The job was the excuse. The dream was the reason. He was curious; he wanted to see what the dream meant, for it remained only vague shadows and shapes to him, and he was pulled—pulled by something unknown. And so he came, and said he was looking for a job. But he didn't care.

A horn shrilled; he jerked his mind back to the present and his truck back into the proper lane.

That had been close. He glanced in the rearview mirror and could still see the other driver's fist shaking at him. He tried to shrug it off lightly, but couldn't. He was breathing heavily, and something was pressing against his chest, and was this fear—fear?—after all these years? Fear of what? Of a would-be accident? Or of something to come?

He swung past a Volkswagen crawling up the grade of Tijeras Canyon, and soundlessly he hummed a tune. Not much traffic heading into the canyon at this time of day. A lot coming out, though, into the city, and he was grateful not to have to watch for other drivers.

He turned on the radio and listened to music and the news. The murders in the mountains were reported, but the police were claiming a bear had killed the picnickers. He wasn't mentioned.

When the news was over, he turned the radio off and drove, thinking of nothing, just directing an occasional look into the mirrors. He passed a few cars and concentrated on getting to the picnic grounds in as little time as possible. Within thirty minutes he was turning off to the Crest. Soon he had pulled up to the same overgrown track he'd seen the day before. This morning the only difference was that the grass had been trampled and tire tracks patterned the dirt.

He passed the flat rock where he had seen the lizard. A fine cloud of gnats danced over a fading flower, darted away as he came closer. He paused under a spruce. Something stirred in the boughs above. Alarmed, he looked up through the gloom of the branches into the round amber eyes of an owl. It snapped its beak, craned its head, hooted sharply and stared. Stared at him, as though it had been waiting for him. Its hoot was again sharp and sent a shiver down his back. Suddenly it flapped its wings and flew away. He backed away.

A bad sign.

An owl stays in the place where people have died, and when it comes it's a sign that someone is going to die, or so the old teachings said.

Ghosts and owls, and those about to die.

Bunk. He tried to smile, failed. His colleagues in the geology department would be laughing hysterically at him now, teasing him about being frightened of a bird.

Not just any bird. An owl.

It was only a bird, not an omen.

Religious nonsense of an old dying religion.

Religious nonsense that had no place in this world, no place in him.

Say it again and again and again . . . and believe.

He walked on, his boots dislodging a pebble. It rolled away, landed on the broad stone with a *ping*, and he felt uneasy at having disturbed the rock. Somewhere in the distance he heard the faint call of the owl again. He kept walking and listened to . . . nothing.

Complete silence. Not even the whisper of the wind in the firs. Not the call of birds, not even of the owl now. He came to the clearing where he'd found the Chicanos. And there was nothing. The cars and vans had been cleared away, the bodies removed, and nothing other than scattered rusty stains on the ground remained to remind him of what he'd discovered the afternoon before. He paced the perimeters of the picnic area, not wanting to step onto the actual surface. He could have laughed at his squeamishness. After all, he'd been in Vietnam; he'd seen worse there, far worse, and yet—and yet he didn't want to touch where the bodies had been.

Why? he thought sardonically. There's nothing here.

Uneasily aware again of the unnatural silence of the mountain forest, he wasn't so sure of that.

He left the picnic area and found himself in a grassy dale surrounded by spindly spruces. The light dimmed and he glanced overhead. The sky had darkened to an intense blue, dramatically unlike the light blue it had been when he'd driven to the mountains. As he watched, it deepened to the shade of midnight. A bolt of lightning ripped open the belly of the sky. Lights, bloodred, swirled in the darkness, coalesced and formed a ball. The fiery ball plummeted earthward.

Toward him.

He reeled back. As he raced toward the protection of the trees, the trajectory of the lightning curved, following him, exploding against the trunks. The drying needles burst into flames as droplets of fire rained on him. With a painful grunt he whirled back toward the open space. His foot slipped on the grass, and he fell faceward, his stomach hitting the ground first. For a moment he was dazed, unable to breathe, to move, aware only of the coiled lightning that flickered above him, around him. He started to rise, was nearly knocked down by a fiery crackling ball.

He flung himself down on the ground and buried his face in the wet grass. Coward. Yeah. He couldn't make it, couldn't get past the lightning. But he sure as hell couldn't stay out here in the open.

The *lightning*. His people called it the arrows of the cloud-dwelling Thunder People. He had always been frightened of it when he was a child; even as an adult he didn't like it.

First the owl. Then the lightning.

Omens. Bad omens.

He risked a glance, his face damp, and watched the display of dazzling lights. The leaves of the trees surrounding the dale burned with a hellish fire. Acrid smoke trailed upward, stung his eyes, forced him to cough. A tree trunk exploded, sending slivers of wood outward and downward. As the lightning sped past, the air crackled; his skin itched, being so close, and he could feel the warmth of it. A bolt of lightning struck a massive evergreen and the ground rocked. Almost as if in slow motion, the branches of the tree peeled away from the trunk, needles raining toward him. Fire blossomed upward.

He flung his face into the grass again, slivers scraping his scalp and his back through the shirt, and bringing blood across the tops of his hands.

A bolt of blue-white fire darted over him, the smell of ozone clogging his throat. A few feet away lightning shrieked as it struck the ground, split into smaller flashes, which in turn split even smaller until it almost touched him. Thunder rumbled immediately afterward—dark, loud booming and rolling sounds that drummed deafeningly into his ears.

Panting heavily, sweating, bleeding from the burns and cuts, he scrambled onto his scraped knees and hands, then onto his feet, and half-ran, half-stumbled toward the shelter of the nearest tree.

Before he reached the spruce, though, it burst into flames, the force thrusting him backward. He landed jarringly on his back, the wind knocked momentarily out of him. Helplessly he watched as an immense ball of lightning, far larger than the others he had seen, diffusing sparks forming a fiery aureole, whirled straight for him. He tried to get up. Couldn't, his muscles and sinews failing him. He watched. Closer and closer it came. He watched the shimmering light, heard the terrifying *snap* as it sped through the air, watched, watched . . . closer and closer . . . and closer, and he heard the whispers, saw the eyes watching him. Closer and . . .

He shut his eyes. Waited. For his death.

Nothing happened.

He opened his eyes.

The lightning was gone. The sky overhead was midmorning blue once more. The leaves and needles no longer burned.

Dazed, he sat up. His hair had come loose, and with a hand still unsteady he pushed it out of his eyes. He brushed brown leaves from his sleeve and stared. None of the leaves, the trees, the grass was singed. There was no sign of smoke.

Nothing.

As if it hadn't happened.

He couldn't have been dreaming—hell, hallucinating. It had been too realistic, too hellish.

He pushed himself slowly to his feet, looking. Again nothing. His black eyebrows pulled together in a frown. It didn't make sense. How could lightning hit almost everything in sight, rain down on the ground, and then there be no sign?

It didn't make sense; nor did the night sky in the day. None of this did.

He searched the backs of his hands. No scrapes there. No burns. No bruises.

His frown deepened as he tried to figure it out, couldn't.

He headed back into the forest; nothing had made much sense since he'd picked up the hitchhiker the day before.

He paused, then:

An owl called, and he heard the whispers, the soft whispers in the bushes, and he ran to the truck.

After he parked the truck, he walked to the convenience store and bought a sandwich and a carton of milk and a Hershey bar, and a newspaper, then returned to his motel room. He read the paper carefully, section by section, as he chewed on his cheese and bologna sandwich. He drained the milk in one long swallow and tossed the carton in the wastepaper basket by the bed. It hit the rim, fell on the floor, but he didn't notice.

This was the early afternoon edition of the *Courier*. Usually slim, it contained news that had occurred after the morning issue had gone to bed, which was generally early the previous evening.

It reported that a number of Chicanos, picnicking in the Sandias, had been killed by a bear, perhaps bears. A similar incident had involved some Texans, who'd been found mauled a few days before.

Nothing was said about his discovery of the bodies. Nothing.

What he had seen with his eyes didn't say that a bear had been there.

And Daltry had claimed it hadn't been an animal.

He crossed his arms on the bedspread, rested his head on his arms and stared down at the worn carpet.

Something was odd, as odd as his experience in the mountains with the lightning had been. Just as odd, just as unnatural.

Common sense told him that.

The radio news had said it was a bear, and he imagined that was the same story on t.v. and in the newspapers.

He didn't believe it.

He stared across at the cracked mirror on the dresser, stared at the reflection of the Western landscape painting above the bed.

Had his eyes, ears, senses perhaps played tricks on him up there in the mountains? No, he hadn't imagined any of it. Not the owl, the lightning, the darkness . . . the whispers. None of it.

Forget it.

Couldn't.

Couldn't stop thinking about it, couldn't keep it out of his mind.

And he had been wrong. Very wrong.

It *was* his business. He *was* involved. He certainly couldn't ignore that. Twice in two days he'd seen something strange in the mountains, sensed the oddness. Not only was he involved; he was caught up in it, and he didn't even know what *it* was.

Except that he intended to find out.

CHAPTER SIX

"Still can't get hold of the Mayor's office?"

Laura looked up from the phone at Bob Fergus, the *Courier*'s city editor, and shook her head. "Nope. They're really mad at me this time."

He laughed. "For the time being. But just wait until they want to look good in the press. They'll come running fast enough." He watched as she swept papers into the center drawer of her desk. "Want another assignment in the meantime?"

"I'd like to pursue this one, Bob."

"Well, until you have another lead, why not look at what I've got? The leader of the National Coalition of American Indians got in today."

She sighed. "Okay. Name?"

"Thomas Yellow Colt is their, you'll excuse the pun, chief spokesman." She didn't smile. "Don't be so intense, Laura. You aren't at the *Washington Post*, for God's sake, and you're not uncovering Watergate."

She pressed her lips together, mildly irritated with him. "I know. I just want to do well."

He leaned across and patted her shoulder, almost in a fatherly manner, except that his fingers lingered a little too long. As he removed them, it was almost a caress. Oh wonderful, she thought sourly. Just what she needed. And him married and the father of three kids and balding and thirty years her senior. It would be just her luck for him to make a play, for her to refuse, and then for him to get her fired.

"Laura?"

"Sorry. I was thinking. Now, where's this Yellow Colt staying?"

"At the Hilton, for Christsakes. These aren't no dirt-poor Indians. Just a bunch of troublemakers who move from state to state, stirring up the locals." He grinned at her, waved a pudgy hand and started to stroll off. "Might make good copy, though, especially as they're planning a protest at the barbecue Friday."

She reached for the phone and made the call to the hotel.

"Yeah?" asked a low voice.

Pleasant sort. She plunged in. "Mr. Yellow Colt? My name is Laura Rainey, and I'm a reporter for the *Albuquerque Courier*. I'd like to interview you this afternoon about your group and your planned protest. Would that be possible?"

He gave a short laugh. "Sure, honey. You come down to the Hilton and we can talk. Okay?"

"Fine, Mr. Yellow Colt. What time?"

"Two."

They arranged to meet in the coffee shop, and after she had hung up, Laura fished her notebook out of her purse, jotted down a few notes, then went to tell Fergus where she would be. Before she left for the Hilton, she called the Mayor's office again. Who knows—her luck just might be changing.

He needed to talk to someone. His university colleagues were out of the question. It had been too long since he'd last talked with them; too much had happened since then. And they would scoff anyway, if he told them what had occurred in the mountains. After all, it was all feelings and senses, and no facts.

He didn't know anyone else in the city. He was completely alone, alone as he had always been, and for the first time he was uneasy about it.

So he had turned to another Indian.

The only Indians he knew were in southern New Mexico, where his family still lived, and he didn't have time to drive down there to visit them. Too, this was hardly something he could talk about over the phone to his parents. His mother would just cry, while his father wouldn't say a word and Ross would be sarcastic.

Instead he had gone to the Indian Pueblo Cultural Center on 12th Street and had explained to the middle-aged woman at the front desk that he needed to talk with someone who knew the old ways. She'd expressed some surprise at this. The whites were forever coming in and wanting to know of the old ways, but not young Indians. She had thought about it for a while, thumbed through a card file, finally jotted something down and handed the paper to him.

He'd thanked her, left and, as he got into the pickup, glanced at the name.

Fedelino Tenorio at Isleta Pueblo.

He'd been to Isleta once and knew it was located about

fifteen miles south of the city. It was so named when the Spanish arrived, for the pueblo was literally on an island at that time, the river curving on each side. Through the years the Rio Grande had found a different route and flowed now only along the eastern side. The pueblo sat on high ground around which the river flowed.

He took U.S. 85 out of Albuquerque, crossed the bridge and drove into the unprepossessing settlement of old adobe and wood houses. Door frames and window frames were painted blue to keep out evil spirits. *Ristras*, the long strands of red chili peppers, hung on the outside walls. Most of the dwellings were one-story high, small, almost ramshackle. Along the river ancient cottonwoods spread rare shade. Dust, as always in that area, swirled in tiny dustdevils through the village as a hot wind swept down the narrow streets. A dun-colored dog raced alongside the truck, veered when he braked in front of one of the adobes. Other dogs, almost the same color as the first, slept curled in the shade of the houses. When he got out, he could feel unseen eyes watching him.

A little girl, barefoot and dressed in dirty jeans and a boy's western shirt, gaped wide-eyed at him. He walked toward her and she ran off. He stopped, waiting for someone to come out. But no one did. So he knocked on the first door, and when the woman answered and politely stood there, he explained carefully that he had come to see Fedelino Tenorio. In poor English she told him where he might find the old man. He was thirsty, but didn't want to ask her for a drink of water. So he graciously thanked her for her help, walked away, knew she still watched him.

He stood in the middle of the dirt road and looked around. Up ahead were the adobe walls of the kiva, the underground ceremonial room for Pueblo Indians. He started to approach it, then stopped. It wasn't his religion. He had no right.

He turned away, searching for the man, and when he next looked back at the kiva, an old man was climbing down the ladder. He watched as the man came toward him.

"You have been looking for me. I am Fedelino Tenorio."

Startled, Chato nodded. "I got your name through the Cultural Center in Albuquerque."

"Ah." Tenorio nodded, beckoned for Chato to follow him.

Tenorio settled in the shade of the eastern exposure of an adobe house so weathered its brick had been worn smooth from the years of rain and wind. Chato squatted a few feet away, and he studied the old man. Tenorio looked to be in his sixties, but Chato suspected he was closer to ninety. The skin around his mouth was wrinkled, as if few teeth remained, and his once black hair was shot with steel, but his dark eyes were still young, still lively, and they continually regarded him with curiosity. And with not a little suspicion. It hadn't been all that long, he thought, as the tribes counted it, that his people had been making raids on the old man's Tiwa family and friends.

"Tell me why you have come to me."

"I had an experience with lightning in the mountains. It was really . . . strange, and bothered me greatly, and I needed to talk to someone else about it."

"A sign of bad things." Tenorio paused.

He knew he wasn't going to get anywhere fast with the man, so he told himself to relax and be ready to spend hours with the Indian. He had brought a pack of cigarettes, and while he didn't smoke, he solemnly handed the pack to Tenorio, who carefully opened the package and took out the first cigarette to light. Wordlessly the pair watched as the same small girl he had seen earlier ran by, the dun-colored dog jumping at her side. The dog barked suddenly, and the girl grinned and waved at Tenorio, who nodded solemnly.

He was aware of other eyes, the hidden eyes, watching him. The Isleta people were curious. Why, after all, had an Apache come to them?

Why *had* he come? Would he find what he wanted—whatever that was? Hardly.

"What sort of bad things?" He rubbed the bridge of his nose and watched the elder.

In turn, Tenorio studied him. Took in the details of his hair, his clothes, his hands. And seemed to make some sort of decision. He rocked back and stared past Chato's shoulder for a long moment, hummed what sounded like a chant, then fixed his dark eyes on the younger man. "You do not believe."

"In what?"

"In what I am saying." Tenorio stubbed out his ciga-rette in the dry sand next to him, and Chato watched as the man drew patterns in the loose soil with the butt. The shapes quickly took form. A man. A mountain. Clouds in the sky. And lightning. The man fell. Struck by the white fire.

Cold sweat trickled down Chato's back. It was too realistic, too much of what had really happened, and he wanted to rub the drawings out with the heel of his hand. As if sensing the younger man's thoughts, Tenorio squinted at him and smiled, the wrinkles around his eyes deepening. Maybe Tenorio was older than ninety. He looked it at the moment. Old and sly, and knowing, and Chato didn't like it at all.

"Why do you come then?"

"I told you. I wanted to know about some of the old traditions. I remember what my teacher said long ago, but I wanted to hear what you might say. About things. Such as lightning."

"It happened to you." Tenorio's voice was low, but its timbre brought a chill to him.

"Yes. . . . And I wondered."

"About the old ways. There is more. You would not have thought of the past if you had not been scared—and—" He stopped, studied Chato. "And because of what is to be for you, for others."

Chato frowned. "What?"

"You are drawn into this, lured by the voices."

"Bullshit."

Tenorio lit another cigarette, sucked on it, shrugged. "You see, I am wasting my breath."

Remotely he felt anger at the old man. "Why are you being so coy? Why don't you tell me? You talk to the white writers and anthropologists who come to you."

"They are different. They are white; you are not. Go home, boy. Go home and ask the grandfathers of your village. Go now while you can."

"I can't. It's too far away. I need to know right away."

"Hurry, hurry. All the time. You are getting white, dreamer of dreams."

Now the anger flared and he wanted to reach out and hit the old man. But he knew Tenorio was right. He was getting white. He didn't have to hurry today; he wasn't going anywhere, didn't have to be anywhere or see anyone, only had to listen to the old man. And find out what he had to know.

Dreamer of dreams. Why had Tenorio said that? How had he known?

"Go away, boy. Look into yourself. Believe. Because what I say will not make sense to you otherwise. You will think me an old fool, and maybe I am. Go away." He shifted a shoulder toward Chato, dismissing him.

He stood, stared at the man for a few moments, then started to walk away.

He wanted to speak, and his fingers curled and uncurled at his sides. He wanted to know why the lightning had come after him, why he had heard the whispers, why he had been the one to find the bodies.

"You are touched."

Startled, he looked back. If was almost as if the old man had known what he was thinking. Like Junior that day. And at that moment a long black-grey cloud slid across the sun.

Tenorio raised his face to the obscured sun, murmured a few words, and in a few seconds the warm sunshine returned.

Coincidence, Chato told himself. That's all.

"By what?"

"The shadows have marked you. Beware. The voices. The eyes. Beware for you and the city. Remember what you have learned."

He walked away without another glance at the old man. You fool. You wasted your time, and now that old man is probably laughing at you with his friends and relatives, and—hell, you dumbshit Indian—what did you expect to find here? Yourself? Your past? It had been, after all, a fool's errand.

But the old man had known what he was talking about. Had known from the very beginning when he had fumbled

with his words, trying desperately to sort out his thoughts
and hoping the old man wouldn't laugh. The old man had
drawn the lightning all too accurately, had known of the
voices and the eyes, even though he hadn't said anything
about them. Tenorio knew. Knew something. He had to.

And he was . . . *touched*.

By the shadows. *The voices. The eyes.*

Beware, the old man had said.

Dreamer of dreams. Just as Josanie had called him so
many years ago. But how had this old man known what
another old man had called him? How? Coincidence? Too
much to believe in this instance.

Beware of what? Of whom? And how, when he was
already involved?

Not involved, one part of him corrected.

Touched.

He slammed the door of the truck harder than necessary;
the powerful engine roared to life and he sped out of the
dusty village. The spinning tires spewing gravel, he headed
back to the city, and tried not to think of the voices he had
heard, of the eyes he had seen in the mountains, of the fact
that he had found no answers.

CHAPTER SEVEN

"The problem," Thomas Yellow Colt said, draping one silk-clad arm along the back of the booth and sipping his Bloody Mary, "is that too many white people aren't aware of the existing living conditions for Indians. Take, for example, the reservations here in the Southwest. No matter how much publicity is given to the reservations, most whites still think my people all live in picturesque Taos pueblo. I know one couple from the East who came here, thinking that the Indians had come back there to live voluntarily—that they dressed in quaint costumes much like the whites in Williamsburg."

Laura only half listened to the man's words. She jotted down a sentence or two when he said something halfway memorable, but for the most part she had her mind on other matters. She had met Yellow Colt at the Hilton coffee shop; they had drifted into the bar, were having drinks, and he had immediately launched into a discussion of his group's politics.

Yellow Colt wasn't tall by Anglo standards, nor was he slim, but he was powerfully built, had commanding dark eyes and a politician's smile. He was well-dressed, too, in expensive clothes. She wouldn't be surprised to learn they bore designer tags. She could tell he was attracted to her and he played on that, smiling a lot at her, patting her once on the arm. And that made her distinctly uncomfortable.

"About the statue, Mr. Yellow Colt." She had to break in so she could talk to him about the protest. "The one you're protesting."

"Fetish," he corrected. "It's a stone representation. That's what fetishes are here."

"Yes, I know," she said a little waspishly, "I've lived in Albuquerque long enough to realize that."

He smiled, not at all disturbed. "Kent has no right to take the fetish away. It's not his or the white people's. It should be returned to us."

"But the people who created the fetish no longer live. They died out hundreds of years ago, and they're believed to have left no descendants. So, who would be designated the caretaker of the fetish?"

"Easy enough. Let us take care of it."

"Us?"

"My group. We're more than willing to handle the fetish."

She glanced up momentarily as a stocky Indian, with long hair tied neatly back, walked into the bar, hesitated as he looked around, then walked out. She watched as he stopped one of Yellow Colt's co-workers. The man pointed toward the bar again. The other man thanked him and entered once more. He waited while his eyes adjusted to the darkness, then looked around until he saw Yellow Colt and headed toward their table.

"I think we would be the best choice because of our politics," Yellow Colt was saying. "What would you say, Ms. Rainey?"

"Oh." She forced her eyes away from the approaching man, from the seductive cat-like way he walked. She smiled at Yellow Colt, who was looking at her as if he knew she hadn't been paying attention. "Yes. Very difficult. I'd like to ask you—"

The man stood by their table now, and she couldn't ignore him. She glanced up at him, then at Yellow Colt.

"May I help you?"

"I'm looking for Thomas Yellow Colt." The second man's voice was low, pleasant.

"I'm Yellow Colt." He raised his head to get a better look at the standing man. Laura couldn't help but contrast them: the new man, with a compact body, dressed in tight jeans, an attractive western shirt, expensive boots, a serious face with high cheekbones; Yellow Colt, on the other hand, heavier, body that would run to fat in only a few years, and a sulky, almost petulant look that this other man didn't share.

"I'm Chato Del-Klinne. I heard about your group on the radio and I wanted to talk to you."

"Sure. Sit down."

Laura started to slide over, but instead Yellow Colt moved so that Del-Klinne was sitting on the outside, almost opposite her, with Yellow Colt between them.

"This is Laura Rainey. From the *Albuquerque Courier*," Yellow Colt finally remembered to say.

Laura nodded at Del-Klinne, who nodded.

"Now, what do you want to talk to me about?" Yellow Colt's tone indicated he wasn't happy about this interruption.

Del-Klinne started to speak, seemed to think better of

93

his words and shrugged. There was something bothering him, Laura knew, and she didn't need to have a journalistic sixth sense to see that. Shadows lay in his black eyes, and there were slight creases along his forehead, recent lines on a face that she thought did not often frown. "Curiosity maybe. I wanted to find out a little more about your group, I guess."

Yellow Colt shot her a glance, an I-told-you-so-and-even-other-Indians-don't-know look.

"In what particularly were you interested? By the way, would you like a drink?"

"Just coffee, please."

The Indian activist gave him an amused look—*keeping away from the firewater, eh, bro?*—and flagged the waitress.

"I don't know what to say, really," Del-Klinne said. "I guess I wanted to find out if you believed in the old ways."

"There are a lot of old ways."

"I know. Nature then. Evil spirits. Portents. Things like that."

The activist smiled genially. "You're an educated man, Del-Klinne. I can tell. What do you believe?"

Laura watched the two men with interest. They didn't like each other, hadn't from the moment Del-Klinne had approached the table. Warily the two men were circling each other. It would be interesting to see the outcome.

"I'm asking you. And yes, I'm educated. I've been to college."

"What do you do now?"

"Various things," Del-Klinne replied, and it was obvious he was uncomfortable with the subject.

"Such as?"

"Look, I didn't come in here to talk about my work and

my educational background. I just wanted to find out some things. Such as what you know about lightning. And dreams.''

But for some reason Yellow Colt wouldn't drop the matter. "A blanket Indian, eh, bro?'' He laughed harshly, looked at Laura. "Is that what you're doin' with your fine education? Is that how you're helpin' your race? By goin' back to the reservation?''

Del-Klinne stood up quickly, his fists curled loosely at his side. "Thanks for your help.'' His tone was sarcastic. He pivoted gracefully and walked straight toward the door.

Yellow Colt laughed. "See what we have to fight, Ms. Rainey? Sheer ignorance on the part of guys like him. What else can I do for you?''

"I think I've got all I want. Thanks.'' She grabbed her purse, tossed some crumpled bills down on the table for her drink because she wouldn't let him pay for it, then hurried out of the bar. In front of it a black wrought iron fence set off a handful of tables with accompanying chairs. At one of the tables a beautiful black woman, dressed in an expensive red dress with a gold belt, lightly swung one leg crossed over the other and nonchalantly studied the businessmen in their dull three-piece suits, the short-sleeved tourists, the serious-faced Indians standing in small groups.

The hookers are out early, Laura thought, and remembered with amusement how shocked she'd first been when a friend of hers told her that those young women weren't waiting for particular dates.

Talk about naive, she thought, and looked around for the Indian who had spoken to Yellow Colt. She saw him in the parking lot and hurried outside.

"Mr. Del-Klinne!'' She waved a hand at him and watched as he stopped. She hoped she'd pronounced his name correctly. God knows, she couldn't give the last part of it the twist he had.

When she reached him, she was slightly out of breath. He was watching her warily. She gripped the strap on her purse tighter and smiled as encouragingly as possible, then took a deep breath.

"Hi. I'd like to talk to you, if possible."

"About what?"

His tone was slightly sour, as if he expected her to repeat what Yellow Colt had said. She couldn't blame him, though, for being suspicious.

"I—well, could we go some place? I'd rather not stand in the middle of the Hilton parking lot."

He smiled then, a pleasant expression. He was a good-looking man, handsome in a way not at all pretty, like most men were nowadays, and she was surprised at herself, because she'd never thought of an Indian in an attractive sense. For all her professed liberalism in college, she hadn't known a single Indian, hadn't sought the company of any, had to admit she hadn't really cared or rarely even thought about their plight. With a sense of irony she realized she was precisely the sort of person Yellow Colt's coalition was trying to reach.

"Okay. We can talk. Hop in." He jerked his chin toward the pickup, and she stepped around to the passenger side. She waited for him to come around and open the door for her; when he didn't, she grasped the handle set almost eye-level with her, climbed into the cab and jerked the door shut. As she watched him back up, she wondered what she had gotten herself into.

He watched her carefully as she finished the last of her green chili cheeseburger. She wiped her fingers fastidiously on the paper napkin, sipped her coke, then looked out the window of the restaurant.

She didn't believe him. He knew she wouldn't, and yet he'd persisted in telling her. Dumb. Dumb and . . . *touched*.

He watched the cars go by on Constitution, heading toward the UNM law school. He had driven to a small hamburger place operated by a Chinese family. Along with great burgers and roasted chicken, they also served a number of Chinese dinners. It wasn't a fancy restaurant, not very big—only about ten tables pushed together in the single room—but the food was excellent, inexpensive, and the service friendly.

He'd found the place when he'd lived in his house, only a few blocks away. So close, and he wanted in one way to drive by and see it again. Yet again he didn't want to, didn't want to see what the new owner had done to it, didn't want to see the improvements or the decay. Didn't want to stir up more old memories. Too many memories were being dredged up recently anyway.

And it was still a mistake bringing the reporter here and telling her everything. He needed to talk with someone. He hadn't planned on telling her, but she had looked sympathetic and had seemed to be a good listener. She'd said she saw he had a terrible burden. She urged him to talk, to tell her what it was that was bothering him, and before he could stop it, everything that had happened had come pouring out. The strange hitchhiker, his missed job interview, the ride to the mountains and his grisly discovery, his trip to the sheriff's department, his second and near fatal journey into the mountains, his visit to Iselta. Everything. Nothing had been left out, no matter how ridiculous it sounded now in this little cafe with the hissing of hamburgers on the grill, the high-pitched voices conversing in rapid Chinese, the scraping of chairs next to their table.

Nothing.

Not even the shadows.

He had thought she would understand. But he was wrong. She had been quiet too long. Her attention had returned to the room and she was concentrating on wiping her individual fingers now with the paper napkin. Maybe she was a cleanliness freak, he thought, amused. Maybe she was wondering how she could escape the nut and get back to her car in the Hilton parking lot.

"The shadows," she said.

The sound of her voice, when she finally did speak, surprised him, and he nearly lost the grip on the coffee cup. He took a quick sip, swallowed the now lukewarm coffee, set the cup down with a slight scrape on the saucer.

"Yeah."

"They chased you."

He nodded.

"And the lightning. Ball lightning is a common occurrence in the—"

"Not like this. I've seen the natural kind. This wasn't." He traced a pattern in the wet ring left by his water glass. Wryly he recognized it was the same pattern the Isleta elder had been tracing in the dirt. He smeared the moisture with his fingertips, wiped his hand on his jeans. "I swear I wasn't—I'm not—on anything. What I saw was real. My detention by the cops was real. And I don't understand any of it. I thought maybe you, as a newspaper reporter, might have heard something that a peon like me wouldn't have." He waited, watched her. At least she hadn't stood up and shrieked that he was a nut who should be locked up. He could be thankful for that.

When she did not speak, he sighed deeply and reached into his pocket to pull out the money. He guessed he hadn't lost much. He'd had some companionship for a while, had been able to talk about what was bothering him, and he only had to pick up her lunch of the burger, fries and coke. He wasn't out much. Except he knew she suspected he was certifiable.

"I believe you."

His head jerked up at that and he stared at her. She was looking at him now, her blue eyes solemn. "Everything I said?"

She nodded.

Laura drank more of the coke, held out the empty glass to indicate she wanted another one. When he returned with a second soft drink for her, another cup of coffee for himself, he sat and drew in a deep breath.

She was still regarding him solemnly. "That sheriff might be wrong. Maybe the guy at the University got mixed up."

"Maybe," he said, sipping the coffee, rolling the hot liquid around on his tongue. "But a bear is a mighty handy scapegoat, if you don't mind the animal mixture. And using the bear as an explanation doesn't tell us why those *things* were at the picnic site."

"Coincidence then."

"No. That's too convenient." He paused to look at her closely. "Maybe it's more involved than we think. Maybe it's really a mass murderer, an escaped convict, something like that. A bear in a killing frenzy would be less frightening to most people than a human killer. Perhaps the city doesn't want that spread around, so there's a news blackout on that. I mean, the news media aren't playing it up; it's their sources."

"Why?" She answered her question almost immediately. "Because of Senator Kent, that's why. At the press conference I asked the Mayor how the deaths would affect the senator's visit, and he adroitly avoided answering me. In fact, he made me look like a fool in front of everyone else."

He glanced out the large windows of the hamburger place, watched an old Chicano, shoulders slumped, head sunk into his neck, shuffle slowly along the pavement, and he was reminded of Junior. They weren't very far from where he'd dropped the hitchhiker off. If he got in the truck and cruised along Central, would he find the old man? Then what? Ask him questions. What would the geezer know? More than he should, one part of him whispered.

"Those bitemarks—not from a known animal," she said suddenly, startling him in the change of subject. "That's what the anthropologist said?"

"Yeah. And the human animal as well. There's something going on here, but I'm damned if I know what. We've gotta do something, though."

He stood up, went up to the counter to pay, then started walking toward the door. Laura followed. When they were in the pickup, and he had backed up onto Constitution and was sitting at the light, ready to turn right into Carlisle, she looked sideways at him.

"Why?"

"Why what?"

"Why," she asked, "do we—do you—have to do something? I mean, it's not your business. You're not a lawman. So what does it matter?"

He stared at her. "It matters because—" Because he had been called; because those voices had stirred something from his past, something he thought he had buried forever, something he knew now still existed. "Because I have to know. Those things came after me; that damned lightning nearly killed me. I'm involved, whether I want to be or not."

"I can accept that, I suppose, but what's your plan now?"

"Beats me."

Without realizing it, he started toward Central and the University area.

He didn't speak for a few blocks, then: "First, we have to compile the facts."

"That's easy enough," she said. She started counting off on her fingers. "Fact: There have been three separate instances of death, all in the mountains. Fact: The deaths might not be related, but they all happened conveniently close in time and location. And two of the deaths have been attributed to a bear. Fact: The anthropologist said the low-riders weren't killed by an animal, so a bear couldn't have killed them. That follows for the campers. And what of the priest? Did he really die from a heart attack?"

"Fact," Chato added, "what I saw sure as hell wasn't bears."

"The inference?"

"Something's going on, and it irritates the hell out of me. Is it part of a cover-up?"

"In Albuquerque, New Mexico?" She laughed. "This is the Land of Enchantment, not Washington, D.C."

"Still, Sheriff Daltry called me, wanted to talk. Why? Because of fear? Or could it have been a warning? *Get out of town before sundown, kid.*"

"A distinct possibility."

"Fact," Chato said, "I saw—found—those mangled

bodies. Fact: I saw those shadows in the mountains. Fact: I was almost killed by the lightning. In the mountains. Always the mountains," he said, glancing sideways at Laura. "Have you noticed that?" She nodded. "The key's there. The murderers are there. I was *touched* there. In the mountains."

She nodded again, didn't speak, but didn't have to. Junior's laugh echoed in his mind, and once more he saw the old half-breed. The man knew more than he had said, knew more than he would say. He didn't have proof of that, of course, but he sensed it. Didn't have to have proof, he told himself.

"I need to find Junior. Somehow he's the key to all of this."

Laura considered, then nodded. "I think you're right. At least I hope you are."

The truck was parallel to the University now, and he glanced at the sidewalk on the south side of Central. Several winos sprawled outside the Frontier Restaurant, their legs outstretched in front so that students walking along the sidewalk had to carefully pick their way through the limbs. He saw more old men tottering down a side street.

Old men. Junior and Tenorio and Josanie. Wisdom came with age, it was rumored. He might believe that of Tenorio and Josanie, but of Junior? He shuddered, remembering the half-breed's ravaged face. Evil, too, could come with great age.

He glanced back down the street at the derelicts and winos. They were everywhere today. All the old men of Albuquerque. Out today to confuse him, to lure him away from the real object of his search.

The hitchhiker. Junior.

He didn't even know the old man's last name. Didn't know what pueblo he came from.

Didn't know, too, how he knew the man was half-breed. Half-breed of what?

He had to find Junior, had to ask him, had to know more.

Before it was too late.

Too late for whom? he wondered. And instantly knew the answer.

Before it was too late for him.

CHAPTER EIGHT

He sat up abruptly, scratched an ear and lifted his nose to smell the wind. The itch persisted and he scratched at it again, his long nails rasping against the scrap of leather around his neck. He bent his head and gnawed at his side, where it itched, too. Then he opened his mouth, his tongue lolling, and looked around.

The shadows moved.

His fur bristled and a growl, from deep within his throat, welled up. Reflexively he snapped his stained and broken teeth. A warning. His gums were pink, blood-stained, and he bared his teeth again, the one long tooth, the only one left in the front, curving up over his grizzled muzzle.

The others in the pack, the females, pups and young males as yet untested by him, echoed his growling, a rolling, low sound that in the past had warned off other enemies, other predators.

But not today.

Grey clouds, their edges smeared with black, drifted overhead, obscuring the sun, and the warmth of the day that he had been enjoying disappeared quickly. Somewhere above there was a flash of lightning, a distant drumbeat of thunder. The wind rose, quickly, strongly, muttering angrily, without warning, as it always did, and brought with it a new scent.

He sniffed again, deeply. The odor was not of Man, but of something older, something not . . . unfamiliar. Decay. Living decay with the fresh, cloying scent of blood. The stench assailed his sensitive nostrils, and one of the pups, not yet weaned, bayed and rubbed its nose along the ground. Its mother clubbed him across the side of his head with a broad-padded foot and the sound ended with a whimper.

The old dog stood up, shook himself, and turned his head this way and that, looking for the scent worse than Man. The evilscent. He heard new sounds, too, in the wind, sounds like the voices of Man. But different.

Bad sounds, sounds so high they pierced his ears, hurt his head.

The shadows crept closer.

His bitch bared her teeth, barked shrilly and padded over to him. She nuzzled him and he snapped at her. She backed away and looked toward the bushes.

The pack had been hunting, and now, with the sun so high and the heat at its most intense for the day, the leader had returned with his followers to their lair. There they would sleep in the shade of the bushes and trees, protected by the rocks surrounding the lair on all sides, and in the evening, once the light was fading, they would go out once more to bring down their dinner. Rabbits and chipmunks, an occasional stray house cat. Later they would

106

return to sleep for the night, and once more, early in the morning, the cycle would repeat itself and they would hunt again.

Hunt or be hunted.

His one brown eye was watchful, the other torn out in a fight long ago. The needles on the branches overhead clicked, and he whirled, teeth bared. The fetor grew stronger. Again the growling in his throat started, his hackles rising as well. His uneasiness increased, and another pup whined. Its mother leaned down to lick it and it soon quieted.

The shadows watched.

He barked once, twice, again—three short sounds. It echoed, clattering against the rocks, and he cocked one ear when he heard something slither down a sandy slope. His keen eye only picked up the sinuous form of a diamond-back rattlesnake. It disappeared with a flick of its rattles down a hole.

The other dogs, sensing danger, huddled around him, forming a rough circle. His trio of pups out of the old bitch waddled toward him, their fat pink tongues lolling. Their stubby legs moved them surprisingly fast and they were soon at his side, their muzzles pulled back in baby imitations of his fierce snarl.

The shadows waited.

Lightning ripped the charcoal clouds above their heads and the dogs cringed, whining in fear. The sky blackened as though it were night, and slowly at first, quickening in a pulse-like rhythm, fat raindrops splashed downward. The rain assaulted them, matting their fur, splattering mud on their feet, blinding them. The leaves shuddered as the branches whipped back and forth.

And the voices still whispered.

And the stench became unbearable.

He barked again at his pack, and they trembled. He nipped at the back foot of the one-eared female, a young bitch who'd borne him many pups, and she whined.

The shadows rustled.

As the rain increased, so did the decaying scent. It assaulted his nose. He rubbed it along the muddy ground, tried to remove the odor. But it didn't help. The decay filled his nostrils, choked him, snapped at him, gnawed his throat.

He shook his head, pawed at it. Nothing helped.

And the shadows leaped.

A pup screamed as sharp claws raked across its muzzle, sliced at its nose. The pup squirmed away, trying to escape the pain in its head. Something dark leaped on it from behind, snapping its spine in half with one meshing of powerful jaws. It shrieked once, was quiet.

The trio of pups backed away from the shadows, alternately barking and whining. One stumbled over a brother; it momentarily faltered, and the shadows leaped. The puppies disappeared under the darkness. Soon their cries were gone.

The bitch circled one of the creatures. Her lips were pulled back into a frozen snarl. She had watched her unweaned pups die one by one, felt even then the milk in her teats dry. She leaped at the shadow and it drew back. Emboldened, she advanced as the shadow withdrew. Closer and closer she came, watching the evil eyes staring at her. She bounded forward, her jaw open to rend the shadow. From the trees dropped other creatures, creatures that seized her legs, her neck, and began biting her, inflicting her with more pain than she'd ever had in any battle. They gnawed at her tail, her stomach, forced her to endure pain, would not allow her to die. Slowly, with their talons, they ripped her belly open, and she heaved a deep sigh as her intestines spilled onto the mire, the pools of water growing pink.

The old dog kicked out with his back legs, raked with his teeth and leaped aside as one of the creatures jumped from a low-hanging branch. The dog slipped in the mud, red with the blood of his pack, and whirled to face his enemies. They ringed him now. Warily he watched. They would go after him in a moment, as they had with the others. Would tear open his belly, slice his throat, pluck his single eye. Out of the corner of his good eye he saw the raw carcasses of what had been his pack. The bodies looked as if they had been stripped of skin, the flesh underneath exposed to the pulsing rain. He slid in the mud and one of the shadows charged. He jumped, coming down on the shadow and something crunched as it gave way under him. A high-pitched scream tore into his ears, and then he was jolted, knocked from the creature by something he had not seen, could not see. He lay wheezing on his side, unable to move, to get up, to defend himself. Above him, around him, he saw the shadows. He snarled as they approached. Pain blazed in his mind, and he blacked out, his teeth still snapping.

Warmth. Someone patted his head. A soothing voice. A clatter of a bowl set on the floor.

He opened his undamaged eye; the rain had stopped. Flies buzzed around the bodies of the puppies, the old bitch, the young one. Chunks of flesh lay separate from the bodies, and already the forest scavengers had begun their work. Overhead, in a calm, blue sky that showed no sign of the recent thunderstorm, three buzzards wheeled in lazy circles. Waiting. Patiently.

He twisted his head to one side, the sand rubbing against the rawness of his hide.

The shadows were gone.

Slowly he lurched to his feet and found only one paw that didn't hurt. The tip of his tail was gone, and blood streamed from the gashes on his back, his sides, his head. One ear was half chewed off; his eye watered so that he could hardly see out of it. He rubbed his face in the grass, could see again.

He limped toward the bodies of his bitch, his pups, but nothing of them remained. None of the others were alive. Only he was. The oldest. The hardiest. The leader.

He turned away, leaving the lair, walking painfully on raw-rubbed pads. He did not look back. He did not see if the shadows watched, if they followed.

He walked, leaving a red trail behind him. He continued walking through the forest, picking his way carefully past the sharp stones and sticks, the broken glass and rusted tin cans, the spent shotgun cases. He ignored the raucous cries of the birds, the curious bright eyes of the ground squirrels. He walked past boulders and trees, and finally past lawns and through streets, walked and walked, into the territory of Man.

He heard the voices long before he saw the humans, long before he had come down the slope. And he had followed them, knowing he would find help. Knowing that from his past.

When he reached the edge of the playground, he sat down on his haunches, whined as pain shot up his back.

"Look! A dog!"

A boy bailed out of the canvas swing and ran toward him. Three other children, two girls and a boy, followed.

The dog started toward them, his tongue out, his nose sniffing.

"Oh, he's been hurt," one of the girls, dark-haired and dark-faced, said. She started to put her arms around his neck.

"Don't, Maria," cautioned the older boy. "You'll get blood on your dress."

"I wonder who he belongs to."

"He don't have tags."

"Maybe he's been running loose in the mountains."

"How did he get hurt?"

They began to pat him slowly and gently on the head. It felt good. One of the girls found an old plastic margarine bowl and filled it with tepid water from an outside faucet. He lapped it up as quickly as if it'd been cold. His single eye closed and he panted heavily, his sides rising and falling rapidly. The sun was warm on him, making him sleepy. And the children were kind, their words gentle. If he slept, the pain would go away, and he would dream of chasing rabbits, and when he woke, the old bitch would be there to lick his face.

"Look. Something's outside the fence," said the girl who had wanted to hug him. She pointed in the direction from which the dog had come.

The older boy squinted in the sunlight, then shook his head. "I don't see nothin'. You're nuts."

"I am not, Carlos. There *is* something there." She looked indignantly at her brother, then stooped to pet the dog.

"Maybe it's another dog," suggested the second girl, who had quickly fetched the water for the dog.

The dog was too tired now to sit. He lay with his head resting on his outstretched paws, his strength, his life ebbing away. The pain was easing now. A fly buzzed around his nose and he didn't bother to snap at it. His eyelid twitched, but he kept it closed.

"Girls are always thinking they see things. That's what Dad says."

"Eee, look, Carlos. Maria was right." The younger boy stared outside the chain-link fence.

The scent of decay floated across to the dog, mixed with the acrid odor of dust and the sweat of the children. That scent. . . . He struggled to open his eye, could not, bared his broken teeth in a silent snarl.

"You afraid? I'm not." Carlos stepped toward the gate.

"No, Carlos, don't go." His sister tried to keep him with them, but he shook her hand off his arm and kept going.

The dog raised his head, nose straight in the air, and bayed deeply, an eerie sound floating across the silent playground. Maria, wringing her hands, followed her brother.

Carlos opened the gate.

And Maria screamed.

CHAPTER NINE

When he got back to his motel room, he kicked the door shut and dropped on the bed, without even bothering to take off his boots. After they'd left the restaurant, he and Laura had cruised the downtown area, checking to see if they could find Junior, but they'd had no luck.

Finally she said she had to return to the paper and get going on her story about Senator Kent's visit, so he took her back to the Hilton to her car. Then he came back here to get out of the heat.

Something seemed to whisper in his mind, but he ignored it, closed his eyes, and thought.

Always the mountains. All these incidents revolved about that location.

But what about the priest?

Natural death or something more?

He frowned, trying to remember where the priest had been staying when he was killed . . . when he died.

He rolled over onto his stomach and reached under the nightstand to get the Albuquerque phone directory. He flipped through the pages, ran his finger down the columns until he found the number he wanted.

It took five rings before someone answered.

"The San Carlos Roman Catholic Retreat." It was a man's voice, placid, gentle, low in timbre. Monkish, he thought, with a half-smile.

"Hi. I don't know if you can help me; I don't really know who to talk to." He tried to make his voice as apologetic as possible.

The man on the other end responded. "That's all right. What seems to be the problem?"

"I'd like to talk to you about the priest who died up there yesterday."

When he spoke again, the man's voice seemed more restrained than it had. Subtly different, he thought. Suspicious. Careful.

"Are you with the press, Mr. uh?"

"Ruiz," he supplied. "Yes."

"This priest was from back East, and simply over exerted himself. It's a sad, but common enough experience, we have found, to our sorrow. They're just not used to the high altitude and low oxygen content. A real problem for us, as you can well imagine."

The voice was still polite, but more than a little curious, he thought.

"I wanted to confirm a rumor I'd heard."

Silence for a moment. "What is the nature of this rumor, Mr. Ruiz?"

"I heard that he had been slashed and bitten and was left in a pretty horrible state. That sure doesn't sound like a heart attack."

114

Some hesitancy now. "Perhaps, Mr. Ruiz, you would like to talk with our prior?"

"No, that's okay."

"What newspaper did you say you were with?"

"I didn't."

"I'm afraid I cannot continue this conversation unless you identify yourself."

Mexican standoff. What next?

"I've got to go now. Thanks a lot. You've been very helpful." He hung up.

He couldn't stop here, not when things were getting mildly bewildering. He would have to make more calls. He called the Sheriff's Department. It was a call he should have made earlier; he shouldn't have waited so long to talk to Daltry again.

But he didn't have to worry about that.

Sheriff Daltry, one of the deputies reported, had gone on vacation. Starting this morning. And no, he wasn't sure when Daltry was coming back, but he thought it was a long vacation. Like two weeks, maybe longer. Could he take a message?

No, he said curtly and hung up.

He called Information, got the number for the Archdiocese in Santa Fe. The priest had suffered a heart attack, the woman there reported.

Did the city handle the priest's autopsy report? he asked.

Silence for a moment; then she asked if he would like to talk with the Archbishop's assistant. Would he care to give his name?

No, he would not, and he hung up again. From the woman's tone of voice, he knew that the man at the retreat had already called the Archdiocese.

He should get the coroner's report on the priest's death.

Find out if the man had had a heart attack. But they didn't let private citizens see those. Maybe Laura could?

He made another call, this time to the University. Daltry hadn't mentioned the anthropologist's name, but there were only two professors who could have been contacted by the Sheriff's Department.

Thirty minutes later he stared at the floor again, the frustration filling in him.

Damn.

Double damn.

The first professor was on sabbatical this year. Obviously she couldn't have been the one contacted. The second one—much more promising, he told himself—was out in the field and couldn't be reached unless it was an emergency. How long had he been in the field? He'd left earlier today.

Too conincidental.

And another dead end.

What was going on? He didn't like all this vagueness, and he shivered as something whispered in his mind, and he sought to shut it out.

Griffen took the call himself, and waited until his secretary left the office. He leaned back in the swivel chair.

"Yeah?"

"It's about the man I told you about earlier," said the soft voice on the other line. "The one who found the bodies in the mountains." The voice paused. "He's been out to one of the pueblos. My friend at the Cultural Center called me."

"There's no harm in that," Griffen said easily. He flipped through his calendar, noted the penned engagements there.

"No. But he was asking her about the old ways."

Griffen looked up. "Old ways?"

"Yes, my friend."

"Do you think he's with that troublemaker Yellow Colt?"

"I don't know about that, although he was spotted with the man at the Hilton, as well as with that reporter Rainey, the one who's been bothering you."

"Yeah, a real bitch. Young and stupid. She doesn't know how to play the game yet."

"He also called the retreat, as well as the office up here."

Griffen frowned. "That's much more serious. But how do you know it was him?"

"We taped the calls. The voices were the same." There was a pause. "What do you want me to do?"

The mayor rubbed the bridge of his nose and stared across the room at a picture of him shaking hands with a president.

"Put someone on his tail. At all times. Got me, Richard?"

"As always, Doug, as always."

The caller hung up, and Griffen looked out the window and drummed his fingers on the desk top. He didn't need Indians, acting on their own or in a group, making trouble for him now—particularly now, and he glanced at his calendar again and the red-ringed date there.

CHAPTER TEN

The yellow eyes stared at him; he heard the harsh whispers. They called him by name, and he tried to brush the murmuring away with a shake of his head, as if the sound were nothing more than flies buzzing in a living cloud around him.

They called, those voices, old and expectant.

And waited.

He saw *them* in the bushes, in the trees, staring at him with their evil yellow eyes, eyes that hated, eyes that lived for fear.

And he waited. He crouched on a large, flat rock in a clearing, and waited.

Like the eyes.

He tried to move and could not. Not even his foot, not even a single finger would respond. Sweat trickled down his face, swept into his eyes, into the corner of his mouth, and he tasted the salt of fear.

They watched. And waited.

Sometime in the past a terrible fire had swept through this part of the forest, leaving stark skeletons of trees. Little greenery showed on the branches, and he wondered why the leaves hadn't come back. A moment before the sun had been shining overhead, but now the sky had darkened, the angry, black clouds appearing out of nowhere. They covered the blue, and thunder boomed off in the distance. Through a rip in the clouds he saw flickering yellow light. An arc leaped from a cloud to a tree; the tree was backlighted for a moment, then exploded, flames shooting dozens of feet in the air.

Still he could not move.

He watched as raindrops fell on the ground, and where they struck the dry, cracked ground, yellow flames leaped up. They surrounded the rock, arched toward him, and beyond the circle of fire he could see the shadow creatures. Behind them was a wall of night. They were coming toward him, those shades, those eyes, those whispers.

And they stood around him and stared and beckoned and whispered. His name. They touched him, caressingly, then ripped their talons across his bare chest. He screamed in pain and tried to get away. But couldn't.

Ribbons of blood appeared on his skin and he watched it seep down toward his navel. One of the creatures leaped forward, its claws clicking on the rock, and it clambered up next to him. It bent its shadowhead down and lapped at the blood, and each long lick sent waves of agony through him. Its tongue was barbed, and it ripped chunks of flesh from his chest. More blood welled out, spurting with each vigorous pump of his heart, and the other shadow creatures joined the first one.

They feasted on his body, and he would not die. Could not. Each touch brought new agony, new hell. He screamed over and over, but no one listened; he made no noise. He pounded his fists, but didn't move.

Then the blackness he'd seen behind the shadow creatures swooped toward him. Enveloped him. Smothered him.

He screamed, knew no more.

And when he woke, he was lying on the bed. The sun had gone down and the room was darkened, the only light coming from the neon sign outside the bungalow. He drew his hand across his chest and felt wetness. Panicked, he lunged at the lamp on the bedside table. In its yellow light he stared down at his hand.

Sweat. That was what he'd felt on his chest. Sweat. Not blood.

It was a dream, he reassured himself. Only a dream. A nightmare. He wiped his hand on the bedspread, rose unsteadily to his feet, staggered toward the bathroom. His hand found the light switch, flicked it up, and he thought he saw something skitter across the tile floor. He stared at the white tub. Along one side, its end tucked into the tub, was a dingy white shower curtain. It concealed half of the tub. Behind it he saw a crouching shadow. Licking his lips, he stepped carefully forward. He was aware of the cool touch of the floor under his bare feet; he heard the ticking of his watch, louder to his ears than ever before; outside a horn sounded; distantly church bells rang the hour. And his breathing filled his ears. He tried to quiet it, so it wouldn't alert the creature.

But it knew he was coming.

And it was hiding.

Then he could hurt it. He didn't have a weapon. Only his hands.

He was past the toilet now. Careful now, careful.

How had it managed to get into his room? He glanced sideways, saw the open window, the torn screen. Somehow it had followed him, found him, then slipped in while he was asleep. It had waited. No, it had been coming out to get him, to kill him, when he had surprised it. He had cornered it in the bathtub.

He frowned. Maybe it wasn't alone? He concentrated on the shower curtain. He saw only one shadow. Maybe the others were waiting outside.

Step carefully. Quietly. His arm rose, his hand reaching out for the curtain. He grasped it, yanked it back, the rings jingling along the rod. And he stared down into the tub.

The bathtub was empty, except for a water stain by the drain.

He could breathe again.

It hadn't been there. Never. Or perhaps it had escaped somehow. No. It had simply been his imagination, fired by his too real nightmare. Breathing deeply, trying to calm the pounding in his chest and ears, he walked over to the sink. He opened on the faucets full blast and splashed water on his face, throat, neck, then took a washcloth and sponged off his chest. As he tossed the washcloth on the glass shelf above the sink, he noticed what looked like red on it. But when he checked, nothing stained the white terry cloth.

Imagination, he told himself.

He grinned at himself in the mirror, and thought he looked terrible. Maybe it was the lighting. All of maybe a 40-watt light bulb. His skin held a grey pallor under it, and there were dark circles under his eyes. His hair was straggling. He combed it with his fingers, pushing back the worst offenders. He'd change clothes, go out for a walk and a dinner somewhere. He'd treat himself, find a halfway decent restaurant, not a cafe, for a change. Order a nice robust meal, not sandwiches, and eat until he'd satisfied his appetite.

That wasn't the only appetite that needed filling. He thought briefly of calling Laura and asking her to join him, but he dismissed it. He wanted to be alone during this meal, and afterward. Alone to think.

Before he switched the light off, he looked once more into the mirror and saw, behind him from the window, Junior's face staring in at him. The old man grinned, showing his stained and broken teeth, and he laughed, a high, wheezing noise.

He whirled.

No one looked in through the window.

Nerves, he told himself.

He'd have a drink at dinner. Maybe two. Or even three. Knock himself out. Sleep a long time. Get up early in the morning and go from there. And try not to dream.

He pulled out a fresh pair of jeans and a cream velour shirt he'd recently bought, then pulled his boots back on. He slipped his wallet in his back pocket and was heading toward the door when someone knocked.

He wasn't expecting anyone, and the only person who knew he was there was Laura. And it was unlikely that she would drop in on him. Not without calling first.

He flattened himself against the wall and tried to peer out the window without moving the curtain, but he couldn't see anyone. Shrugging, he gave up. It was probably the manager or someone visiting who'd come to the wrong room. He pulled the chain off, grasped the knob, opened the door.

The shadow creature stared at him, its yellow eyes glinting from the light of the neon motel sign. He shrieked once, fell back and tried to push the door shut before it could get in. Something thudded against the door, and he was knocked away. The door flew open and the shade slipped across the floor. Its claws ripped into the thin carpet, and it whispered his name.

He tried to rise, but its evil eyes pinned him in place and he was paralyzed. He opened his mouth and screamed and screamed, hoping someone would hear him, but he made no sound. It leaped onto his chest, knocked him onto his back, and his head hit against the floor. With one wide swing of its claws it tore open his new shirt, leaving the soft material in shreds. Talons flexed scant inches above his face, and the creature stared at him. He knew it laughed; it whispered his name again, and as it reached down to gouge out his eyes with its terrible claws, the phone rang.

He raised his head. His cheek was sore from resting on the rough bedspread and one hand was numb from his lying on it.

The phone kept ringing, and rubbing the other hand across his face, he reached over to answer it.

"Hello?" His voice was a little shaky.

"Chato? Laura here. Can we get together sometime tonight?"

"Sure." The sound of her voice brushed away the last fragments of his sleep. "What's up?"

"Nothing really. I just thought we could have dinner together."

"Fine with me. I haven't eaten yet."

"Are you all right? Your voice sounds strange."

"Yeah. I just woke up out of a doubly bad nightmare. The eyes from the mountains." She didn't say anything,

124

but he could hear the unspoken sympathy. "Let me shower and I'll pick you up. Or we can meet, if you like." He didn't want her to think he was putting the make on her. He wanted to, but not right now, not after his near brush with death in his dreams.

"Come get me, if you wouldn't mind the drive. Are you sure you're all right?"

"Yeah. Just fine. I've got a few interesting things to tell you, too. Give me—" he glanced at his watch—"thirty minutes and I'll be there to pick you up."

He jotted her address down on the pad of paper by the phone, and after they hung up, he stared around at the room. Shadows leaned in the corners. Furniture cast dark shadows that stretched toward the bed. Shadows hunkered in the half-opened closet. He ran his hand through his tangled hair. He was afraid to look too closely, afraid of what he might find.

He went into the bathroom, stared for a moment at the shower curtain, then quickly crossed the floor and pulled the curtain back. The tub was bare. He washed up, changed clothes, looked somewhat ruefully at the cream velour shirt in the closet and headed for the door. He reached his pickup without incident.

As he pulled away from the motel, he glanced into the side mirror. A black car eased out into the traffic behind him.

CHAPTER ELEVEN

Her apartment faced Montgomery, where so many apartment complexes had sprung up in the mid-70s'. The eastern United States had experienced the gasoline shortage and a series of extremely harsh winters; Albuquerque experienced an influx of cold and disillusioned Easterners, and the apartments, usually high-priced and shoddily built, became the answer to the housing boom. The complex was huge, and he drove around for a few minutes, easing over the unpainted speed bumps until he found the right building. Her apartment was on the second floor, and when he knocked twice, she promptly answered the door.

Laura's home consisted of an entryway, a pullman kitchen, a living room, and a bath between two bedrooms. She was a little nervous, he noticed, as she politely showed him around. She wasn't a collector and didn't have many knickknacks standing around. A few posters, of the Santa Fe Opera and art galleries in Taos, adorned the walls in the living room and one bedroom. Otherwise the white walls were left bare. Her bathroom counter was orderly; no nylons adorned the shower rod. He had to admit the furnishings were in perfect taste, but somehow it left something to be desired. He couldn't live here. It was too perfect, too well-kept, and it was almost as if she'd decorated the place after seeing a photo in a magazine.

The second bedroom contained two large, unfinished bookcases, a small student desk, a black metal typewriter stand with an IBM typewriter on it, a four-drawer filing cabinet. On the walls he noted her diploma from the University and several certificates of merit for reporting. The desk was not as orderly as he'd expected, with papers scattered across the top, books piled here and there, and pencils and pens and erasers within easy reach.

"Writing a novel?" he asked, looking with interest at the one stack of orderly papers.

She shook her head, her hair fanning out. "No. Journalism essays. I'd like to do a column sometime. So I'm trying my hand at some freelance assignments." She brushed a hand against a typed paper. "It's difficult, though, to come home after work at the paper and try to write."

"Maybe you should take up stamp collecting instead."

She shot him a strange look, as if puzzled by his attempt at humor. She was so serious, and he was uncomfortable with that. He liked Laura. He really did. But. . . . That intangible "but" stayed in his mind.

Once they were back in the entry hall, he helped her on with her light jacket, then paused with his hand on the doorknob.

"I think I'm being followed now."

"What?' she asked sharply.

"This black Buick's been on my tail since I left the motel. Can't be a coincidence."

"What are you going to do?"

He shrugged. "What can I do? Just go on as I had been."

"How did they find you?"

"Probably through the Sheriff's Department. I had to let the cops know where I was staying." He shrugged, and they left.

As they drove up Montgomery he checked for the black Buick. But it was hard to see in the darkness with all the lights, and he couldn't tell.

They decided to get dinner at Carrow's, an all-night restaurant that served fairly complete meals for little money. It was just a few blocks east of her apartment. They didn't talk much while they ate, he steadily attacking a plate of huevos rancheros. He watched her closely as he mopped up the chili with a torn bit of flour tortilla. She kept her eyes down, concentrating wholly on her meal. She tended to nibble a little, then pushed her food around with a fork. When they were finished, after the waitress had taken their plates and they were sipping coffee and Laura had lit a cigarette, he leaned back in the booth.

"I've got a little more information." He nodded to the waitress when she came by with a coffee pot. He watched her pour more coffee. "You want to hear it?"

"Sure." She pushed back a strand of hair from her eyes, sipped her coffee.

He glanced out the window and thought he saw a black Buick turn into the parking lot.

"I called the San Carlos Retreat in the Sandias, then the Archbishop's office. Both were remarkably tight-lipped about that priest's death. Sheriff Daltry, I was informed by one of his colleagues, had just gone on vacation, and no one seems to know when he'll be back. Also the anthropologist just went out into the field. Damned odd timing, I think.''

He signalled the waitress. As he was talking, he watched the door of the restaurant. A couple, laughing and kissing, entered, then five teen-age boys in El Dorado High School letter jackets, an old man with a brown cane, two women in shorts and halter tops, a middle-aged man in a plaid shirt and dirty jeans.

Was one of these the occupant of the mysterious car? He studied them. But beyond a few cursory looks, except for the two young women who grinned at him, no one seemed interested in him.

Maybe the driver was here—he couldn't tell—or maybe the driver was waiting outside for him. And what then? Would the car's engine be turned on, and would the driver try to run him down? Or would it simply slide into the lane behind his pickup and follow him?

It would follow, he thought. Nothing more sinister than that.

They sipped their coffee in silence for a few minutes; then Laura looked up. She frowned a little, her brows drawing together, then pushed her hair back. For the first time he noticed her ears were pierced and she wore tiny diamond studs.

Fancy. And he began to suspect she might well be out of his league.

"It just doesn't make sense," she said. "I mean, I don't know where all of this is headed."

"You and me both, sister," he said. And regretted the words as soon as they were out. This wasn't a woman he could joke with. "Look, Laura, it's not going to proceed nice and neat. I guess we just play it by ear. I hope neither of us proves to be tone-deaf," he added in an undertone.

He stood, slapped down a tip and then briskly walked to the cash register.

Outside the warm night air smelled of cars and dust. Across the street the Los Altos Twin Theatre was just letting out, and half a dozen teen-agers stood around laughing about the newest Burt Reynolds comedy they'd just seen.

Laughing, he thought, when there's been so much death. But they didn't know, didn't understand. He shivered as a cool breeze touched the back of his neck, forced the suggestion of the whisper from his mind.

"What now, Laura?"

Her voice was deceptively calm. "Oh, I didn't have anything really planned. I just thought we could talk some more. You know. Maybe have some drinks."

He grinned. Yeah. He knew.

"But what about—"

With a sharp gesture of his hand the tall man cautioned the other to silence, and the three men waited until Maria, the serving woman, set the glasses and decanter in front of them and left the room. She didn't speak English, but it was good policy not to discuss too much in front of the servants.

Senator Robinson Kent smiled amiably at his two guests. Across from him sat Douglas Griffen, Mayor of Albuquerque, and Richard de Vargas, Archbishop of Santa Fe. They sat in the den of his retreat, on the back road to Santa Fe, behind the Sandias. The house was a traditional adobe with vigas and an interior courtyard. Colorful Navajo blankets decorated the whitewashed walls and brick floors. The furniture was Spanish colonial, dark and heavily made and expensive by all accounts, and on a table not far from the fireplace sat a fetish.

Kent tossed a piñon log on the fire and watched as the sparks flared up. He turned around to the others and eased his long frame down into a comfortable chair not far from the fire.

"Now, what were you saying, Doug?"

"But what are we going to do about this Yellow Colt character? He'll be there Friday when you *officially* arrive."

Kent smiled his politician's smile, the smile that had won him many votes in the last election. He had arrived just a few hours ago from Denver, where he had been attending a Western States' Governors' Conference. He'd landed his Lear jet on the private airstrip in back of the house, and as soon as this clandestine meeting was finished, he would be getting back into the jet to return to Denver and in two days time would be publicly arriving at the Alburquerque airport, and no one would be the wiser for his quick trip back here.

"Sure, he'll be there. I expect that, Doug. He's been making noise for a long time, but that's all it is—noise. When was the last time anyone listened to him?"

He took a long swallow of his bourbon and water.

"I don't know," de Vargas said doubtfully in his soft voice. He toyed with the ice in his drink. "This time he could do more than make noise. I don't trust him. And then there's that other Indian as well, the one I'm having watched."

Kent chuckled. "You worry too much. From all you've told me he's a nobody, a bum who can't make up his mind whether he wants to hide on the reservation, teach, or drink himself blind like the rest of those Indians."

Griffen glanced over at the fetish on the table. "It's just that we've come so far. . . ."

Kent followed his gaze. "And we'll be going farther, Doug, I guarantee it. Fifteen years hasn't been all that long to wait, considering the rewards. Everything," he said with a glance to de Vargas, "except for that damned priest, has gone just right. We can't lose now. Nothing can go wrong. In two days time you give me that—" he nodded toward the fetish—"and I'll smile and thank you from the bottom of the taxpayer's heart, and I'll take it back to Washington and give it to the Smithsonian and make New Mexico look like a real good guy.

"And then—" he paused to take a sip of his bourbon, and his eyes strayed back to the fetish—"my friend at the museum will see to it that it quietly disappears one night. And after that, my friends . . . well, after that we have nothing to worry about. *It* will give me the power to do whatever the hell I want, and, gentlemen, when it puts me in the White House, whatever I want is . . . whatever I want."

Griffen squirmed at the dark look on Kent's face, and Kent caught him.

"You afraid?"

Griffen shook his head, too fast.

Kent laughed without mirth. "Doug, you have no ambition, you know that? All you want is to be governor of this sandhole and rake in the loot as fast as you can open your pockets. Well, *it* and I are going to give you that, you know it, and you'd better get used to it."

When there was no contradiction, the smile broaded and he raised his glass. "A toast, gentlemen, to power even the damned Russians will wish they'd never seen."

Griffen drank deeply, refilled his glass and drank again,

ignoring the looks the other two gave him. Courage was what he was after, and when he'd found it, he shook his head. "That damned priest. He could have spoiled everything."

"Father Lopez has been taken care of," de Vargas said with a slight twist of his lips.

"Indeed," said the senator, "indeed." He leaned over and took the heavy iron poker in his hand and jabbed at a log that had fallen off the others. He chuckled again. "I understand that the monastery he's been sent to discourages talking."

"Yes, and they believe in heavy penance. I think he'll do well there."

Griffen glanced over at the fetish, dark and squat, and shuddered.

They would use it for their purposes, but that didn't mean he liked the thing. It was ugly . . . and alien, the creation of a mind he neither tried nor wanted, ever, to understand. Fifteen years ago they'd made the discovery, and for fifteen years they had lived with the knowledge of the thing's existence, and even after that time, it still made him uneasy, fearful. Rob laughed at his fears; he couldn't.

Of course, it had been Rob who'd first discovered that the thing contained some sort of power. Kent had been working on a law case and had to talk to an archeology professor at the University. The professor had been sorting through various objects found at some half-forgotten pueblo. While the man was out of the room, Kent had examined the fetish and had accidentally dropped it. Nothing had happened—it hadn't even chipped. Intrigued, he'd slipped it into his pocket. The professor had never noticed, and he'd left.

That night he showed the statuette to his two friends. He

told them what had happened earlier in the day, and then he'd gone out to his kitchen to get a hammer. He battered at the thing for almost an hour. And still it remained unscarred.

It's special, he had said, his hands cupping the black stone, and he'd stared, awed by it. De Vargas had nodded, saying he knew many Indians still believed in the powers of fetishes, but Griffen had said nothing. Those old Indian religions had long ago gone the way of the buffalo, he thought. The fetish didn't mean a damned thing, and didn't contain one bit of power. It was just stone.

But you're wrong, Rob had said, as though reading Griffen's thoughts. It does have the power, and he had held it out to Griffen, who had taken it reluctantly. And then he knew. Ice-cold pricklings had shot through his hands and his arm to his chest, and his hands had begun to sweat, and he could scarcely breathe, and even as he held the damned thing, he could feel it pulsing through him. *The power*. The raw, untapped power of the fetish. Panicked, he'd flung the stone at Rob, who'd deftly caught it with one hand and who'd laughed at his friend's dismay.

That night they had begun to make their long-range plans. The fetish had been given into the hands of their priest friend for safekeeping. And it had gone with de Vargas as he climbed up the ecclesiastical ladder to his present position. But then the damned priest, one of de Vargas' many assistants, had found the fetish in its box, and had gone to the press and made the stone public. Thinking quickly, de Vargas had announced that he'd uncovered the fetish in one of his trips to Albuquerque and that he planned to present it to Mayor Griffen, and Griffen had said he planned to give it to their senator for the nation.

135

CHAPTER TWELVE

It was inevitable, he thought as he watched the sleeping woman, that it would lead to this. After they'd left Carrow's, they'd driven to a market where she'd bought some eggs and cheese and milk and some vegetables, and then they'd come back to the apartment. She had invited him in; they'd had a few snacks and some drinks, talked, kissed a little, and somehow—he wasn't particularly clear on the method, but wasn't particularly surprised either—they'd ended up in her bedroom.

There she'd gone all shy on him and had looked away. He'd walked over to her, placed his hands on her shoulders and gently pushed her down until she was sitting on the blue bedspread. Carefully he'd undressed her, slowly unbuttoning her blouse, allowing his fingers to trace the smoothness of her chest above the line of the bra. She'd arched her back and, impatiently grabbing his hand, moved it to the snaps in the back. He'd chuckled, had undone the snaps and taken her breasts in his hands. He'd kissed each one, caressing the warmth of the nipples with his tongue, and she had moaned and lain back on the bed.

She had watched as he unbuttoned his shirt, pulled off his boots and pants. He had stretched out next to her, kissed her mouth even as he ran his hands down her stomach. She made love as precisely as she spoke—capably, but without fireworks. Later they had talked, until her eyelids had dropped and she'd fallen asleep. His head propped on his hand, he studied her face in the dim light coming through the drapes, then concentrated on the dark spot of a picture on the wall.

His thoughts were mixed—of her, of the creatures he'd seen in the mountains, of the black car. He thought he heard a noise, and for a moment thought of the shadows. He cocked his head and listened. Nothing now. His attention was drawn away when she stirred, stretched and yawned.

"Did I sleep? I'm sorry."

"It's okay. You've obviously had a long day."

"I haven't been a very good hostess."

"You've been just fine." He dropped his head, kissed her shoulder, brushed its softness with his lips.

"I've never made love to an Indian before."

"Neither have I."

"You're joking!"

"A little. Just a little." Because of the closeness in the tribe, he'd avoided entanglements with the Apache girls he knew. His libido had been almost completely centered on the white girls, who'd thrown themselves at him while he was a University student, and later, when he was a professor.

"What do we do now?" she asked.

He shrugged, then realized she probably couldn't see the gesture. "Don't know. We've got to find Junior sometime.

Somehow. I need to talk to him. Everything began to happen after I picked him up.'' He was quiet for a moment, then: ''What about I call you at work early in the morning?''

''Fine.''

She slipped her arm around his neck and pulled his face down to hers. They kissed long, open-mouthed, and he brushed a hand across her breasts, stroking her already aroused nipples. He bent down to her breast, then straightened abruptly.

''Kent,'' he said.

''What?'' Her hand on his buttocks dropped.

''You mentioned doing a story on Kent's visit. Why's he coming here? Just to make lots of political brownie points at the Balloon Fiesta?''

''Oh no.'' He knew she was regarding him oddly in the darkness. ''You have been out of touch, haven't you?''

''Yeah. Never was much interested in politics anyway.''

''Oh.''

Strange, he knew, for her as a journalist to comprehend.

''Friday evening the Mayor is having a gala affair, as they say on the society page, where he will present our junior Senator with an Indian relic, which the good Senator in turn plans to present, with all good intentions I assure you, to the Smithsonian.''

''Grave-robbing, eh?''

''That's what Yellow Colt said, too. But it's an old one, Chato. I mean it's been out of the ground for a long time, so there's no claim on it.''

Obviously she didn't see it the same way he did. It didn't matter much to her to see artifacts belonging to New Mexico Indians removed from the state. What had happened to her veneer of liberalism?

139

"What sort of relic is it? The bones of someone's great-grandfather?"

"Don't be sarcastic. No. Just some kind of a stone figure. I can't remember what animal it represents."

A fetish, he thought, and recalled all the whites from out of state who'd grinned at the word, aware only of the usual English meaning. In the Southwest a fetish was a representation of an animal, a bird, bear, turtle, in stone, turquoise, bone, ivory. Sometimes they were hung on thongs around the neck; others were made into necklaces or earrings. Fetish necklaces were particularly popular, he knew, among white women, and he recalled one of his geology students, who'd come to his class, her sweatered chest almost entirely covered with necklace after necklace of coral and turquoise and shell fetishes.

Generally the Pueblo Indians made them, and they were thought to ward off evil spirits or witches.

To ward off—

Touched.

And he knew then they were not alone in the apartment. He had heard a sound earlier, had ignored it, and now, and now— He leaped from the bed.

"Chato!"

He ran into the living room, flipped on the light switch and saw the curtains blowing in through the open sliding glass doors. Cautiously he stepped out onto the balcony, stared down at the wide expense of lawn behind the apartment building, and saw something, in the lights from the swimming pool, slip past a lawn chair.

Something dark.

Touched.

Something touched his elbow.

He whirled, startled.

"What's the matter?" she whispered.

He turned back to stare down at the lawn. After a moment he realized they were both nude and standing on her balcony.

"Let's get inside before we get arrested for indecent exposure."

Once back in the living room, with the doors firmly locked—*again*, he thought—and themselves dressed, they sat down to hot coffee and some frozen doughnuts she'd popped into the oven.

"You did lock the backdoor earlier?" His hands were spread around the cup, as if he could warm himself that way. He needed it; all the warmth had been sucked out of his body and he was bone-cold. He heard the whispering voices in his head, and he didn't know if he was remembering them or actually hearing them now. He shook his head, trying to clear it.

"Of course. I always do. It's second nature for me. You know how traditionally paranoid women living alone are. Why?" She frowned, bit into a sugary doughnut and waited for him to speak.

"Someone got in."

"Oh God." She dropped the uneaten part of her doughnut on the plate. "How?"

He shook his head, trailed a finger through the crumbs of his doughnut. "I don't know. I didn't hear anyone break in, and I never did fall asleep. Maybe it was just your average garden-variety apartment thief."

"But how did he get the doors open?"

"That's simple enough for someone experienced at that sort of thing."

It also made a hell of a lot more noise than he'd heard. He frowned suddenly. Maybe there had been more noise than he'd thought. What if he'd drifted off without realizing it and had only heard the slight noise when he was once more awake. A good explanation. Only he didn't buy it.

C'mon, Chato, you know it wasn't human. You're just putting off your conclusion; you don't want to admit what you saw.

What he saw.

A shadow.

And it had been in the apartment with them.

CHAPTER THIRTEEN

"Says here that the cops shot the bear that's been killing people." He looked at her over the top of the newspaper.

"Right." She sipped her coffee and nibbled at her toast.

"It says so in black and white." His laugh was bitter. He finished the last of his eggs. "I have something for you to consider."

She raised her eyebrows.

"What do you say to writing an article about what I saw in the mountains? You could interview those kids at the school as well. If the newspaper ran that, maybe it'd shake the damned politicians out of their complacency." He waited while she considered.

"You might be right. I have some meetings to cover today, but when I'm finished with them, I could start on the article."

For the first time that morning he saw some animation light her face. In fact, he had to admit that she looked more alive now than she had the night before when they'd made love. Oh well, he thought wryly, we can't all be Don Juans.

They parted ways, and outside he breathed deeply. It was already warm this morning, even though it wasn't yet ten. He could see one balloon hanging over the Rio Grande valley, and that reminded him again that the Balloon Fiesta was only a few days off. He rolled the windows down on the truck, sat for a few minutes with the engine off. So, he was going to look for Junior, eh? Where? He watched a grey cat stroll across the sidewalk.

Central, as he'd said to Laura. And if he struck out there, well, there was a long list of bars in the phone book. Providing the old man haunted the bars.

He started the truck, backed up and pulled out onto Montgomery. He glanced into the rearview mirror and froze when he saw it.

The black Buick.

He stopped at a traffic light and it drew up behind him. He tried to see the driver, but the glare of sunlight on the glass of the windshield prevented that.

Had the driver stayed all night and waited for him to appear? He was damned tired of being followed. The shadow creatures and now this car. What had he done to deserve all this attention?

He drove east on Montgomery, toward the mountains, then turned onto Juan Tabo. Then he took a right onto Menual, speeded up for a mile or more, pulled into the right lane, then back into the middle lane just in time to dodge a parked car in front of Ho La Ma Restaurant, before turning down Louisiana Boulevard. He drove until he got to Osuna, took a left down to San Mateo, then a left again.

Still the black car followed him, neither losing him nor gaining on him.

He speeded up, the accelerator hitting 60. He cut in and out of lanes, nearly sideswiping a pickup filled with bales of hay. He took the corner onto Montgomery wide, tires squealing, and he glanced anxiously around for patrol cars. Saw none.

Then he pushed the pedal down hard and hit seventy. Looked in the mirror again. Still no cops.

He pulled into the parking lot at Laura's apartment, jumped out of the cab and ran to the street just as the black Buick started to pull off the street. He ran toward it and had just reached the handle of the door on the passenger's side when the driver realized what Chato was doing.

The car slammed into reverse. Chato hung on to the handle as he was dragged backward. He managed to keep his fingers curled around the handle, and when the driver saw he was still there, the car was shunted into first. It shot forward as the driver floored the gas pedal. Chato felt as though his arm were being ripped from the shoulder socket. His feet were knocked out from under him, and then the car was pulling him along on his knees. He could feel the pavement shredding the denim of his jeans, and he looked up just in time to see a speed bump rushing toward him.

He let go, and tumbled backward, landing sprawled across the pavement. He rose slowly to his feet, unsteady from what had happened. The Buick stopped, backed up. It was coming straight for him. He dropped and rolled under a parked Chevrolet. The Buick slammed into the '57 Chevy. The car above him shuddered once, then twice when the Buick hit it again. He didn't move. Prayed, too, that the Chevy didn't spring a leak in the gas line.

Apparently the Buick driver was frustrated that he couldn't flush Chato out. After a moment of its engines being

145

gunned, the car shot away and he watched as it eased out onto Montgomery. From his position on his stomach he could see it cruise slowly by. He waited, knowing it wouldn't leave soon. Minutes passed. The grey cat he had seen earlier peeked at him under the bumper and hissed, its back arched.

"Don't blame you at all, kitty," he whispered. "I'd be pretty wary, too." He knew he must look a mess. His hair had come loose, and damp with sweat, it was plastered across his face, down his neck. His jeans were torn, his knees bloody, and his shirt, face and hands were covered with dirt and grease from the pavement.

The Buick drove by again.

He chuckled softly to himself. He'd wait until he thought it was turning around down the street, then run like hell to the pickup. He waited for the Buick to pass, and as soon as it was out of sight, he rolled out from under the Chevy, jumped to his feet, smiled briefly at a startled woman who was walking toward the car, keys in hand, and ran for the truck.

Crawling into the cab, he crouched down on the floor.

When he thought it was safe, he looked out the back window. The owner of the Chevy was staring at him, and the black Buick was driving past again.

When it was gone, he slid behind the wheel, started the engine up, and instead of driving out onto the street, he went farther back into the complex. An alleyway led to another apartment complex, and that in turn led to a side street in a residential area. He reached that street, and there was no sign of the Buick.

Probably the driver thought he'd left by Montgomery. Good.

He glanced at himself in the mirror, wrinkled his nose at what he saw.

Time to get back to the motel, shower and change. Time to do some thinking before he went looking for Junior.

Do some thinking about the driver.

He had seen the man behind the wheel of the Buick, despite the efforts of the driver to keep him from seeing anything.

Yeah, he'd seen him all right. Seen him, his dark suit—and the white Roman collar.

CHAPTER FOURTEEN

She paused, her fingers curled over the typewriter keys, and reread what she'd just typed. She started typing again, finished that page, started another.

When she had a stack of nearly twenty pages, she finally picked up a pen and began going through the text, correcting the typos. There weren't many this time. She read quickly, thoroughly, pleased with her words.

She wanted it to be effective, hard-hitting, moving. And when it was published in the *Courier*, well, then no one—not the Mayor himself—could deny what had been happening.

In her article Laura detailed the murders in the mountains as well, describing the similarities between them. She told about the priest, the campers, the low-riders; she wrote about what Chato and the kids had seen.

All the grisly deaths. All the strangeness—creatures included.

She retyped one page with a few typos on it, then

straightened the sheets. She crossed the large city room, made copies of the article, returned to her desk. She glanced at the clock.

10:45.

There wasn't another person in the room, and the only sound was the click of the teletype at the other end. She put her copy of the article in her desk, closed the drawer and picked up the original and her purse, which she slung over her shoulder.

She'd drop the article in Bob's basket, then be on her way home.

She'd have liked to have talked with him about it, but he wouldn't be in for a few hours and she really wanted to go home and sleep. Sleep, nothing more. Didn't want Chato to come over. Didn't want to sleep with him. Didn't want him around.

She wanted to be by herself.

She walked past the rows of desks, opened the door to Bob's office and dropped the article, its pages stapled together, into his basket. She started to leave, then hesitated and returned to take a slip of paper and write a note to him. She told him she'd get in touch with him early that morning. After she'd paper-clipped the note to the article, she left, closing the door behind her.

Chato hadn't called, and she wondered why as earlier he'd said he would. Maybe he'd found out something about the old man. Maybe he'd forgotten. Maybe he'd just said that.

She didn't know why she wanted to stay away from him tonight. But she did. It was enough, she thought, that she had written about his experiences in the mountains. She'd given him that much, after all. Tit for tat. Payment for last night.

She slowly walked down the stairway of the building that the *Courier* shared with the two other Albuquerque dailies. Her footsteps echoed in the stairwell, and above her a door opened and someone walked out onto the landing. She continued descending, deep in her thoughts.

Why did he make her so uncomfortable?

Because he was Indian?

Maybe. Maybe not. There was more maybe than maybe not, she suspected. But why should that particularly bother her? She wasn't a racist. So what was it?

He'd been a good lover, too; it hadn't been a bad experience for her. No, he'd been thoughtful and kind and always considerate.

Yet . . .

Yet what, Laura? she demanded of herself.

It was, she decided at length, because he was a man obsessed. Obsessed about this mountain thing. He had to know all the time what was going on, had to talk about it all the time, wanted to find out everything about it. She knew he didn't understand why she wasn't wholeheartedly pursuing it. She had other articles to write, other stories to cover. She was intrigued by the murders; she wanted the killer to be caught, but it wasn't her story.

He didn't understand.

She was afraid.

Afraid of those shadows he'd mentioned, afraid now that she had talked with the little girl about them that the shadows did exist. At first, when he'd told her about his experiences in the mountains, she'd thought he might just be a gentle crackpot. But going to the school had changed that. It had become reality.

She should report it. She should dog the story, demand of the Mayor to know what was going on and why he claimed that it was a bear that killed those people. She knew all this. Just as much as she knew she wouldn't do it.

To find out too much would lead to harm. It was a good way of getting hurt, just as getting to know Chato too well would end in pain. It always did. This time would be no different. Cut him loose, she thought, before it's too late.

The footsteps behind and above her quickened, and she glanced up into the shadows. And saw nothing.

Maybe it was her imagination. No, probably it was one of the night shift people from one of the other papers. But why didn't they use the elevator? For that matter, why didn't she?

She needed the exercise, and maybe the other person did too, she thought with a quick smile.

When she reached the ground floor, she pushed through the door, crossed the lobby. It wasn't large, not like the ones in New York, and soon she was out on Silver. She looked up and down the street, so quiet at this time of night, and breathed deeply. The coolness of the night air cut into her lungs, but she didn't mind it. In fact, it felt good after the stuffy confines of the news room upstairs. Her car was parked in the lot behind the building, set aside for the papers' employees. She started walking toward it.

As she reached the corner, she heard the footsteps behind her. She stopped, glanced back, saw nothing.

She was letting things get on her nerves, she told herself. Chato was making her nervous. Made her jump at shadows. Made her afraid.

And she resented that. She was strong and determined, and had never been afraid of the dark. But he was doing his best to subvert that.

Leave it to a man, she thought irritably. They were

never happy with an independent woman, always wanted the "girls" to run to them to be protected. Well, she wasn't about to do that.

Something moving caught her attention out of the tail of her eye, and her breath caught in her chest. The top of a trash can clattered to the pavement, and a plaintive meow sounded.

A cat.

That was all.

She laughed aloud, nervously, shifted the shoulder strap of her purse.

She was getting as bad as Chato. He was superstitious, and now he was trying to make her the same. Well, it wasn't working. Nope. She had better things to do with her time, and that wasn't one of them.

The footsteps continued behind her, and she quickened her pace.

She could see her car, a late model Datsun, straight ahead. It was parked under a street lamp, sitting in an arc of light.

A few blocks away a car's horn honked, and she heard the rumble of a truck. Music drifted faintly down the street from a radio, but she realized she was the only one out. No one else was in sight.

Only her . . . and the owner of the footsteps.

Tomorrow Senator Robinson Kent would arrive at the Albuquerque International Airport. In the afternoon there was to be a cocktail party, and in the evening a barbecue, in his honor. She'd managed to wrangle an invitation to the barbecue, and she intended to get close to the senator and ask him some questions. Kent planned to hold a press conference when he arrived, and he would speaking about the gift to the Smithsonian.

The Indians.

Oh my God. She could have groaned aloud.

She had totally forgotten about Yellow Colt and his group. They would be there, no doubt, protesting to the top of their lungs about Kent removing something that belonged to them. Incredible. They'd never owned that rock; neither had their ancestors. They were so quick to pick a fight, even over a bit of inconsequential rock now.

But worse—she had dropped the ball. She should have kept in touch with Yellow Colt. Was it too late to call him? She checked her watch. After eleven. She didn't think he'd be going to bed early. She could always drop by the Hilton. It wasn't all that far away.

Or maybe she should go back to the office now and call him. She turned. The footsteps stopped.

"Hello. Is anyone there?"

Her voice showed her nervousness. After all, in the past few weeks there'd been several rapes in the downtown and University areas. She secured her car keys between her fingers, waited for someone to answer. She peered back into the darkness. Saw no one.

She would keep going to the car, drive over to the Hilton, try to talk with Yellow Colt. And tomorrow she'd attend the press conference and the barbecue.

And tomorrow there'd be Chato.

And tomorrow she would worry about him.

She quickly unlocked the car door, glancing over her shoulder from time to time as she did so, aware that since she'd spoken aloud the footsteps had not resumed.

Maybe she had scared whoever it was off.

Maybe they were waiting . . .

She slid into the seat, hit the lock with the heel of her hand. She looked out toward the building, still saw nothing.

Something scratched along the side of her car.

She shrieked. Fumbling with her keys, she pushed them into the ignition. The car rumbled to a start.

The scratching continued.

It was on her side. Just below the level of the window. On her side. So close to her. Just a matter of a few inches of steel, not even that. Between her and . . . it.

The car's engine fluttered and died, and her breath caught. She flipped the ignition on again, threw the car into reverse. She had to get out of here. Had to get away from whatever it was that had stalked her, whatever it was that was scratching her car.

The Datsun roared backward, and she glanced at the spot where the car had been sitting.

Nothing.

What if the thing were stuck to her car?

She shuddered. Glanced at all the windows. They were, thank God, rolled up. It could have been summer; she could have left the windows down as she normally did.

She shuddered again.

The scratching began again, still on her side.

She wanted to see what it was. She wanted to lean her head against the cool glass, stare down and see. See it. And see it staring up at her. No.

She put the car into first gear, then threw it into reverse. She kept doing this, hoping the creature would fall off. How was it hanging on? The sides of the car were smooth. There was nothing for it to cling to.

The car rocked back and forth, and then she listened for a moment. She couldn't hear the terrible scratching sound.

She was breathing hard, her mouth open to get more air, and she was so hot, so suffocatingly hot in the closed car. She wanted to open the window, but didn't dare. Instead she opened the vent. Air, not much cooler than that already in the car, flooded in.

The scratching was gone.

Breathing more easily now, she shifted back into first and directed the car out of the lot. She glanced back at the parking lot. And frowned.

She could see nothing on the asphalt.

Puzzled, she turned her head.

And looked into yellow eyes staring at her through the glass.

She shrieked again, jerked the wheel to one side, and went to shove her foot on the brake. Instead she hit the accelerator and the car shot forward. The eyes still stared, unblinking at her, and she threw the car to one side, trying to dislodge the creature. The steering wheel slid out of her hands, spun, and too late she saw the parked truck.

The Datsun slammed into the larger vehicle, the awful sound of metal scraping along metal rasping in her ears. She was thrown forward, her forehead smacking against the steering wheel, and before she sank into the blackness, she had the satisfaction of knowing that at least the creature had been crushed between the car and truck. She smiled. Fainted.

And the unblinking yellow eyes continued to stare in at her.

CHAPTER FIFTEEN

The road was dark, unlit, and he jounced along on the pickup's seat. A tree loomed in the beam of the headlights as the lane curved. He glanced up at the black sky, where no moon was tonight. On the dashboard the luminous hands pointed to five before midnight.

Earlier he'd called Laura at the newspaper, but the first time there'd been no answer. The second time some man had answered, snapped a quick no to his inquiry, and slammed the phone down before he could leave a message. The third time no one answered. She wasn't home either. She could be anywhere. She didn't have to check in with him.

His day hadn't been very successful. He hadn't found Junior, hadn't found anyone who knew the old guy, and he was beginning to think Junior might well be a figment of his mind.

Dreamer of dreams.

He had gone back to his hotel and taken a nap, had

awakened after dusk from an uneasy sleep filled with odd dreams. Dreams that left him uncomfortable even now that he was awake. He felt a little lost tonight, and didn't know what to do now that he couldn't reach her.

Just knew he had to do something quickly, quickly before the shadow creatures caught up with him, before the car and whoever had sent it caught up with him.

Tenorio. From Isleta. He had to see the old man again. Tonight. Had to talk with him.

Now he pressed the accelerator down, watched the needle creep up to fifty, past fifty-five. Faster. He had to get out there quickly. Had to find the old man and talk with him. He glanced back over his shoulder, as though he expected to see the shadow creatures or the black Buick, but there was nothing behind him but night. He'd managed to elude his tail, for the car had been gone when he'd come out of the motel. Now he rolled the window down, coughed a little in the dusty air, and kept driving. He might as well be on another planet, for all the strange shapes that loomed out of the darkness as he swept past. There were no sounds either, except that of the truck's engines and its tires on the dirt.

Alone. He was alone except for—

A figure stepped off the shoulder onto the dirt lane, directly in the path of the truck. He slammed on the brakes and the truck fishtailed as he sought to control it. Finally he straightened it, and when he'd thrown on the handbrake, he jumped out of the cab.

The figure still hadn't moved from the center of the road.

"I knew you would come, dreamer of dreams."

It was Fedelino Tenorio.

"Goddamn, old man, I could have killed you!"

"You would not have."

Tenorio stood still, didn't come closer.

He felt a prickling along the back of his neck. Nerves; he dismissed it. Chato came around to the front of the truck and studied the old man in the beam of the headlights. He had on a sweater against the coolness of the night. Otherwise he looked the same as the other day when Chato had gone to see him.

"Turn out the lights."

For some reason he couldn't determine, he found himself obeying. Maybe it was because for many years he had been told how wise old people were, how they were to be obeyed in all things, listened to and revered. Maybe there was something more in the old man's voice. Something that made him want to obey.

When it was dark all around him, the old man beckoned to him. He could just make him out faintly, still standing in the middle of the road. He walked up, until he was just a few feet away.

"Look, my son. Look into the sky."

He threw his head back and stared up into the blackness. Here, so far from the city and lights, the stars shone brighter. Cold and distant, though. Red and white, gold and blue.

Minutes passed as he stared up at the stars. "What am I looking for, old man?"

"See the vastness; know that you are touched. I am an old man. I am a believer in the old ways. You ask yourself, what can this old man know? I do not know books as you do. But I know myself. I tell you again, you must believe in the old ways. You must hunt for the end in the past. You must."

A cold breeze, slight and slow, had sprung up, bringing

159

with it the soft fragrance of the night flowers. He stamped his feet, blew on his hands and rubbed them together.

"You keep saying that."

"Yes."

"I can't . . . that is, to believe in the old ways, to accept the superstitions—"

"White men call them such."

"But ghosts—and witches. I. . . ." His voice trailed off and he felt the darkness close around him.

"And the evileyes. What is the explanation for that? What does science tell you? Are they animals? What animal has that cunning, that viciousness? Only one? Man. And it is not Man who does this. You know that. It is the evileyes. The shadoweyes."

Shadoweyes.

He could feel the hairs along his neck prickle, and he felt as though he were being watched. Suddenly he wanted to get out of there and return to his warm hotel room.

The past tugged at him, flooded him with memories of Josanie and their many hours together.

"Know that even now they are meeting, that they seek the power, that power which is to be yours, that power which only you can control." Chato said nothing, trembled as though chilled. "You have much to do, and little time in which to do it. First you must find a medicine pouch, which will carry all those things which you need to—" And for a moment he could not tell who was talking. Josanie or Tenorio.

"A medicine pouch? I'd be laughed out of the first store I went into."

The Pueblo Indian remained silent; uneasiness mantled Chato. He shifted position, stuck his hands in his pockets, cleared his throat.

"I am finished. Go back to your motel. Go back and be killed."

That last chilled him more than the night breeze.

"You know damn well I don't want to be killed."

"I do not know it. I see a man who sees the answer before him—in him—and yet will not see it. I can say no more to you. I can do no more. I have warned you. I have tried to help. That is all I can do."

He hobbled away slowly.

"Come back, Tenorio."

The old man continued on his way.

Something flapped its wings overhead; flinching, he looked up.

An owl, he guessed, even though he saw nothing now.

He stood there for a few minutes more, scanning the darkness, trying to see Tenorio, but he couldn't. Maybe he should go after the old man.

No. He remembered too well the lightning in the mountains.

He got back into the truck and turned on the headlights; he saw nothing but the empty land. Did I dream the meeting? he asked himself on his return to Albuquerque. Dreamer of dreams, the old man had called him again.

"How does he know?" Chato cried aloud, and only the noise of traffic answered him.

He knows as I knew to go to him.

He shivered, and pulled into the parking lot of the motel. And when he walked into the room, the light on his phone was on. He called the operator and found someone had left a message.

Laura wanted him to call her.

She was in Presbyterian Hospital.

*   *   *

She wasn't badly hurt—a few bruises, mostly on her forehead—and he took her home and stayed with her the night. In the morning, on their way to the airport to meet Senator Kent's airplane, he told her what had happened to him. She said only that she was in an accident.

She'd picked up a newspaper as they were leaving the apartment complex, and she was glancing through it now. For a long time she didn't say a word, then finally: "It's not here."

"Your article?"

"Yes. The one I worked on last night. I don't understand."

"Maybe they didn't have enough space. Or maybe it's been slotted for a later edition."

"No. I know Bob would have put it in this edition. That's very strange."

"Call him when we get to the airport."

"I will, if we have time."

He didn't pay much attention to the posted speeds, but kept an eye on the rearview mirror for flashing red lights. He didn't have to worry, though, for they arrived with minutes to spare.

The day was already hot, the sky clear and blue. There were no signs of clouds yet. To the east he saw a faint grey, like rain clouds, approaching the mountains. He hoped they'd hit the city with a cooling rain. It certainly needed the moisture.

He thought he saw something dark move under one of the cars in the parking lot, but when he passed the car, he saw nothing.

Imagination. It was getting away from him. Old Tenorio was certainly spooking him. And probably enjoying it one hell of a lot.

162

Once inside the main building, they checked the arrival board, found that the Senator's flight had been delayed slightly due to bad weather in Washington, D. C.

"All this after we nearly killed ourselves getting here," she said.

"Of course. It's Murphy's Law."

He took the newspaper from her and sat on a bench inside the terminal as Laura left to make her phone call to the *Courier*. He leafed through the paper, not really reading the articles. He stopped and frowned when he came to a small two-inch report buried in the back pages.

An elderly Indian man had been killed along the highway by Bosque Farms the night before. The police reported he'd been killed around dusk, the time of day when it's hard for motorists to see pedestrians. Apparently he had been walking on the shoulder of the highway, had strayed into the path of an oncoming car. Killed instantly, he'd been thrown thirty feet.

The Indian's name was Fedelino Tenorio.

He stared.

Killed at dusk.

And he had talked with the old Indian at midnight.

CHAPTER SIXTEEN

"Damn him!" Faintly, as though his head were enveloped in a thick fog, he heard the click of her high heels on the tile before she spoke. "Can you imagine what he said? Chato?"

He was still looking at the article about Tenorio's death. Still disbelieving. But here it was. Printed in the newspaper. And he knew he'd talked with the old man. Remembered it well. Remembered, too, the time of the meeting. The old man . . . dead . . . when Chato had seen him. Dead. A ghost. He shuddered. He had talked with a spirit.

He heard distant laughter, faint, mocking . . . the laughter of Junior.

Somehow he managed to find his voice. She did not notice the strain in it. "What did he say?"

"He pulled the article because he thought it would, and I quote, panic the populace even more than it already was, and he didn't want Senator Kent's visit spoiled. It's censorship!" She sat, tossed her address book into her purse and glared at her shoes. She didn't ask what was troubling him, although from his expression she could tell something was wrong.

They sat for a few minutes in silence. Chato was cold, as though he'd stepped into the midst of a snowstorm, and when he raised his hands to rub them together, he saw they trembled. At that moment the loudspeaker crackled, announced the arrival of the plane from Washington. They started toward the escalator to take them to the TWA satellite.

They walked without speaking; Chato, deep in dark thought, kept his eyes down. It was true; all of it was true, true, true. He had turned his back on all of it, and now he realized he had been wrong.

The TWA area had been cordoned off and closed to regular pedestrian traffic, but Laura flashed her press card, told the guards Chato was with her, and they walked through the metal detector and into the satellite. The room, decorated in what Chato thought had to be the ugliest southwestern-style furniture, was filled with reporters and cameras. Smoke curled above the heads of the crowd, and it seemed everyone was talking as quickly and as loudly as possible.

"Is he off the plane yet?" he asked, shouting to be heard.

Laura stood on tiptoe, looked around, shook her head. "No. Not yet. I wonder where the protestors are. They were supposed to come to the airport. At least that's what Yellow Colt said." The door to the tunnel was opening. "Oh, here he comes."

A tall man in his late forties strode into the room. He was smiling and had his hand raised to greet the reporters. Several other men, obviously aides, accompanied him.

Robinson Kent looked like a nice man, Chato thought. A man you could trust. A man you would want to vote for and to have represent you in Washington. His face was broad and plainly handsome, fair-skinned, but his brown eyes were sharp, and they moved constantly about the room, assessing what he saw.

It was the first time Chato had ever seen a U. S. Senator up close. He didn't feel as impressed as he knew he should. The news of Tenorio's death had taken the edge off everything.

Still smiling, Kent walked up to the podium set at one end of the terminal. He waited for the journalists to quiet, then spoke into the microphone.

"It's great to be back in Albuquerque again." He acknowledged the smattering of applause with a nod of his well-groomed head. The hair at his temples was just beginning to silver, and it lent him an air of distinction. Here, his demeanor clearly said, was a potential elder statesman. "And I want to tell you how much it means to me to be here just in time for the International Hot-Air Balloon Fiesta." There was even more applause at that and Chato had to smile. Albuquerqueans seemed to like their balloons even more than their senator.

"As you know, the primary reason I'm here today—" He stopped, looked toward the back of the room. Gradually the others in the audience became aware of a noise that was growing in intensity, becoming shouts. Kent glanced back at his audience, started again, but once more faltered to a stop as the yelling increased in volume and gradually drowned out his voice. Chato turned to see what was going on, as did the reporters around him.

The security cops at the doors were struggling to keep a handful of people from pushing their way into the room.

One was already halfway in, and he was twisting and turning, struggling, in a cop's hold. He recognized Thomas Yellow Colt.

"You have no right to take what's rightfully ours!" Yellow Colt shouted. He squirmed loose from the cop, shoved forward before the man could stop him. The crowd of reporters fell back, letting Yellow Colt pass through their middle. It was almost as if they feared him. Cameras followed his progress as he headed straight for Kent. When he was almost nose to nose with the senator, the white man did not fall back as Chato had expected. Yellow Colt's companions were still at the door, held back by the police, but they shouted their support. There weren't more than ten or twelve of them. A mightily pathetic number for a protest movement. Was it apathy that had kept others from the airport? Or fear?

"And you are?" Kent asked smoothly, as if he hadn't just been shouted down.

There was just the slightest hint of condescension in the senator's voice, and Chato thought that very few would have noticed it. Maybe only himself and Yellow Colt. And they were more accustomed to hearing it than the white and Chicano reporters.

"Thomas Yellow Colt. Founder of the National Coalition of American Indians." He met Kent's gaze. "We demand that you do not take what doesn't belong to you. That fetish belongs to New Mexicans, and even more than to them, to the Indians. It should stay here. It has no right to be in Washington. It belongs here. With the Indians."

"A very pretty speech, Mr. Yellow Colt. But the fetish is a wonderful example of pre-Conquistadoran Indian craftsmanship that should be shared with the American people as a whole." He smiled at Yellow Colt, a full six inches shorter. "We, as New Mexicans, cannot be selfish."

"Bullshit."

For a moment Robinson Kent looked surprised, but he quickly masked it. "There's much that New Mexico has to offer, and this is just one of many—"

"You whites stole it forty years ago. It's bad enough that it's not in its rightful pueblo. Now you want to take it back East. We've told you before—I wrote you letter after letter, Kent, and all of 'em you ignored—that the fetish is an intensely religious article used in sacred ceremony. It should remain with its people. It has no right—"

"You speak of rights, Mr. Yellow Colt, and I think you are denying the right of the American people to share in the glory of our wonderful southwestern heritage."

Strong applause met the senator's words, and he smiled, basking in the acknowledgement.

Yellow Colt shook his head, then lunged at the senator. Kent fell back, away from the podium, and tried to thrust Yellow Colt away from him. The three men standing by Kent seized Yellow Colt and grappled him to the ground.

Chato watched the Indian struggle on the floor with the three men. Yellow Colt was putting up a pretty good fight, although severely outnumbered. One part of Chato wanted to help, wanted to get Yellow Colt back on his feet, because he believed in what the man was saying, but another part warned him to stay away. It wasn't his fight.

And yet. . . .

Not wanting to miss a second of the violence, the reporters pressed closer to the scuffle in an effort to get a better view. The cameras continued to roll. Camera bulbs winked continuously.

At that moment the Indians being restrained by the

security cops chose to start struggling. One broke through their lines and rushed toward Yellow Colt. One of the cops chased him, grabbed him by the collar and hauled him back to the door.

Laura edged closer to him. "Is there going to be a riot?"

Chato watched the fight at the front of the room, the fight at the back of the room. Because of this fetish, this fetish he had never seen, never even heard of till two days ago. Something tickled in his mind, and he shrugged, as though that would push it away. He couldn't be getting strong feelings here. There wasn't any reason. Or was there?

Yellow Colt was still putting up a good fight, having knocked one of the aides to the ground. He jerked away from the other two, got to his feet, and lunged for Kent again. In the back the handful of Indians screamed as one, a sound that made Chato's spine prickle, and they surged forward. One of Yellow Colt's followers fell back against a local television cameraman. His mini-cam slipped from his shoulder, fell to the floor, shattered, littering the tile with glass.

"Goddamn it!" the cameraman said as he bent to look at the wreckage. Another reporter backed up, didn't see the kneeling cameraman, and tripped over him. He fell into several other reporters, grabbed at them to break his fall, and they all stumbled.

At that moment about fifty passengers from a plane that had just landed in another satellite straggled through another door, completely unaware of what was going on here, and stopped, staring at the brawl. Chato kept edging Laura closer to the wall, well away from flying fists and kicking feet. One of the security cops swung his nightstick toward a slim Indian, who ducked. The nightstick landed across the face of an elderly woman passenger, breaking her glasses and cutting her lip and forehead. The young man with her launched himself at the cop, and they toppled to the floor, the young man punching the cop first with his left, then with his right fist.

At that moment more cops, both city and airport security, poured in through the doors from downstairs. Guns ready, nightsticks raised, they went after the protestors. One of them headed for Chato, started to grab him by the arm, thinking he was a protestor, but Laura shoved the man away.

"He's with me!" she screamed, trying to be heard over the noise. He glanced at her, nodded, moved off to go after another Indian.

Within minutes the police had subdued Yellow Colt and his followers, handcuffed them, and were ready to remove them. They weren't going to go quietly, though, and they were chanting. As he passed Chato, still by the wall and out of the way, Yellow Colt glanced at him, and smiled with an ironic expression.

"It's up to you now, bro."

Chato stared, not knowing what to make of Yellow Colt's words.

Then Yellow Colt and his followers began shouting. He could hear the words as they faded into the distance.

Medics had rushed in to take care of the wounded, and the elderly woman was removed on a stretcher, the young man, his face a bloody pulp, tagging after. Several others, cops and reporters and one of the aides, were taken out of the room.

The two remaining aides conferred momentarily with their boss, who smiled a little shakily as he smoothed back his hair. "Well, enough of the interruptions now," he said into the microphone. Only the aides laughed. "I'm going to my hotel now, but I'll see you all later at the barbecue. Adios."

Chato and Laura waited until everyone had left the room before they headed for the escalators. Yellow Colt's words remained with him. What did the man mean?

"What's this fetish that everyone's talking about? Is it some kind of closely guarded secret?"

The fetish . . . When he thought of it, he heard faint whispers and moans, and thought he heard an old man trying to talk to him, as though his voice were coming from very far away. He shook his head. Too little sleep last night and not enough to eat today.

"It's no secret, really," Laura said, as they started downstairs. "The Mayor has it right now. After all, he's the one who'll present it to Kent."

"Have you seen it?"

She shook her head. "No, just heard about it."

"Wouldn't it be funny," he said as they headed toward the car rental counters, "if it really didn't exist, and all this trouble was for nothing."

But it did exist. He didn't have to see it to know that.

He waited while she rented a car to replace the one wrecked last night. The airline ticket counters weren't doing much business, and only an elderly Chicano woman, dressed in a shapeless sweater and a nondescript dress with low black shoes, waited on one of the benches. She watched him as he went by, and watched him again when he walked past her from the opposite direction. Everyone was suspicious in Albuquerque these days.

The airport had already been cleared of the reporters and protestors, and it seemed to have returned to normal. All this trouble . . . because of the fetish. And suddenly he wanted to know more about it.

They walked toward the outside doors. "Do you think the newspaper has anything on it?"

"It?" she asked absently, as she thrust the papers into her purse.

"The fetish."

"I don't know. There's probably something in the morgue. I'll call you later if I find something." He nodded. "By the way about last night. I want to thank you for coming and staying with me. That was very kind." She paused. "There was more to my accident than I said." She rubbed a finger along the leather strap of her purse. "I was being followed when I left the office. In fact, I heard something behind me while I was going down the stairs, but thought it was just another reporter. Outside I couldn't see anything, but i could hear something. I finally got to my car and started to pull out. Something climbed onto the car. It looked in the window at me. It had such . . . such evil eyes, and it was staring at me as if it wanted to reach out and—"

"Shhh. It's okay now, Laura."

"That's when I wrecked the car." She paused. "What does it mean, Chato?"

"I don't know, really. I guess from this and from the one I saw at the apartment that they can go wherever they want. They aren't confined to the mountains."

"I didn't want to hear that," she said quietly.

"Neither did I."

173

CHAPTER SEVENTEEN

The phone was ringing as he entered the motel room. "Hello?"

"Hi, Chato. I've got your information. Plus some more."

There was an edge of excitement in Laura's voice that he hadn't heard before.

"Where are you calling from? It's really noisy."

"I'm in a phone booth around the corner from the newspaper. I didn't want anyone to overhear me, so I left the office."

"What have you got—national secrets?"

"Just about." She paused only the slightest of moments. "The fetish was actually fairly simple to research. There's not much on it, but it was discovered in the Pueblo de Sombras."

"I've never heard of it."

"Not many people have. The archeologist who excavated it was a professor at the University and found the fetish, along with some other artifacts, back in the late sixties. But it came up missing shortly after that. He's dead now, died just a few years ago, but I did manage to track down one of his assistants from that time. She's with the Museum of Albuquerque now and remembers the fetish well, and how excited they were at its discovery. And she said, well—now get this—she said the professor noticed the fetish was missing right after a young lawyer visited him on a federal case. Guess who the lawyer was?"

Coldness seeped through him. "Who?"

"Robinson Kent."

"The senator?"

"The very same."

"Why doesn't this woman protest or something, try to get the fetish back?"

"Well, she no longer works there, and they never had time to tag it. And she has no proof. It's just a coincidence."

"Sure it is." He was silent for a moment, then: "But if he stole it, why does the Mayor have it now, and why is he about to present it to him to give to the Smithsonian? None of this makes much sense."

"Well, it was rediscovered last month in Santa Fe. In the Archibishop's office."

"Now what the hell was it doing there, after Kent had it?"

"Don't know, although the priest who found it has been sent packing to a strict monastery up north, one where they frown on everything, including life. De Vargas then declared that this valuable object had to be given to Albuquerque's mayor—because, he said, *he had found it in Albuquerque*—and he gave it to Griffen. And almost immediately Griffen announced his intention of handing it over to Kent, who said right away that the Smithsonian had to have it.''

Chato frowned.

''Are you there?''

''Yeah. Just thinking. There's something fishy about all this. That fetish must be worth more than everyone thinks. Or something else.'' Something that nibbled gently away at his mind, tickled; he tried to brush the slight discomfort away.

''And that's not all.''

''More?''

''When I arrived back here, Bob apologized about suppressing my article, said he felt bad about it—as he damned well should. Believe me, I played on that, too. Later he took me aside and gave me this. Said I couldn't use it right now, but he wanted to make up for my article.'' She paused.

''Yes?'' His voice trembled slightly. What was she going to say?

''There is reputed—reputed only, mind you, *but* by a confidential source in the Mayor's office—to be a survivor of the attack on the campers.''

''Jesus. Who? Where is he? Why haven't we heard from him?''

''Bob didn't say any more. Maybe he didn't know. But the Mayor's office, or whoever, is keeping this person— and it's a woman, incidentally—under wraps.''

A survivor, and they hadn't known—no one had known— about this woman.

''Just thought you'd like to know.''

''Thanks, Laura.''

''Don't forget—I'll be at the barbecue later on, and I don't know when I'll get back. Maybe you should just wait for me to call you.''

He agreed, and after he hung up, he continued to sit on the bed, his hands flat on his thighs, and stared down at the carpet.

A survivor.

The fetish.

From the Pueblo de Sombras. Roughly translated as the Pueblo of the Shadows.

Shadoweyes, Tenorio had called those creatures.

Shadows. Shadoweyes. Survivor.

He was missing something, something that would tie things together for him, something that would make sense of all of this.

Something.

Where did he begin to look? De Vargas, Griffen and Kent. There was a tie there. But why?

He picked up his denim jacket and headed for the door. It was time he met the mayor.

"What may I do for you, Mr. Del-Klinne?" Mayor Griffen asked, smiling.

He had come downtown, given the secretary his name, and even before he'd handed her the lie he'd thought up on his drive there, the Mayor was telling her to let him come through.

And that surprised him. Or maybe it shouldn't.

Griffen indicated for him to sit down, and he did so. The Mayor's office was tastefully furnished in heavy wooden furniture, with the American and the New Mexico flags behind the desk. One wall was filled with photographs of Mayor Griffen with country singers, with rodeo stars, and with several presidents. A glass-enclosed cabinet opposite that wall contained a number of Santo Domingo pottery bowls, a metate, and several ears of colored corn. One shelf held a number of intricately painted kachinas, most of them of Hopi design. He didn't see a fetish, wondered where Griffen kept it.

"I'd like to talk to you, Mr. Mayor, about the recent murders in the mountains."

"The bear has been caught and destroyed."

"I don't think a bear did that. More than one would've had to be around to do all that damage—I found the bodies of the low-riders."

"I know who you are, Mr. Del-Klinne."

And that shouldn't have taken him by surprise, but it did. He remembered the black Buick that followed discreetly behind him.

"Are you having me tailed?" he demanded.

"Why should I do that? You're no one, Mr. Del-Klinne." Griffen's smile widened.

"Well, somebody thinks enough of me to have put a black Buick on my tail."

"Perhaps you're imagining things. Or perhaps you have an angry creditor."

"I owe nothing to anyone," Chato said quietly.

The two men eyed each other for a few minutes, and Chato could hear the soft clicking of the air conditioner.

"What about the things in the mountains? I saw them; other people have as well. You can't explain those away as bears."

"Things in the mountains?" The mayor's eyes seemed to flicker with some interest. "What precisely have you seen, Mr. Del-Klinne?"

"Shadows. Shadow creatures. I saw them in the mountains after I found the bodies."

"I see." Griffen relaxed and smiled. "It is rather hot, Mr. Del-Klinne. Heat can produce hallucinations."

"Those weren't hallucinations."

"So you say."

"Why won't you listen?"

"I have listened. I've listened to a crackpot. You can leave now."

Chato stood and scowled. "You don't give a damn about your constituents. Something's going on; people are dying in terrible ways and no one seems to be doing anything or finding out. There could be more. I mean to find out what's going on." Chato walked to the door, grasped the knob. "I just hope you manage to survive." He opened the door. "One of those deaths I'm talking about could be yours."

He left before the mayor could speak, got into the elevator, thumbed the button for the ground floor.

Well, he thought, what the hell had he accomplished? Not a whole lot, that was for sure. And again in the back of his mind, almost at the subconscious level, he could hear the tiny whispers, pushing him, urging him. Toward what? For what?

He should get in his pickup and pack his clothes and leave the city, and not come back for a long, long time. Get out while he still could.

"That Indian was here," Griffen said into the phone. "No, the other one. Asking questions." He paused, listened to the other line. "I'm going to take care of him, don't worry. I've already made a call. It's just. . . ." He stopped, took out a handkerchief and wiped his forehead. Unease filled him. This afternoon that *thing* would be out of his possession; it would be the last time he ever saw it, thank God. "He mentioned something he saw up there. Shadows. Used the same words the woman did. Just like the kids talked about, too. Rob, I know this is crazy, but you don't think it has anything to do with the— No? You sure? Okay. Okay. I won't worry. No, you're right. I shouldn't. I'll see you later. Yeah. Bye."

He hung up, leaned back in his chair and closed his eyes. But Kent's soothing words hadn't comforted him. He couldn't dismiss from his mind that there had been too many murders in the mountains—odd butcherings that no bear could have done—and that three people, in separate incidents, had seen something, something like no one else had seen. He didn't like it; he didn't like it one bit, didn't like it because he didn't have an easy solution for it.

And mostly he didn't like it because all of this seemed to have started about the time they decided to move the fetish out of New Mexico.

And that was too much of a coincidence.

Outside the municipal building on Marquette, Chato paused to get his breath, for it was a shock coming from the icy offices to this oven of unseasonable heat. The air was lifeless, without a breeze to stir it. The sun was still high, beating down unmercifully, and the peak temperature hadn't been reached yet, would not for another couple of hours. He wished he could be in a pool now. He thought longingly of the one at Laura's apartment complex.

A quick trickle of sweat slid down his back, and he shifted uncomfortably. He needed to go back to the motel and change his shirt, and maybe lie down for a nap for a while. Just get out of the heat and the sun.

He started down the street and grew aware that two Albuquerque cops were heading toward him. He looked around for the mysterious black Buick, but didn't see it.

CHAPTER EIGHTEEN

The cell was small, dirty, smelled of Lysol, urine, unwashed bodies, vomit, stale sweat and liquor. There were two other occupants besides himself. They were winos, unshaven, heavily clad despite the heat in the cell, and they still reeked of alcohol fumes. They had been asleep when the door had opened and Officer Bristol, the younger cop, had escorted him inside. They hadn't bothered to stir, and now, hours later, they were still dead to the world.

After the cuffs had been snapped on, the older cop had read him his rights. They'd pushed him into their squad car, then driven the few blocks to the city jail, and there he'd been booked and taken to the cell.

He had been allowed one phone call. He'd called Laura at the newspaper. She was out, a woman who answered her phone said. Frustrated, he had asked for her to take a message and had stressed that it was urgent that Laura get back to him right away.

What if she couldn't bail him out? What if it were too

much money? But what did it matter if he spent a night or two in jail?

Loss of time is what it meant. And time was something he knew he couldn't waste.

He thought back to an hour before. The booking had been routine, and the cops had seemed almost apologetic, as if they weren't totally convinced of his guilt. Which confirmed what he had been thinking about Griffen. Not many of his underlings seemed to like him. He did not inspire trust.

Tiring of standing in one spot, he paced the small cell, taking care not to disturb his snoring cellmates. He supposed he could trip over them and they still wouldn't wake, so deep were they in their besotted dreams. Still, he didn't want to talk with anyone. He wanted this time to think.

He rubbed a hand across his face, smearing the sweat and dust there, and grimaced. He should have watched his mouth in the Mayor's office. He'd been as dumb as shit to make those remarks.

You don't give a damn about your constituents. I just hope you manage to survive. One of those deaths I'm talking about could be yours.

Damn him; damn the Mayor. Griffen knew what he meant, knew he wasn't threatening him. But it was convenient for the Mayor to get the troublemaker off the streets.

And how the hell had Griffen known who he was? The man following him was a priest. What connection did Griffen have to a priest—and why was a priest tailing him, after all?—and . . . .

Too many questions, not enough answers.

He smoothed down his hair with both hands, wished he could change his shirt. The sweat on it had dried and on his body as well, and he felt uncomfortable. The cell was without the benefit of even a fan, and he was surely contributing to the pungency of the air. He leaned his forehead against the coolness of the bars and waited. It was dark here, as several of the lights had burned out in the cell, and one in the hallway was gone as well. Typical efficiency of the police department. It would probably be months before the bulbs were replaced.

He was glad his parents couldn't see him. His father was proud of how no one in the family had ever been arrested, and now he was here. At least, he thought, his lips twisting into a wry grimace that was almost a smile, it wasn't for DWI.

Down the corridor a door slammed; one of the drunks snorted, rolled over and fell heavily asleep again, and he heard two voices coming toward him. He stepped back into the shadows of the cell, not wanting to be seen.

"I don't know anything more about it, Manuel. Just what I told you," said the first voice.

"Who do you think she is?" the second man asked. His voice was slightly accented. "And why *there* of all places? That's weird, man, you know?"

"Hell, I don't know why that guy does anything. Maybe she's the Mayor's mistress."

"That son-of-a-bitch?" The second man laughed. "He couldn't get it up with the help of a balloon."

They both laughed. The two men were approaching his cell, and he pressed himself flat against the far wall, held his breath, waited.

"Yeah. You know, there's a lot of weird things going on recently, Bernie. All that hush-hush stuff up in the mountains, and now this broad. Bet the brothers are having one hell of a fine time. So much for chastity vows, eh?"

The other man laughed coarsely, made an obscene gesture with his hand, and his friend chuckled.

"Hey, isn't she the one who lived through the—"

"You guys down there taking a leak? You going to talk all day?" a third man called down the hallway.

"Mother-fucker," Bernie muttered under his breath. Louder he said, "Comin' right there, George."

They walked past Chato's cell, toward the other door at the end of the corridor.

"Well, isn't she?"

"The survivor? Yeah. You remember last weekend up there—"

The slamming of the metal door cut off the rest of the man's words.

Survivor.

A woman.

The brothers. With vows of chastity. Monks.

A woman had survived something last weekend and was now with monks. Laura had mentioned that the woman who had made it through the attack on the campers was reputedly being held somewhere; the attack on her friends had been last weekend.

It had to be the same woman. It was too much of a coincidence otherwise. And he didn't believe in coincidences. Not this time, not now. Not with these circumstances.

So, she was being held at a monastery. But which one? How many could there be? Local or otherwise?

He had to find it, had to go there. Hurry, whispered a gruff voice at the back of his mind. Hurry, there isn't much time.

He slammed his fist against one of the bars, ignoring the pain that shot through his wrist and lower arm. When would Laura come to get him? God, he hoped it wouldn't be too late.

Impatiently he waited.

"I got your message just in time," she said.

He stopped at the desk, collected his wallet and pen-knife along with the other contents of his pockets. "Yeah?" They walked out of the building and he frowned in the sudden brightness.

"I was on my way to the cocktail party and wouldn't have been back till late tonight. I just decided to stop by the office."

"Good thing for me." They reached her rented car, got in. "Thanks again, Laura. I'll pay you back as soon as I can. I—"

"It's okay. I know you're good for debts."

They reached the lot where his truck had been impounded. She drove off, and he presented his ticket so he could reclaim his pickup.

He was heading for Central when he remembered. Damn! He'd forgotten to tell Laura about the woman at the monastery. Too late now. He'd tell her later.

He reached the motel, cleaned up, changed into a fresh shirt and jeans, then gobbled down the sandwich he'd picked up at the store around the corner.

What now?

Scowling, he glanced in the mirror on the dresser to brush back his hair, and he slowly sank onto the bed.

The face of Tenorio was staring at him.

He closed his eyes, willed the face to go away. When he opened his eyes again, it was still there.

"Boy," said the face in the mirror. "Boy, you must hunt them." Chato said nothing, was afraid to admit that he would be talking aloud to someone who was dead, had been dead for days. "Boy." The voice sharpened. "Do you hear me?"

Chato nodded.

"You must go to their lair in the mountains. Destroy them there. Only you can do this . . . you and the fetish. Believe, too, dreamer of dreams, believe in yourself or you will surely die." The old man's voice faded to a whisper and the image in the mirror wobbled.

Chato's eyes closed. He jerked them open. He didn't have time to sleep, had to get going, had to find—

He slept.

CHAPTER NINETEEN

Every real and would-be politician in the thirty-two counties of New Mexico must be attending, Laura thought, surveying the crowd of well-dressed, well-groomed people who were mingling, talking, drinking and laughing at the Piñon Flats picnic ground, which was located on the northeast fringe of the city. And it only served to remind her that this was election year. How could she forget, with all these aspiring statesmen and stateswomen present?

She sipped at her drink and caught a young man from one of the eastern counties staring at her admiringly. She smiled a little. He might be a peanut farmer in Portales, but he certainly had good taste.

And she knew she looked good—she'd dressed with special care. She wore a low-cut velveteen dress with a wide gold belt that emphasized her narrow waist. The ivory of her dress contrasted strikingly with her dark hair and blue eyes. As for jewelry, she had selected only a simple single gold chain for her neck and gold button earrings.

Simple, yet elegant.

She wanted to make a striking appearance. She knew the senator had an appreciative eye for pretty women, and this couldn't hurt her chances of getting close to talking to him.

What an opportunity that would be—an exclusive interview, and a chance to find out what was really going on. It would have been easy to contact the wire services, to have blown the whole thing open, but not yet, not before she got all the facts, before she got all the credit. She smiled to herself. Laura Rainey—say good-bye to cub reporter, hello to investigative reporter.

The afternoon cocktail party had begun after lunch, which in this instance meant one p.m., and it was supposed to continue until the early evening, when the barbeque began in earnest. She wasn't sure how one could really tell the difference between the two, although at the barbecue they'd finally get around to serving the substantial food—the ribs, chicken, and other meats that would be cooked over the barbecue pits. Already some of the chefs were setting up their kitchens.

It had almost been called off, this great political affair, because of the recent deaths. People were spooked, afraid to go out, but Griffen had maintained publicly that the barbecue would be good for everyone's morale, and so the show, as it were, had gone on.

For the gala occasion, footed by the Mayor's and Senator's political party to prove what good sports they all were, several local mariachi bands in Mexican costumes had been hired to stroll through the crowds. Also performing were some puppeteers from the University, as well as the collegiate glee club, directed by their roly-poly leader. A

scar-faced country singer, who had been born in New
Mexico and came back yearly for the State Fair in
Albuquerque, had drawn a sizable crowd in one part of the
picnic grounds. One of the city councillors, who was an
amateur magician, was enthralling a number of city government employees who oohed and aahed over his sleight of
hand. In a little while hot-air balloon demonstrations would
be given by balloonists who'd volunteered their time. Free
rides would be given to those who wanted to go aloft, and
already there was a substantial waiting list.

Sometime, in the midst of all this circus-like activity,
Mayor Douglas Griffen, in a ceremony expected to be
fairly informal and quite down-home, was scheduled to
present the Indian statue to Senator Robinson Kent, who
could be depended on to act like a senior statesmen. She'd
seen the articles on Kent's arrival before the paper had
gone to press, and he had—not unexpectedly, she thought—
come out looking quite good. Better than Yellow Colt,
who was sitting in the city jail at the time, unable to raise
the steep bail that had been set.

Laura took another sip of her drink and looked around.
White tablecloths covered the cement picnic tables in a
futile effort to make the surroundings look more elegant
and less what they really were—a huge picnic grounds,
ideally suited for company picnics or political party social
bashes. The tables were laden with every possible kind of
snack, from fancy crackers and olives to dips and tasty
cocktail sandwiches, and by each table stood a smartly
dressed high-school-age boy and girl, volunteers, courtesy
of the Albuquerque Public Schools, just waiting to help
someone. The standing joke at the *Courier* was that APS
hoped to impress the legislators into putting more money
in the schools' budget.

Off to one side, almost in line with the mountains—she looked at them shimmering in the afternoon heat, shivered as though she had been chilled, and gulped her drink—a pavilion had been erected in the unlikely event that the weather might turn adverse and everyone had to take shelter. Rain hadn't been predicted by the various television forecasters, but after so long of a heat spell at the wrong time of the year, it wouldn't be at all strange for a cloudburst to explode without warning. In that case, she thought wryly, a pavilion wouldn't be much protection with the torrent of water that would come swooping down off the slopes of the mountains.

Close to the pavilion a bandstand, painted white and trimmed with patriotic bunting, had been built, and there one of the mariachi bands played their trumpets and guitars. On the other side of the bandstand was a platform, at the front of which was a podium and a microphone system. Two immense speakers had been fixed on each corner of the platform. Metal chairs sat in a line behind the podium. For the distinguished guests, who after hours of walking around and meeting the public and shaking said public's hands, would no doubt be glad to sit a spell.

The oddest thing about all of this, she thought, was underfoot. Someone concerned about long hemlines and shined shoes had thought of spreading an artificial covering that looked like grass across the grounds. It was soft underfoot, and cool, and it eliminated the possibility of rising dust, unruly ants and unsightly weeds.

She wondered how much it'd cost the Albuquerque tax-payers.

A burst of laughter drifted toward her in the hot, lifeless air, and a burly man pounded another on the back. It was more like a fiesta than a cocktail party, and before the evening was out, it was going to get a lot more boisterous. The Chamber of Commerce had generously donated the liquor for the occasion.

She could feel the sweat gathering at her waist, where the belt cinched her tightly. The dress was warm, too, far too warm for the unnatural heat, and she wished she'd worn something lighter. She pushed back a curl which had fallen over one shoulder and paused to look toward the mountains. The sun's low position had thrown part of the Sandias into shadows. She licked her lips nervously. She didn't want to look at the mountains, tried not to, but couldn't help it. She was drawn to them. Drawn to the shadows. She had to keep watching, almost as if she expected to see something happen. She remembered the creature that had clung to her car; she shuddered.

She forced herself to watch what was going on around her.

Everyone who was anyone was attending. There were state senators and representatives and the lieutenant-governor; the governor had sent his regrets, another engagement having kept him away. In reality she knew the governor hated the sight of Senator Kent and had once sworn to a number of aides that he'd far rather be dipped in horseshit than appear with him in public. Thus far he'd kept his promise. She recognized several prominent artists from Taos and a playwright from southern New Mexico, whose play had been running on Broadway for over a year; there was the local owner of the largest liquor distribution center in the state, as well as a world-famous race-car driver, the manager of the public service utility, the heads of both political parties, the president of UNM and the director of the Albuquerque Museum.

And of course there was, making himself known without appearing to do so, Senator Robinson Kent, his entourage having increased to include people from the Mayor's office along with those who would be expected to dance in attendance for such an occasion. There were bank presidents and senior law firm partners, Santa Fe opera directors and t.v. station owners, several former mayors, an ex-governor, and a couple of influential ranchers.

She sipped her now-warm drink and watched as Mayor Griffen hurried over to Kent. She didn't know when to approach the Senator. It had to be the right moment, for she'd only have the one chance.

Kent and Griffen conferred for a moment; then the two politicians walked toward a third man. She frowned when she recognized him. Richard de Vargas. The Roman Catholic Archbishop of Santa Fe.

Intrigued, she edged past one of the refreshment tables, snagged a handful of tortilla chips and continued to watch the three men. They were talking earnestly now, well out of the earshot of any intentional listeners, such as herself. Griffen seemed agitated as he gestured broadly with his hands. He was obviously upset about something. Kent was calm, and she thought de Vargas looked fairly sinister dressed in his churchly black. A faint smile rested on his thin lips, and it widened just slightly when he looked up at that moment and caught her looking at him.

She looked away. She didn't want to attract attention. Griffen was now looking at her, obviously after de Vargas had said something. She strolled casually back to the refreshment table.

They had to be talking about the recent murders and the coverup. It made sense. Especially after Chato had met with such resistance with the Catholic Church. But why? And why were they concerned that she'd been watching? They weren't doing anything after all, only talking. She edged away from the refreshment table, deciding she needed to put more distance between herself and the three men. At least for a while. She still planned on talking to Kent, but wasn't sure how she'd manage it. His bodyguards hovered a few yards away from him, and so far none of the journalists who'd approached him had been allowed to pass the protective circle. Apparently he was out to enjoy himself tonight and didn't want to be bothered with the press.

The subject of her thoughts had left the Mayor and Archbishop to talk with one another, and he was now chatting with a group of state politicians. She strolled past the bandstand, listened for a few minutes to the brassy music, then began picking her way carefully through the throng, always managing to keep him in sight. She was slowly, though inexorably, angling her way toward him. She stopped behind a cluster of well-dressed women, whose throats and ears and fingers glittered with gems. A small fortune in jewelry was walking around the picnic grounds, and she wondered what would happen if someone lost a ring or cuff link. They'd probably tear the place apart for a gem that cost more than she got in a year at the paper.

Kent was too busily engaged to notice her. But his aides weren't. Everyone wore name tags, but all members of the press had been required to wear ones with "PRESS" printed in large type above their names. Not what she would call discreet. And the bodyguards had spotted her name tag. The two men looked at each other, then at her, but she kept on going, refusing to give up when she was this close to the Senator. Throwing back her shoulders, she walked toward him confidently.

But she never reached him. A hand, beefy and large and very strong, shot out and caught her arm.

"Let go of me!" she said in a low, angry tone. How dare they treat her in this manner!

"I suggest you turn back, Miss Rainey, and let the Senator be." The speaker, his voice filled with affable humor, was a good six inches above six feet, as was his companion. The one who'd nabbed her seemed to be the friendlier of the pair; the other one scowled at her. They both looked like ex-football players, and probably each weighed well over two-fifty.

"Be what?" she asked sweetly. "Secretive?"

He didn't say anything, just let her go and folded his arms across the expanse of his chest.

The silence grew louder.

"Okay, I'll leave." She shrugged and promptly tried to move past him. The second man stepped forward, blocking her way. She threw back her head, stared up at the immense, unsmiling man and felt a small shiver of fear. These men were very big, and if they got mad . . . No, they didn't have to even be angry to hurt her.

"Miss Rainey. Please," said the first bodyguard, still faintly smiling. "Don't be difficult."

"I just—"

"We know what you want, Miss Rainey," he said. "Now go on back and have another drink. Enjoy yourself. And let the Senator enjoy himself."

Shrugging, she whirled away and returned to the bar, where she ordered another tequila sunrise.

There had to be a way to get to Kent. She wasn't about to give up now. Those apes didn't know her. Sipping her drink, she scanned the milling crowd, searched the faces. Now, whom did she know who could introduce her to the Senator?

The *Courier*'s publisher was there, but she wasn't precisely on a first-name basis with him. She didn't play tennis with the manager of the public utility or any of the upper-class citizens. Someone who owed her a favor. But who? Certainly not the Mayor.

The crowd shifted, formed into new conversation groups, and she saw a solitary man, looking a little lost as he stood by the pavilion. Narrowing her eyes, she recognized the thin form with the horn-rim glasses. Eagleton Haas, a political science professor at the UNM. He'd written numerous books and articles on the American political system and several on New Mexico politics; he was a popular lecturer and the state government's leading authority as well. While at the University, she'd signed up for several of his classes; after she was out of his classes, she'd reviewed his books for the campus newspaper.

And she knew he knew Kent. Haas knew everyone in New Mexico politics.

She took a large swallow of her drink, tucked her purse under her arm and, wearing a warm, but determined look, advanced on the unsuspecting professor.

"Professor Haas," she said, smiling even more widely now and extending her hand. Haas had always liked his female students, and she certainly wasn't above using a little charm on him.

It wasn't lost either.

"Ah, Ms. Rainey. What a delight." He stooped to read the letters under her name. The position also gave him a better view of her bosom. "I see you're with the *Courier* now. A superior newspaper."

"Thank you, Professor. We think so."

"No, no, Laura. Now that you're out of school, please call me Eagleton. We can be much more informal now." He smiled.

"All right . . . Eagleton." What a mouthful. She studied him over the rim of her glass. "What do you think of all this political hoopla?"

He was in his element now. "I think the Mayor knows it's an election year and he wants to help his good friend Senator Kent, who in turn just might be able to help him politically. Did you know they were at the University together?" He shook his head, swallowed some of the dark liquor in his glass. "You couldn't get much more of a contrast than those two. I've been toying with the idea of examining the relationship of political friends, tracing their beginnings to their school days. For my next book," he added quickly, as if she'd ever doubted his meaning.

"Like the British system," she said. "You make a friend in school, and after that it's just a matter of the right connections."

"That's right." He was obviously pleased with her. "You must be doing well yourself lately. Are you covering this for the paper, or are you here more for your amusement?"

"A little of both, really." She thoughtfully watched the Mayor, now deep in conversation with three women city councillors. "I have to confess that I've never liked Griffen—too much the typical politician for me. But Senator Kent, on the other hand, seems like a decent fellow. But maybe that's the PR I'm been reading and not the real man."

"He is pretty good. Politics-wise and human-wise." He

198

watched the senator speaking to a small group of men and women, which included the country-western singer and the playwright. At the moment they were laughing at something Kent had just said. "Still, he's the political beast at heart. He knows he's up for election, too. It's apparent in everything he's done this afternoon. And of course there's all this nonsense about the Indian statue." Haas shook his head. "It should make for an interesting book, if he wins."

"He certainly is elusive. I've been trying to get closer so I could talk with him, and those big lunks lurking around him won't even let me get within spitting distance of him." She waited, hoping he'd take the bait.

"Would you want to meet him?"

"I'd love it, Eagleton. If you can manage it—and only if it won't be any trouble."

"No trouble at all," he reassured her. "I'm sure it can be arranged." His tone was faintly dry.

"Thank you." It was easy, so very easy.

"C'mon then." Without any prompting, he took her hand in his.

As they cut through the crowd, Haas talked of his latest project, a survey of current politicians in the state and the breakdown of the influence of their regional backgrounds, and when at last they reached the Senator and his group, Haas stood for a moment, listening to Kent speak about the demographics of voters, before he broke in.

"Utter bullshit."

Startled, Laura stared at her companion.

Kent, a frown forming on his face, swung around to respond. The expression softened when he saw Haas.

"My God, Eagleton, I didn't know you were here."

"Couldn't keep me away. Have to get more notes for

199

my book, y'know." He chuckled as he extended his hand. "How've you been, Rob?"

"Fine. Just fine." He flashed on his politician's smile. "Couldn't be better. Things are looking good for the Party this year."

"You always say that," Haas said now, grinning at what was an obvious in-joke with them. "If it got any better for the Party, it'd be in control of Arizona as well."

Both men laughed, and Laura tried not to stare at Haas. Rob? He was on a first-name basis with the Senator? She was surprised, but pleased by the unexpected intimacy. It made her introduction to Kent all the safer.

"Rob, I have a young woman here—she's a former student of mine, in fact, and a good friend as well—who's been dying to meet you. Isn't that right?" He gestured to her, and she stepped forward.

Privately she would admit that this close Robinson Kent was even more impressive than at the distance she'd seen him before. She had the feeling that this was a man destined for greatness. Maybe even the White House. She smiled dryly. She'd been reading too many Allen Drury books lately; she'd better cut out the nonsense and get back to the real world. The real world that included Senator Robinson Kent.

But he *was* impressive, and very handsome. A real heartbreaker, too. The type of man some women—and also men—would vote for because he was so good-looking, because he looked the part, because with his face and bearing he couldn't be anything else but a legislator. And the charm was there as well. She could feel it, and it was obvious that even Haas had been affected. It was a real presence, something she was sure Kent counted upon to help him.

She looked at him, waited.

"Senator, this is—"

"Ms. Laura Rainey. Yes." The smile broadened, and she knew his grey eyes held amusement. "I've heard a lot about you, young woman."

CHAPTER TWENTY

When he awoke, he felt refreshed, felt better than he had in days. He rubbed his eyes, and as he left the room to get a soft drink from the machine by the office, he glanced at the mirror. Saw only himself.

Tenorio had come to him from . . . wherever . . . to tell him to hunt the creatures in their lair. Twice he'd seen the old man after his death. Ghosts, and Josanie long ago, did not always leave when the body died.

It was also considered bad luck to see a ghost.

He took a healthy swig of the soft drink, sat on the bed and thumbed through the phone directory. First things first—where the hell was this monastery? As he expected, Roman Catholic monasteries weren't listed in either the yellow or white pages.

Randomly he picked one of the Catholic parishes, and when he had the secretary on the line, he explained he was writing a book about the Catholic Church and needed to know the names of some of the monasteries in the state.

He jotted them on a pad of paper as she gave him the names and locations. Afterward, he stared thoughtfully at the list, tapped the pencil on his knee.

He could rule out the monasteries way up north and way down south. Same with those either too far west or east of the city. He figured he was looking for a monastery somewhere in the Albuquerque area. Close to the Mayor. Someplace where she could be reached, could be moved quickly.

Only two matched those requirements. One was the Holy Innocents Monastery located behind the mountains; the second was St. Basil's out on the West Mesa.

So which one was it?

Did he have time to go to both? He had to select one. What if his first choice were wrong? He'd still end up going to the second one.

Choose one.

And only one.

Around and around goes the wheel of chance. Pick one. Only one.

He took a long swig of Dr. Pepper, stared at the now-reduced list. Hurry, one part of him said. Stay, the voices whispered, and he shook his head, trying to force the sibilant voices away. But they wouldn't leave. They stayed and made his head hurt and he couldn't think and—

NO!

He thrust them away, forced his mind to a dark blankness, and when all was quiet, when his head no longer throbbed, he breathed deeply, evenly.

The decision couldn't be put off any longer. He had to decide. The decision of your life, one part of him said.

West Mesa or behind the mountains?

Was there ever any choice? he wondered, laughing without sound as he drained the last of the soft drink and headed outside for the truck.

Holy Innocents—behind the mountains—it would be.

As he drove toward the mountains, the voices grew louder. Again he slammed them away, and in response he heard a whining laughter. Of the black Buick he saw no sign.

When he reached the exit for state Road 14 in Tijeras Canyon, he turned south. The woman had said to go fifteen miles until he saw the sign. From there it was straight down the road. She didn't say how far, but he knew it probably was more than a few miles.

More than twenty minutes later he saw the freshly painted wooden sign. Its wide red arrow directed him onward to the Holy Innocents Monastery. As the distance narrowed between himself and the monastery, something clawed at his stomach. Nerves, he told himself, concentrating on the narrow dirt road, liberally provided with chuckholes and deep ruts, the results of erosion and flash floods.

It was the charge of the U. S. Cavalry, this time played by the Indians, rushing in to rescue the fair maiden, and—and he didn't know how to do it. He couldn't exactly stroll in and announce that he'd come to rescue the woman the monks were holding. Not unless he wanted to end up in jail again.

He'd have to sneak in. In broad daylight. And he didn't look much like a monk.

The odds were definitely against him.

Would there be much outside activity? How large was the complex? How many brothers would there be? How was he going to do this?

And there it was, shimmering in the heat. The Monastery of the Holy Innocents proved to be a small group of stucco buildings, surrounded by fir, elm and piñon trees.

Honeysuckle wound its fragrant way up the walls. There was plenty of shade and overgrown bushes in the front that would provide cover for him. To the south, connected with the main building by a breezewalk, was the chapel, a large white cross atop its flat roof. The cross blazed starkly in the sunlight. Even from this distance he could see the muted colors of the stained-glass windows. Not the richest monastery he'd ever seen, but a fairly respectable one.

He parked in the dirt lot that sat to one side, studied the grounds. Where would the woman be held? He could automatically discount certain areas right away. The cafeteria. The laundry. The chapel.

A handful of monks in brown robes came out of the chapel and walked over to the main buiilding; a few minutes later several left through a different doorway there and headed toward a smaller structure behind the main building.

The sun beat relentlessly through the windshield, making him hotter, making him sweat, and he shifted to get into the slight shade within the cab.

He was aware of the clock ticking in the dashboard, ticking away the minutes, ticking away the time until he was discovered.

He had to do it.

He had to brazen it.

It had to be now. He couldn't waste any more time, couldn't stall.

Now.

As though he moved in slow motion, he opened the door, jumped out and, taking a deep breath, headed for the buildings of the Monastery of the Holy Innocents.

CHAPTER TWENTY-ONE

"Excuse me, Eagleton," Robinson Kent said smoothly, "I'd like to talk with Ms. Rainey alone." He smiled to take away any sting to the words.

Obviously none had been felt, for Haas waved jauntily and strolled off in the direction of a refreshment table.

"This way, Ms. Rainey," the Senator said.

She didn't have much of a choice, for he'd clasped his hand on her elbow and was steering her toward the seclusion of the pavilion. She hated it when men did that, and she particularly did not like this man doing it. She brought her elbow up sharply, then snapped it closer to her body, breaking his grip.

Unruffled, he smiled at her, didn't try to touch her again. He pointed to the pavilion, and when they reached it, he indicated for her to sit. He sat opposite her, steepled his fingers, stared thoughtfully at her.

"Now, Ms. Rainey, I think we should talk."

"Precisely why I wanted to see you, Senator. Although

it certainly was hard to reach you." She nodded toward his two bodyguards, who had trailed after them. They stood at a discreet distance. She didn't think they were pleased that she'd managed to get to their boss. Their boss. She studied the lines of his face, the strong jaw, the determined eyes coolly appraising her. Why had he wanted to talk to her? How had he known who she was? She thought she'd let him do most of the talking.

"You seem to be doing well, Ms. Rainey. I understand you were graduated not long ago from my alma mater, UNM." He smiled at her.

"That's correct."

"You're probably wondering how I knew that."

Her silence didn't seem to disconcert him in the least. "I make it a point to know about various members of the press. Especially those promising ones. Ones who might be interested in involving themselves in a political campaign sometime. And I don't mean as a member of the press." He paused, straightened his cuff. Still she said nothing. "You take my meaning—may I call you Laura?"

"No."

"Really, Laura, let's not make this difficult. All right?"

"I don't know what you're talking about, Senator. I'm here simply to cover the barbeque. I thought this would be the perfect opportunity to meet you and conduct a simple interview. That's all." She hoped her face was as deadpan as her voice.

"I've heard otherwise." Again she said nothing. "I see you are going to be hardheaded. You're young, very young, and inexperienced, Laura. You aren't playing the game."

"I know. I've been told that before. It hasn't stopped me, as you can see."

"It will someday. You have to give in. Go with the

system. Otherwise it'll eat you up. There'll be nothing left."

"We'll see."

"You certainly are the defiant one. A very liberated woman, I take it."

She met his eye then. "I manage."

He said nothing, simply studied her, shifted his position in his chair.

"About the interview, Senator."

"Come now. We know that isn't your real reason for being here."

"What is my real reason then?"

"You are trying to harass the Mayor and to publicly embarrass him."

She stared, quickly recovered. "I don't have to do that. He does it well enough by himself."

He smiled. "Spirited, with a barbed tongue."

"I don't like being called a liar by the Mayor. I don't like getting the run-around. I don't like having one of my articles suppressed. I don't like coverups. And I particularly don't like what's been going on lately."

"Sometimes there are very good reasons—"

"What about all those deaths in the mountains?" she asked.

"I really don't know anything about that, Ms. Rainey. I just flew into the city today."

"So you won't say anything about them?"

"How can I speak uninformed?"

She stood. "That's almost a requisite for being a politician." She saw his darkening face and knew she'd made another enemy. The list was growing longer and longer. "Good day, Senator."

She walked out of the pavilion without looking back.

The bodyguards stepped toward her, but obviously Kent waved them aside and they let her pass.

Well, another avenue was closed to her. First the Mayor, now the Senator. There didn't seem to be many people left who might be able to tell her what was going on. Somehow, though, she told herself, she'd find out. Somehow.

And wished fervently there was a patron saint of journalists.

He reached the main building without anyone stopping him or, for that matter, seeing him. He thought. He hoped. He paused, his heart pounding, his breath short. *Hurry, hurry, hurry*, urged the faint whisperings. He stared hard at the bushes. What did he expect? Something sinister? Something that looked like eyes? But nothing was there. They were plain bushes, simple and very unsinister honeysuckle, dozens of bees buzzing around the delicate blossoms.

He pressed himself flat against the stucco and waited, wiped sweat from his cheek, wondered if he could pass as the gardener. No, that was probably one of the monks. For a moment he regretted his long hair and wished he'd brought a hat. But a hat would be noticed right away inside.

He should have waited until night, when no one could see him. But no, that had its dangers, too.

He peered around a corner toward a second and smaller structure. No one in sight. Couldn't see anyone at the windows. Walked quickly, purposely toward it. The large one in front probably housed offices and the like, and he didn't think the woman would be held there. She'd be kept in a dormitory, perhaps, away from most of the monks.

The second building had two wings and could possibly

210

provide more isolation. Also, now that he was closer, he saw the other structures were a garage and a shed for gardening tools. Beyond that was a vegetable garden with cornstalks nodding in the heat, a patio with benches, and a basketball court.

He reached a double wooden door. Carefully he tested the handle, twisting it to one side. The door opened easily and with little noise, and he breathed a sigh of relief. He hadn't prepared himself for locked outer doors. He slipped in and found he faced a long corridor. Doors lined both sides all the way down to the end of the hallway, where there was another door.

He'd been right. This was obviously the dormitory.

From where he stood he couldn't see where the other corridor crossed, but it had to be there. He started walking. Each door had a grate set at eye-level, and he peered into the first. Nothing out of the ordinary, and unoccupied as well. The same with the second, the third. Minutes were ticking by. He glanced at his watch, licked his dry lips. He had to find her soon.

He was just crossing to the fourth door when he heard a door close somewhere in the building. He stopped, his breath caught, and waited for someone to appear. No one did, and he inched carefully until he came to the transverse corridor. Left or right now? He listened, thought he heard something faint from the left-hand corridor.

Carefully he peered around the corner. At the far end was a straight-backed chair—occupied by one of the brown-clad brothers of the Holy Innocents Monastery.

He had found her.

He pushed back his hair, rubbed his chin, considered. The monk didn't look armed; surely he didn't have a concealed gun. And the man didn't look particularly sturdy either. He swallowed a few times, took a deep breath and headed boldly down the corridor. His boots tapped loudly on the floor, the sound echoing through the hall. He wished he were barefoot, but it was too late. The monk had heard him and was already standing, a puzzled look on his face.

"Griffen sent me," he said, trying to look fairly bureaucratic, and knowing he wasn't succeeding. The man was Chicano, and when he saw Chato was Indian, his puzzled look became a frown. "I'm here to—"

"I don't recognize you," the monk said curtly. "I don't think you should—"

He never finished his sentence.

Chato leaped forward, rapidly traversing the few feet separating them, and solidly slammed his fist into the man's abdomen. The monk grunted and doubled over, clutching his stomach. Then Chato gripped his left hand with his right and brought them down together across the back of the monk's neck. There was a thud as his hands hit his mark, and the monk toppled to the floor.

"Sorry, Brother."

He tried the doorknob. Locked. Damn. More delay.

Outside he heard a noise. Voices. Someone was coming. His heart pounding, he quickly knelt and searched through the monk's clothing until he found a key. He fumbled, dropped it, picked it up again.

Calm down, he told himself. No one would come in; no one would find him.

Inserting the key, he turned it, and the door swung open. He stepped into a room that looked precisely like the others he'd seen. There was a cot along one wall, a table under a high window, and a single lamp next to the table.

A chest sat to his right. On the table was a tray with several dishes on it. Nothing had been touched.

A blonde woman, dressed in a man's shirt, jeans and cowboy boots, lay on the cot, her hands tucked behind her head. She was staring up at the ceiling, and when he entered, her head tilted his way. She obviously expected the monk. Slowly she sat up, bringing her feet down to the floor with a thud.

"Look," he said slightly breathlessly. "I don't have much time, and I know this may sound crazy, but are you the woman who survived the attack in the mountains?"

She stared wordlessly at him, and he began to think he'd made a mistake. God, let her be the one. Don't let her be someone's swept-away mistress. "I said, miss—"

"I heard you." Her voice was low and pleasant. "Yes, I survived an attack in the mountains. I thought you knew all about it." She stood akimbo, looked him up and down. "What's it to you?"

"I'm here to rescue you."

CHAPTER TWENTY-TWO

Martin Landsman, who was the butt of a lot of good-natured kidding from his ballooning buddies because of his name, cursed fluently in both Spanish and English, and threw in a few words he'd picked up when he'd been stationed in Wiesbaden.

The damned balloon was going down.

He threw out more ballast, watched as the sandbag hit the ground twenty feet below. The hot-air balloon lurched upward slightly, and he fell against the basket.

He shouldn't have gone up today. He'd known it was going to be bad from the moment he'd rolled out of bed that morning, realizing he'd overslept and missed the mass ascension. His crew had been waiting for him at Cutter Field, had been for hours, and he'd arrived just as the other balloons were lifting off. By the time the envelope was filled, everyone else was in the air. Then he'd gone up and a crosswind had hit him, carried him away from the others, driven him way far along the mesas, and he'd come down earlier than he'd wanted do—and had barely missed an immense tangle of electrical wires in doing so.

Damned day. Damned Fiesta.

It didn't really start until Sunday, but just about as many balloons went up the few days before the Fiesta as on the opening day. And there were the usual tests and games as well.

He should have scratched this year, forgotten the whole thing until next year, and maybe just given up the balloon. It was expensive, God knows, and everyone he knew always expected him to give them free rides, as if it didn't cost a cent for him to operate. And then his partner, wonderful friendly Sammy Griego, who was everyone's good buddy, had run off with the bank account they kept. Last the police had heard from him, the sucker was running east through Texas. And they didn't think they'd be able to get the money back.

Then he'd gone and volunteered to be one of the balloonists at the political barbecue, and it wasn't even his party that was throwing the wingding.

So why was he doing this? Masochism, he decided. It was the only explanation.

He blasted the propane burner slightly; it hissed and air inside the orange and yellow nylon heated. The balloon rose a little, and he smiled, feeling some of his tension fade.

He still wouldn't miss this for the world. He liked the sound the balloon made, though otherwise the flight was virtually soundless; he liked the freedom from the earth and the magnificent views. It made all his problems seem so small when he was up in the balloon. He couldn't stay mad or upset for long.

Coming up quickly below him was the Cibola National

Forest. He could see the forest ranger's station and outlook, the sunlit lines of the tramway and the restaurant at top, and across from him, on an outcropping of granite, he saw a herd of mountain goats. He grinned. Probably were wondering what the hell kind of bird he was. He waved. The sudden movement set them off. They blurred; dust rose, and when it settled, the goats were nowhere to be seen. By the Crest a hang-glider, trusting in the theories of aerodynamics, stepped off into space that ended well over five thousand feet below him, and his blue craft caught an air current and slowly, gracefully rose.

And behind Martin—he turned carefully and stared, feeling just great now.

To the west spread one of the most panoramic scenes he'd ever seen, and he'd travelled a lot with the balloon in his forty-six years. The air was so clear he could see Mt. Taylor, a full sixty miles west of Albuquerque. The city, all in shades of grey and beige and cream, stretched toward the river, and there he saw the band of green and gold of the great cottonwoods, trees that had stood since Coronado's time. Beyond that were the muted colors of the desert of the West Side, the dusty black of the volcanic Seven Sisters, and beyond that stretched even more desert until the eye reached Mt. Taylor. The highways, bisecting the city, were thin ribbons, dotted with tiny specks of light—cars, the sun reflected on the metal.

He could look northward and see the immense mountains, the Sangre de Cristos, around Santa Fe, snow already falling on the peaks. To the south were more mountains, and he could pretend he saw those by Socorro.

Thousands of miles of scenery—all up here within sight— and it was glorious. He never tired of looking at it. Couldn't. It was always changing with the days, the seasons.

He unzipped his jacket a little, leaned his hands on the edge of the basket, smiled and waved to some folks below at the barbecue. Then he glanced back at the instrument panel and his smile faded.

He'd dawdled too long and the air inside the bag was cooling too rapidly. The balloon began to descend again, and his good mood evaporated.

Damn. There was always something.

He opened the burner wide, but it was too late; the balloon kept sinking, kept going down at an angle until it was headed straight for a strand of tall trees.

CHAPTER TWENTY-THREE

"Rescue me?" she asked, her voice amused. "Is this some sort of trick?"

"I really don't have time to explain." He was talking fast, knew someone would discover them soon, or that the monk outside the door would come around. "Will you come with me?"

"Why should I?"

God, why was she being so stubborn? "Do you want to stay here for another week or however long it takes them to decide what they're going to do with you?"

That seemed to hit a responsive chord, for she shook her head, her long hair fanning out.

"Come on then." Without waiting for her to come to him, he reached out, grabbed her by the hand and edged out into the corridor.

The monk still lay sprawled across the floor, unconscious. She stared down. "Did you kill him?"

"Just knocked him out." They were walking cautiously

toward the main corridor now, and Chato was listening carefully for any voices.

"Where are we going?"

"Back to Albuquerque. By the way, I didn't catch—" He stopped. A door had opened. The door to the outside. Footsteps echoed down the hallway. Coming their way. "Look, there's a door to the left at the end of the hall. I want you to run to it and get outside however you can. Get into the green pickup in the parking lot. I'll be right behind you." Then he shoved her toward the junction of corridors. She darted to the left.

"Stop!" a man's voice shouted.

He heard her running, and heard someone else running up the corridor toward the junction. Just as the monk came abreast of him, Chato leaped out, grabbed the monk by the sleeve, whirled him around and slammed him into the wall. He slid down. Chato turned to follow the woman when the outside door opened again.

He knew he'd been spotted.

He reached the door, found it opened into a men's lavatory. A window, about four and a half feet off the ground, was open. She'd obviously gone through that. He jumped up, grabbed the sill just as the door swung open. A hand got hold of his heel, and he kicked out, hard. His boot hit something soft, and there was a groan. He squirmed through, jumped to the ground, almost fell, and started running. Through the trees he could see the woman. She had almost reached the parking lot.

And she was heading for the wrong truck.

There was a second green truck in the lot.

"No!" he shouted, all caution gone now. He heard men running after him. He glanced back, stumbled a little, saw two men behind him. They must have come through the window as well. He looked toward the lot and cupped his hands. "Hey! The other truck!" He pointed hard toward his pickup. She looked back over her shoulder, nodded that she understood and veered toward the right one.

As he ran, he pulled out his keys. God, he should have given her the keys, let her start it. As it was, if he could outrun the monks, they would just barely make it. They had to. So far they'd been damned lucky, and he wasn't about to let that change. She climbed in and pushed open his door. In a matter of seconds he reached it, started the engine. Then he closed the door, slammed the truck into reverse, and roared backward, knocking down a monk.

"Oh Jesus," he said.

"I don't think you killed him," she said. She was looking out the back window. "The other monk's helping him up. Must have just grazed him."

She was a cool one, he had to admit. She hadn't screamed when he struck the monk, hadn't gotten excited. He liked that.

The speedometer hit ninety as the truck roared out of the parking lot and down the road, flinging gravel out from under its tires. A long plume of dust spewed upward behind. He pressed the accelerator down, and the speedometer edged upward. Ninety-three. Nine-five. Wavered. Then one hundred.

He risked a glance sideways. The wind streamed in through the open window, blowing her blonde hair across her face, but she was calm, not scared like many women— and men—were at high speeds. He checked the rearview mirror. So far no one was following. Good. At least they had a head start. Maybe they could get back to Albuquerque and lose anyone who might be following them.

Probably right now someone was on the phone to the Mayor, or whoever was responsible, and was telling him the girl had been sprung.

The wind screamed past them, and the woman rolled up the window on her side. He didn't dare take one hand off the wheel. Not at this speed. Not on this road. The truck hit a pothole, reared up, and the wheel threatened to jerk out of his hands. He clamped his fingers tightly on the hot plastic, grimaced, and wrenched the truck to the right and out of the hole.

"Do you want to explain now?" she asked, once the truck was under control again. She was slightly amused, and he grinned.

"Sure. I owe you that much. My name is Chato Del-Klinne. Bear with me—it's a strange story. Just a few days ago I was walking through the mountains and found some dead people." He proceeded to tell her everything that had happened. And he told her how he'd come to hear about her and how he'd figured out where she was being held. "I was determined to get you out," he concluded.

"Why?" She was genuinely curious.

"Because I've seen the shadow creatures, too."

He sensed, rather than saw, her shudder.

"Please."

"Is that what you saw?"

"Yes. They were . . . horrible."

"How did you escape?"

"I woke up and saw their eyes. I managed to roll down the slope just as they . . . they crept out of the bushes." Her voice broke momentarily, and it was the first time he heard emotion in it. "I ran then, ran for what seemed like

miles and miles. I must have tripped somewhere along the
way and hit my head on a rock. The next morning I woke
up and there were some policemen standing around me.
They told me I'd been found by a passing motorist and
that everything was all right, and then I was brought back
there."

"Do you know what you saw?" he asked.

"Our guide, Junior Montoya, said—"

"Wait a minute." His voice was sharp. "Junior Montoya?
Was he sort of elderly, greasy looking, with bad teeth?"

"Yes. Do you know him?"

He laughed shortly. "Not precisely. I met him, though,
the first day I drove into Albuquerque. He was acting
weird then, but I didn't really think anything of it. Go on.
Sorry for the interruption."

"He said there was a pueblo nearby that was haunted. I
asked if there were ghosts there, and he said it was haunted
by something worse than ghosts. He said they were Indian
spirits. And that the pueblo was built by a people dead
before Coronado came through. And that the spirits were
evil. I found that out." There was nothing in her voice
now, and he knew she was thinking of what she had seen.
He had never seen an attack, only the aftermath.

The pueblo again. And the spirits.

They were silent for a few miles, and then: "You
know," he said, trying to break some of the heaviness
inside the truck, "I don't know your name. And here I've
gone and rescued you. Some fine knight I'd make."

"Sunny Mae Foster. Isn't that terrible? They call me
Sunny, though. From Lubbock."

He didn't think she sounded a bit Texan, but he didn't
say so. And he also thought she was very pretty, from the

223

small glimpses he'd gotten. Mostly he hadn't had time to look at her.

"What now, Chato?"

"There's a common element to both our stories."

"Junior Montoya."

"That's right." He braked as they approached the highway back into town. "I think our next step should be to find him. Wherever he is."

CHAPTER TWENTY-FOUR

Laura watched as the orange and yellow balloon lifted away from the trees. For a few minutes she thought it would crash, but then the pilot seemed to get control again, and the balloon rose.

She didn't really care much for balloons, certainly wasn't the ballooning fanatic that so many people in Albuquerque were. She liked them only inasmuch as they were newsworthy. If the pilot had crashed, that would have been news, much like the time a few years before when some out-of-state balloonists had decided to try to fly over the Sandia Mountains. Any local balloonist would have warned them about the quirky air currents by the mountains and told them it was sheer folly, but the balloonists hadn't bothered to consult any of the natives. So they'd made their attempt. And they'd all died as a result. The first fatalities at the Balloon Fiesta, although it hadn't been a Fiesta-sanctioned activity. *That* had been news.

She lost interest in the balloon, which was now headed

back to the picnic grounds, and strolled once more toward a refreshment table for another tequila sunrise. It was her third; she had a slight headache, and she didn't give a damn.

So what the hell was she supposed to do now?

The sun was setting, and she could smell the piñon wood in the barbecue pits. Dinner should be ready any time now. She'd have to leave around eight to get back to the office in time to write up her account, and she still didn't have an interview with Kent. She had a story, sure, but her damned editor wouldn't run it. He'd just refuse to print it, the way he did with the other one. Damn him. Briefly, as she glanced at the mountains, more shadows on them now than earlier, she wondered where Chato was, then decided she really didn't care.

Damn him, too.

Damn Kent.

Damn all of them.

She looked down at the glass in her hand. She had finished her drink already. She got another one and sipped it, the soft warmth spreading through her. She brushed by a short, dumpy woman, her bright red hair obviously dyed, almost knocked the flaming redhead's drink out of her hand, apologized curtly and kept on going.

Had to get control of herself. There was nothing worse than a drunken woman. Wasn't that what men always said? Damn Kent and his little remark about her being liberated. Probably thought he was being cute.

She heard the hissing of a burner overhead and looked up. That dumb balloonist was heading straight for one of the refreshment tables. Why didn't he lift the silly thing up? She raised her glass to her mouth, then paused, not drinking. Had she seen something move along the edge of the gondola? It wasn't the pilot. At least it didn't look like him. In fact, where was he?

She swallowed a large mouthful of her drink and shivered, but not from the ice-cold liquor.

The something.

No. It wasn't like that at all. It couldn't be.

Others around her had become concerned about the rapidly descending balloon, and some of them were shouting at the balloonist.

"Get up! Get up! You're coming down in a crowd! Watch out!"

"Hey, Martin," a man dressed all in western garb shouted, his hands cupped around his mouth, "what the fuck are you doing?"

"He's in trouble," a woman with iron grey hair said to Laura. The front of her black dress was covered with twenty or more strands of silver heishi jewelry. She touched Laura on the arm. "I've been to every one of the Fiestas, and I know trouble when I see it. Oh, my goodness."

Laura's news interest was piqued now, and she knew she should get closer to what was going on, but something kept her in place. As the gondola dropped closer and closer to the ground, Laura stared. Her fingers numb, the glass slipped from her hand, shattering on the ground.

"Oh my," the matron said, concerned.

Laura's stockings and shoes had been splashed with the liquor, but she didn't notice. She watched as the shadows clambered up from the inside of the gondola, and she felt the shriek rising inside her.

"Get out, get going," she said, grabbing and shaking the woman's arm. A turquoise nugget on one of the woman's numerous bracelets cut into her hand, drawing blood.

"What?" Her companion was startled.

227

"Run for your life!"

Four men, obviously the ground crew for the balloonist, had started toward the balloon.

They had to be warned. They had to know. Before it was too late.

"Leave him alone!" Laura shouted, trying to be heard over all the noise. "Get away!" But the band was still playing, and no one, except the old woman next to her, heard. No one.

Oh God, she couldn't watch. Couldn't stay here . . . not when—

They leaped from the basket, flinging themselves on the ground crew. The men shrieked as they fell to the ground, writhing, clutching at the shades that covered their faces and necks. Some of the people standing nearby to watch the balloon's descent heard the men scream, realized something was wrong, and they turned, but by that time there was nothing they could do.

It was too late.

Too late for all of them, Laura thought.

The balloon landed; the gondola fell over, and the great expanse of nylon collapsed. Flames shot up as the burner ignited the material.

Shadows spread across the ground, stretching outward in an ever-expanding ring of darkness, lapping at the feet of the observers. Men and women alike screamed as the creatures touched them. Laura felt the surge of evil from the things on the ground, expanding, coiling, reaching, and her stomach turned. She backed slowly away from the horrors in front of her without looking behind her, kept moving until her back hit something. She screamed, groped, found the side of a portable toilet. She pressed herself against it, and stared ahead.

Now she was rooted to the ground. She couldn't flee, even though she knew she might die. All she could do was watch, and cry.

The burning balloon ignited the ground covering, and flames burst outward in all directions, radiating rapidly away from the original fire. Between the columns of flames and smoke, she saw the shades as they stalked and attacked the people.

The older woman who had talked to her had finally fled, screaming, but she tripped over a prone figure, its eyes torn out, and tumbled to the ground. As she struggled to get to her feet, the shadows reached her, touched her. Her screams cut off abruptly as her body disappeared under the shadows.

By the pavilion Eagleton Haas was beating at something in front of him with a chair. His pants leg was torn, and she saw blood streaming from a terrible gash. Darkness reached out to him, pulled him inside, and he cried out once.

The red-haired woman, her hands gone, ran past, shaking her bloodied stumps in front of her. The creatures, their yellow eyes intent, pursued at her heels.

Nearby the country-western singer sprawled, as though drunk. His flesh had been peeled from his chest, and there a handful of the creatures feasted.

Stumbling toward her was a man on fire. A hot, stinging, bitter taste rose in her throat as she recognized him. It was Douglas Griffen. His eyes were mad, and clinging to his legs, oblivious to the flames, shadows gnawed on his bared flesh even as he tried to escape them.

He saw her, stretched out a charred arm in petition, its sparks flying outward, and tried to call to her. The sound was a hideous shriek. Blood spurted outward as flames hissed, and he collapsed face down, not more than a dozen feet from her. The shadows swarmed over him, fire shooting up between them.

She clapped her hands to her nose and mouth, tried not to vomit. The odor of burning flesh assailed her nostrils, matted her hair, coated her skin, filled her with nausea. She struggled to free herself from her lassitude.

She had to get out.

She had to live.

She couldn't see Kent, didn't know if he'd escaped. Didn't care now. Cries of terrible agony filled the evening air, and she heard a few cars starting up. Someone must be escaping, getting out, and she knew she had to get there, had to find someone to help her.

Everywhere she looked she saw the spreading flames, punctuated by the yellow eyes, the evileyes she had seen before, and they were staring at her now, as if noticing her for the first time. They were coming after her. Slowly moving toward her. They knew she had escaped them once before. Knew she would not again.

Sobbing, Laura turned and ran, tripped over a tiny child curled in death. Her knees almost brushed the ground as she began to fall. She managed to push herself up with her fingertips, scraping the skin from them, got her balance and kept going.

She knew they were behind her, close, too close. The creatures of hell. The things with the sharp teeth and the sharp talons, and those horrible eyes. Those hating eyes that stared and ate her soul. She stumbled toward the parking lot.

Just as she reached it, a gust of wind swept flames toward the front line of cars. The gas tank of the closest car ignited and it exploded, sending metal flying hundreds of yards away. The fire leaped from car to car, one explosion following another. One of the cars just pulling out stopped, and the driver stared mesmerized at the scene in front of him. She tried to yell at him, tried to warn him, but he didn't hear. Flames touched the car, then it was gone in a burst of fire.

She watched as the cars went one by one. Oh God. She couldn't get out. She was doomed. They were going to kill her. Strip her flesh. Eat her. Before she was dead. Oh God.

No. She wouldn't let them.

Still they came toward her, those horrible shades. Sliding across the ground, through the flames, the gasoline, beckoning they came.

Dazed, she stumbled toward them, then stopped, remembering what Chato had said about them. With a great effort she turned, and ran—ran for her life.

CHAPTER TWENTY-FIVE

The sunlight was rapidly fading from the sky, the heat retreating with it, and on Central the neon lights over the bars and motels and adult bookstores and hockshops came on, casting a garish gleam on the otherwise undistinguished street. Up and down the street car headlights glimmered in the greyness of the dusk.

He put the truck's lights on, changed lanes and glanced sideways at his companion. She was staring out the window, watching an elderly man and woman walk into Goody's restaurant.

They hadn't talked much since coming into town. They had passed the house-trailer sales lots, the crumbling restaurants, the used car lots of East Central without saying a word, and it was only when they were getting close to the University area that he decided that their best place to look for Junior would be in the bars downtown.

It was a Friday night, and the places would be crowded.

233

They might have a hard time finding the old man . . . unless he wanted to be found.

"You know," she said, her soft voice breaking into his thoughts, "it's almost as if Montoya knew what was going to happen that night. He had to. I can't believe it was just coincidence that he left ahead of time."

"Yeah. It struck me that way, too. And that means those creatures don't always attack and kill humans. Somewhat encouraging."

"Somewhat."

They were now parallel to the University. The main parking lot, adjacent to Yale Park, was empty of cars. Usually on a night like this it filled rapidly for a concerts at Popejoy and Keller Halls or for some athletic event at Johnson Gym. But now people were afraid; they were staying home, he thought. Another siren wailed in the distance, and he could see a flashing red light up Central. They'd heard a lot of sirens since getting back into the city, and there had been a yellowish glow to the north. Some fire, he thought, and dismissed it.

"You know, Sunny, when we go looking for this old guy, well—" he paused to look sideways and saw her profile outlined from the lights in the park—"I mean, it could get pretty rough. And those guys there are going to stare at you. There will be a lot of rude comments made as well, I'm sure."

"I've been stared at before." He could hear the amusement in her voice, and it puzzled him. "I would think you might be worried too, Chato. They won't take kindly to an Indian being there."

"Yeah, I've been thinking about that. But there are several bars where the clientele is more Indian than anything, and Junior said he was a half-breed. It's a long shot, but we might give it a go there first."

"I'm game."

Again he heard the amusement.

"What do you do in Lubbock?" he asked, suddenly curious to hear more of her voice. Since he'd rescued her, he'd learned virtually nothing about her beyond her name and where she came from. Curiosity was only natural. And he hadn't seen a ring on her left hand.

"I'm in public relations. The personnel department." He could see her smiling now.

"Oh. With a company." He was beginning to get an idea of what she did, at least of what he thought she did.

"You might say that. It's very small, though. Not many employees. The wages are just dandy, however."

She laughed aloud then, a rich laugh that he liked. She didn't go on, and her silence confirmed his guess.

He lifted his foot from the gas pedal, aware that the needle had inched over forty-five and that they were in a thirty-five zone. Hurry, hurry, hurry, came that inside whisper. I *am*! he cried silently, and only laughter responded.

"I was a professor of geology at the University."

"Is that so?"

He couldn't tell if she were serious.

"I quit a few years ago. Felt a little out of place. Wanted to roam around, find myself, as they used to say."

"Did you?"

"I guess."

"Do you enjoy what you do?"

"Yeah. You?" He sensed the shrug, didn't see it in the dark.

Hurry, hurry.

They passed Presbyterian Hospital and saw two ambulances pulling into the driveway by the Emergency Entrance.

He thought about swinging by the paper to see Laura, but glanced at the clock. Not yet seven. She said she wouldn't be leaving until eight, so there was no sense. They could drop by her apartment later. Good God. He needed to find a place for Sunny to stay. Maybe Laura wouldn't mind if the other woman stayed with her.

"You know," she said, "we talk about these creatures and the murders they've committed, and we don't know why or what makes them do it. We don't know what they are. Except evil."

A gust of wind blew in his window, and he shivered with the sudden coolness.

"Evil," he murmured, as though echoing her, and the urgency within him clamored. "I have to do something. I don't know what."

"About the creatures."

He nodded. "Tenorio came to me—after he was dead. Told me. I turned my back on my religion many years ago. I have to turn back to it."

She was silent. Any moment he expected her to jump out of the truck, shrieking that he was a madman. But she didn't; she just sat there, her head slightly tilted as she listened.

"They can be anywhere, I guess. But they haven't done much in the city, as far as I know. It's almost as if they're waiting . . . for something. For someone." And he felt chilled at his own words.

They'd left the business section of downtown Albuquerque far behind now and had entered a section less prosperous, much older. It was darker here, too, with fewer street lights, fewer house lights on. He swung the truck into a small, crowded dirt parking lot before a bar, whose sign out front had been broken so that only two *e*'s and a *t* were still lit. The Schlitz sign, however, was intact. Iron bars had been placed across the windows and the adobe on the outside was chipping; out back a garbage dumpster was spilling over with uncollected garbage.

"Charming," the woman said as she got out of the truck and looked around. "You certainly know how to pick them."

How different from Laura, he thought, as they walked toward the front door. Laura would have pursed her lips disapprovingly and probably refused to set foot in the place.

Even outside they could hear loud rock music, and when they stepped through the door, heavy cigar and cigarette smoke swirled thickly through the bar's warm air. The room was dimly lit and fully occupied, and no one looked their way. He paused at the bar, glanced casually around as his eyes adjusted to the lack of light. Sunny was also looking around.

He knew they were being watched, and the main topic of conversation seemed to be a fire that had started earlier in the evening. He shut out the heavy voices, concentrated on looking for Junior. After a moment he said, "Do you see him?"

She shook her head.

He walked up to the bartender.

"Yeah?"

"Looking for Junior Montoya. A half-breed. Broken teeth."

Keeping his eyes on him, the man shook his head. "He not been here tonight."

"Thanks." He dropped a five-dollar bill on the counter, walked outside. She followed.

"How do you know he was telling the truth?" she asked once they were back in the truck.

"I don't. I just have to take his word. If he knows where Junior is, he'll let him know I'm looking for him."

He glanced up at the mountains, saw the lights of the restaurant atop Sandia Crest shining faintly through a haze clinging to the face of the mountain. It was a hushed night. Expectant. Waiting without breath. The only sounds in the city were of the cars racing past on Central and the distant fall and rise of sirens.

The second bar wasn't far from the first, and it was a repeat performance. No one had seen the old man. They drifted from bar to bar, each one seemingly worse than the one before, and the hour crept closer to midnight.

He pulled into another lot. "Okay. This is it. If we don't find him here, I give up for now."

This bar was farther out west on the highway than the others they'd been to; in fact, it was almost out of the city limits. Its rough sign was hand-painted. Only a few trucks and older model cars sat in the field that served as a parking lot.

There were no lights out here to break the darkness of the night, and he again thought how still everything was.

As if something . . . they . . . were waiting.

They walked into the single room, and found it remarkably quiet. Just a handful of Indians sitting at a bar, drinking and saying very little. There were no video games, no pinballs, no television. Just the eerie silence. And the dimness. The seats of the booths were red vinyl, now cracked with hard and long use and mended with electrical tape. Candles in green bowls set on the tables served a dual purpose—to light the table area and to keep insects away. An old jukebox in one corner was quiet for now. The bartender, a dark man with a bulging belly, glanced in their direction, didn't speak.

Sunny tugged at his sleeve, and he turned to look where she pointed.

And in the back of the room, he saw Junior Montoya.

CHAPTER TWENTY-SIX

Four empty glasses and a full one sat in front of the old man, and he looked as though he'd been expecting them. Probably had, Chato thought dourly.

"So, boy, we meet again. Heh, heh."

The light from the candle caused the ruins of his face to look like the ravages of a canyon. He was just as old, just as seedy-looking as Chato recalled.

"Ah, señorita," the old man said, staring at Sunny with obvious recognition. He noticed Junior's eyes had widened when he saw the woman. He was apparently surprised to see her still alive.

She didn't speak, and he knew she must be recalling the horrible events of that night when her friends had been killed and she'd barely escaped.

Chato sat without waiting to be asked. Sunny pulled her chair away from the table, away from Montoya, who leered across the table and cackled.

"You're in a fine humor, Montoya."

"Si. Meester Chato, I tell you I am doing fine."

"You remember my name."

"I remember much about you."

"And what about your friends, the shadoweyes?"

For a moment Montoya looked surprised, but he covered it by leaning forward, the light playing across his face, making it even more hideous.

"You have met them?"

"Yeah. Right after they killed the low-riders."

"Dumb shits. Those people." Junior shook his head, hawked, spit on the floor. Chato's disgust increased. Being with the old man was like having turned over a rock and finding something best left in the dark dampness of the soil.

He glanced at Sunny. She was staring down at her folded hands. Listening, but not looking. Montoya saw his expression and grinned again, winked.

"You got good taste, boy. Last time she was with a rich Texan and he—"

"That's enough, Montoya," he said quietly. "I'm not interested."

At that moment the bartender wandered over to them. "You want something?" he asked Montoya.

Chato shook his head, as did Sunny. The man shrugged, returned to his post behind the bar.

"Why don't we talk about your friends?" Chato suggested.

"How do you know they are my friends?" Montoya grinned at him, scratched his chest through a long rip in the material.

"We're not stupid, Montoya. No matter what you think." He continued to stare at the half-breed, noted that in the yellow light Montoya's face unpleasantly reminded him of a jack-o-lantern. Teeth and all. "After I saw you that day I found those Chicanos; later on I found out about the dead campers Sunny was with, and then a priest. All from those creatures. And I've been given the royal run-around by the Mayor and his people, who are scared shitless this'll drive business away, or whatever. So tell me about them, Montoya. Tell me about this mysterious pueblo. This Pueblo de Sombras."

The half-breed swallowed some of his drink, wiped his mouth with the back of his hand. "Such a clever boy, eh? You learned much at the University. You're not a dumb Indian like these, eh?" He jerked his head toward the Indians at the bar. "No. You're better than them. We all know that."

"Montoya," he warned.

The half-breed grinned. Held out his hands. "Eh, all right. You are so smart to find me. I will tell you." He drank some more beer. Chato watched as some of the liquor trickled down Montoya's chin. The old man made no move to wipe it away. "The pueblo is old. Very old. So old that all record has been lost of it."

"How did you find out about it?"

"Ah, I am a guide. It is my job, Meester Chato, to find these things out." He grinned. "So old the people were gone long before Coronado came through."

"You said that before," Sunny said, speaking for the first time.

He simply cackled. "There are guardians there of great treasure, it is said. And the guardians have been disturbed. They do not like it."

"The shadoweyes." When the old man did not answer, he pursued. "Is that what you mean by guardians? Are the shadoweyes the guardians?"

243

Montoya's lips pulled back in a grin that was a grimace. "The shadoweyes. Very old."

"They're the guardians?"

"They've got to be," the woman said, "or the old fool wouldn't keep repeating himself." Her voice was sharp. It was fear, he thought, that sharpened it. The fear that he felt, too.

"They are the ones who watch. And wait."

"For what?"

"Si. They wait."

Senile old fool. What a waste of time it had been looking for Montoya. He hadn't told them anything they didn't already know.

"Wait for what?" Sunny asked.

"Wait for him to come."

Chato frowned. Montoya wasn't making sense. "What about the fetish?"

The old man's eyes flicked. And for the first time he noticed how dark and flat they were. Rocks. Without emotions. Like a reptile's.

"Fetish?"

He didn't believe Montoya's innocent act. Not for a minute. Not from this man. "Yeah. What's its connection with the pueblo?"

"There is rumored to be a fetish from the pueblo. Found by a white archeologist a long time ago. But it has no value other than what the whites put on it." He winked. "Let them play with their pretty rocks and pebbles, eh? We have better things, you know?"

"The fetish."

"A plaything. Nothing more."

And of course that meant it wasn't. But it also didn't tell him what the fetish's significance was. The mysterious fetish. There *was* a connection. He just didn't know how it connected. Junior knew, but wasn't about to tell him. And he didn't like guessing games, so he wasn't about to sit here all night pumping the geezer.

On the other hand, he really didn't have much choice, did he?

He decided to change his tactics. "Won't you help us?" he asked. "We're your people. They aren't. They'll turn on you in the end, and you'll be hurt—murdered—just like the others. They can only use you for so long. Come on, Junior. Help us. Okay?"

Junior blinked at him, took a sip, blinked some more. The flame of the candle wavered with a sudden current of air, and the smell of wax and sour sweat from the old man drifted over to him.

Chato folded his arms and leaned back, waiting for Junior's cooperation. He had a hunch it might take a while. They'd just wait. The air in the bar was getting warmer, heavier, choking him, and he wished someone would open a window to let the breeze in. Where had that one draft come from? Probably someone opening the door. He was tired, too, and he stifled a yawn. He wanted nothing more than to go to bed—and sleep.

His eyelids were heavy, and they kept dropping, as if he had no muscle control.

"The shadoweyes wait for you," the old man whispered, and Chato nodded sleepily. Suddenly Montoya cackled, and Chato jerked up in his seat.

The half-breed was gone.

He stared at the empty chair, turned to Sunny. She was asleep sitting up.

He touched her arm, and she flinched, opening her eyes. "What?"

245

"We fell asleep. He's gone." He rubbed a hand across his face and looked around. Most of the customers had gone. In fact, except for the bartender and one man who had his head resting on the bar, they were the only ones left in the room.

"How long were we asleep?"

He looked at his watch. "Jesus. It's been hours. It's after midnight." He stood a little unsteadily, as if he'd been drinking a lot. He ached all over, too, and his head pounded. "Let's go. We're not going to find out anything else tonight."

The air outside had grown remarkably cool, or perhaps it was the contrast with the hot, sullen air of the bar they felt. For a few minutes they stood and breathed deeply, let the night air cool them. His head began to clear, and the muscle ache eased. The stars were faint tonight, as if the haze by the mountains had seeped across the sky. He wondered if it would rain later. The city needed it, needed to have the stench of death and fright washed away.

They got into the truck and pulled away from the bar, and when they got back on the highway, he thought he saw something scamper across the road. Something with bright eyes.

A finger traced ice down his back. He looked at Sunny to see if she'd noticed, but her eyes were closed. He decided not to say anything.

She yawned, then with a puzzled tone to her voice, said, "That was so strange. Both of us falling asleep like that, and for so long."

"Yeah. I don't like the idea of someone exerting some kind of control over us. And I don't understand it either. He doesn't seem like someone with"—say it, Chato, he told himself, say the word out loud—"powers."

"I know," she whispered.

Powers. The old man had power. The shadoweyes had power. Didn't anyone have power against them, power to stop them from what they planned?

The shadoweyes wait for you, the old man had said. For you. For you. For me, Chato thought, the knot of fear twisting inside. For me alone.

Remembering what he'd seen—or thought he'd seen— run across the road, he quickly rolled up the window on his side.

"We're going to Laura's apartment now. We'll talk with her. Maybe she saw the fetish at the presentation."

"Sure." Her hand reached out, switched on the radio, and they listened to the country music as they drove on the freeway.

When they reached the Montgomery exit, a newscast came on, and he automatically tuned it out as he thought about their encounter with Montoya. Then he thought he heard something about the barbecue, but by that time the music had returned.

"What'd they say?" he asked.

"There's been a ballooning accident at the barbecue," Sunny replied quietly. "A fire started and dozens of people have been killed or injured. Including the Mayor. I mean, he's dead."

Griffen dead. A fire. That's what the men in the bars had been talking about. That's why there was the haze over the mountains. That was the yellowish cast to the sky he'd seen to the north earlier. That's why there were so many ambulances out.

He had been a fool not to suspect that something was wrong. An absolute fool.

Oh my God. Laura was there.

247

He pressed the accelerator down hard and the truck jumped forward with a scream of its engine. He swung wildly past a station wagon, cut sharply in front of it, ignored the blast of the horn.

He had to get to her apartment and find out what had happened—find out if she were okay.

If she weren't—maybe she hadn't—

No. He wouldn't think of that. Not now.

And in his head, in the cab, he heard the horrible cackling of Junior Montoya.

CHAPTER TWENTY-SEVEN

He knocked loudly, heard hesitant footsteps behind the door; then they became running steps, and the door was thrown open.

Laura stood there, framed against the light, and he'd never seen her look so bad. In fact, she look horrible. Her hair was windblown and tangled; she had soot on her face, and blood streaked her ripped and stained dress; her eyes were red from crying. And her expression was one of absolute terror.

She gave a muffled cry when she saw who it was, started toward him, then stopped when she noticed Sunny. She backed away as they entered the apartment.

"Laura, what happened?" She was acting so odd, so unlike the confident woman she was.

She flung herself in his arms then, burying her face against him. She tried to talk, but could only make pitiful mewing sounds. Finally he just hushed her, held her and rocked her gently.

"I'll get her something to drink," Sunny said quietly, slipping past them and heading for the kitchen.

He nodded and stroked Laura's dark hair. He let her cry, feeling her body shake against his chest. The tears became sobs that racked her body, and still he just held her, was a warm comforting presence. Finally, when the sobs had diminished, he led her by one hand, as though she were a child, to a chair in the living room. She stood numbly by it, did nothing, and so he carefully placed his hands on her shoulders and pushed her gently, forcing her to sit. Offering no protest, she sank onto the cushion and leaned back, her eyes closed. There were deep dark smudges under her eyes, and soot had worked its way into the tiny lines around her mouth and eyes. He didn't see any signs of burns, so she probably wasn't injured. But what was wrong? More than the fire had disturbed her, he thought.

Not more than a few minutes later Sunny, who'd waited until Laura was calmer, brought a glass of whiskey to her. She accepted it with hands that shook, drank it in great gulps.

Chato waited until she had almost finished the drink, then asked again, "What happened?"

Laura took a deep breath, passed a hand over her face and stared at the blackness that came away on her fingertips.

"They came out of the balloon, and—and—" Her voice choked.

"Take your time, Laura," he urged. He got up and poured a second drink for her. She gulped that one just as rapidly as the first.

Then, in a small voice so low they could barely hear her at times, Laura told them her story, from the moment she had arrived—told them of seeing Eagleton Haas and meeting Senator Kent, of watching the descent of the balloon, of the horrors that followed afterward.

She refused to look at them as she talked of the creatures. He reached over and brushed her cheek with his fingertips. She flinched, and immediately he withdrew his hand. After she had run away, never once looking back, she explained, she found herself on a busy street—Juan Tabo, she thought, although she couldn't recall now. She recalled seeing ambulances and fire trucks speeding by, but time seemed suspended to her, and she didn't make the connection. She stood by the curb and waved her arms, and at length a kind-hearted motorist stopped and gave her a ride back to the apartment. The man had asked her what had happened, but she'd only said there'd been a fire. When she got back to the apartments, she'd had to go to the manager's to get a pass key—her purse and everything in it had been left behind at the picnic grounds.

The mention of the picnic grounds brought back the horrors for her, and tears welled in her eyes again, seeped down her streaked cheeks. "I've never seen anyone killed before." She hid her face in her hands and he once more took her into his arms to comfort her.

Sunny had said nothing during Laura's recitation, but had simply sat on the sofa and listened. He knew she must be thinking of her own encounter with the shadoweyes; her face, though, held no emotion.

After a few minutes, when Laura had quieted, Sunny stirred. "I think we ought to put her to bed. She needs to rest, needs sleep."

He agreed and slowly helped Laura to her feet, then into the bedroom. There they managed to get her out of her ruined dress and stockings and into a clean nightgown. Sunny returned to the living room, while he gently wiped

Laura's face, arms and hands with a damp washcloth he'd retrieved from the bathroom.

When he started to get up, Laura grabbed him with frantic hands. So he sat again, and said nothing, and watched her as her eyelids closed while he stroked her hair. After a few minutes her breathing became regular and he knew she was asleep. He quietly left the bedroom.

Sunny was sitting in one of the chairs. "What now?" she asked tersely.

"I don't know." He slumped into one of the chairs. "I wonder who had the fetish. We'll ask her tomorrow, when she's rested. We should go to bed now. It's late, and I think tomorrow's going to be busy."

"I don't know if I can sleep," Sunny said.

"Try. It may be the last we get for a long time," he said.

They found extra pillows and blankets in one of the hallway closets and made a bed for Sunny on the sofa and one for him on the floor of the living room. When they were finished, they stood for a moment almost touching, and he could feel the desire growing inside him. He wanted to hold her, to kiss her, to make love to her, because tomorrow . . . tomorrow he might not be here. He forced himself to draw away, kissed her chastely on the forehead.

He checked once more on Laura, saw that she was soundly asleep and would not, he thought, be disturbed by nightmares that night. The whiskey had helped there. He returned to the living room, found Sunny already settled on the couch. He switched off the light, glanced out the sliding glass doors and remembered when he had seen that dark shape run across the grass. Had it been only days ago? It seemed like weeks.

He yawned, stretched and lay down, pulling the blanket up to his chin.

But he couldn't go to sleep.

He saw the eyes that stared, unblinking. They stared. They watched. Him. He heard them whispering and they were calling his name.

And he heard Junior's laugh. He moaned aloud and heard a rustling noise in the room. He tensed, waiting for the shadow to appear.

Something warm slid under the blanket next to him.

Sunny.

He reached for her, and she came easily into his arms. Holding her against his chest, he felt the steady beat of her heart, her life. Her arms slipped around him, and he kissed her mouth; her firm lips parted under the pressure of his. Her hands gripped his shoulders then, the fingers strong and urgent. Gently he unbuttoned her shirt, pulled off her jeans, and lay down next to her, his mouth already on hers, his hand on her firm breast. She wrapped her arms around his neck, pulled him close, and he lost himself totally in his arousal. He thought of nothing but this woman and himself, and for once the terrible images of the shadoweyes were driven from his mind.

Afterward she slept peacefully in his arms, and he drowsed, content, staring up at ceiling, and saw there the round yellow eyes. And heard the siren call. Whispering softly, beckoning for him to come to them.

He closed his eyes, forced the image from his mind. Sunny stirred, as if sensing his disquiet. He stroked her hair, murmured to her, twisted a curl that lay across his arm. She fell asleep again.

Again he shut his eyes, and saw death beyond them, and all sleep faded.

He might die soon.

Death . . . He had faced it in Vietnam ten years before. Had been injured, left to die, but had crawled back to safety, and had been patched up so they could order him back into the jungles, and he had managed, despite the sanguinary desires of his commanders, to come home alive and whole. You didn't much like it, didn't like being so close to death, but in a war you expected that. You didn't expect to find death in these hideous forms from the mountains. You didn't expect death this way. Facing shadow creatures with talons and fangs, creatures that could tear you to shreds in minutes. That would rip out your throat. That would kill you in agonizing ways.

Ways . . . the Old Ways.

The old Isleta Indian had said look to them. Believe in them. Follow them. He said to make a medicine pouch.

The old ways. Who remembered them? Long ago he had turned away from the shaman Josanie. Now he wished he hadn't. He wished he had listened and learned all that he could from his teacher, wished because he knew that he would face the shadoweyes, that the burden he had feared so long had finally come to settle upon his shoulders. Like a great eagle, it dug its talons into his shoulders and clung to him. The talons of the shadoweyes.

Junior was right. They waited for him, and he would go to them. But not tonight. Tonight—what was left of it, for already he saw the sky beginning to lighten—tonight must be rest.

He closed his eyes, seeking sleep, willing it. And finally it came.

Silver, cold and dark and silent, surrounded him, and it was very misty, as if a fog had crept over the city. No noises of the city disturbed his concentration. His brow was furrowed as if he were deep in thought.

The voices coaxed.

And he responded.

The jingling. Keys in his hand. He could not see where he was going. Did not know where he was going. It was not important. It was only important that the eyes were before him, the voices calling, and that he—

Someone called his name. The woman.

Again, louder this time: "Chato!"

Her voice. Soft and concerned and perplexed. Whispering. Whispering to him. Urging him.

He did not look back, did not want to see her in the moonlight.

The door of the pickup. Keys out. Keys—

His arm shook. "Chato! What are you doing?"

The silver fog disappeared and the whispering faded; he opened his eyes. Sunny was standing next to him, her hand on his arm. He stared at her, unable to speak. What had happened? What was she doing out here? What was *he* doing out here? The last thing he'd recalled was falling asleep. He frowned. It was almost dawn, and somehow he'd managed to get dressed, get down the stairs and out to the parking lot in front of the apartment building.

She touched his cheek. "I woke up when you got your keys out. I called to you, but you just kept going. You didn't even look back. I knew something . . . funny . . . was going on, so I followed. Are you all right now?"

He took a deep breath, stuck the keys in his pocket. "Yeah. I was dreaming."

She put an arm around him and they moved back toward the apartment. He paused at the foot of the staircase and stared at the blackness of the mountains to the east.

They had been calling him, had been drawing him to them. And they had almost succeeded. If it hadn't been for Sunny. . . . He shuddered, turned and swiftly kissed her. Her lips were cool and sweet-tasting and they widened under the pressure of his. For a moment they were held together in the embrace; then a cool wind drifted across them and they separated.

Holding hands, they started up the stairs.

CHAPTER TWENTY-EIGHT

They ate a hasty breakfast, the three of them, shortly after eight and stared at the *Courier*. The banner headline read, "FRIDAY FIRE KILLS MAYOR, ARCHBISHOP," and beneath it were the photographs of the prominent dead and articles about Griffen, five professors from UNM, a former governor, the liquor distributor, the country-western singer and the leading playwright. Over a hundred people were reported to be dead or injured. The deaths were blamed on a balloon mishap. The out-of-control balloon, reported the account, had come down in the midst of the partying crowd. The balloon had caught on fire and the flames had spread across the artificial ground covering. People had panicked and chaos had resulted.

Nothing was said about the shadoweyes. A horror too great for anyone to talk about, Chato suspected. Most survivors would probably be all too glad to repress the memory of the hellish shades.

"Kent's name isn't among the list of dead," Sunny said, looking up from her section of the paper.

"Then he must be alive," Chato said. He frowned, looked at Laura. "Did Griffen ever get a chance to present the fetish to Kent?"

"Yes. That happened just before the balloon started to go up. It was scheduled for later, but the Mayor seemed like he wanted to get the ceremony out of the way."

He must have suspected something about the fetish, Chato thought, and wanted it away from him. "Wait a minute. If Kent isn't dead—although we don't know that for sure, and if he had the fetish with him when the shadoweyes attacked—"

"Then there could be a connection," Sunny supplied.

"Damned right. Where was the Mayor when the creatures attacked?"

"With Kent and de Vargas," Laura said.

"They died; Kent didn't. My God! But the only way we can find out for sure is—"

"—is to find him!" Sunny said.

"Do you mind explaining to me?" Laura asked, her voice a trifle acid. She had showered this morning, and washed her hair, and dressed in clean slacks and a blouse, and except for the dark circles still under her eyes, Chato could not tell that the night before she had faced horrible deaths and mutilations.

"It could mean," the other woman said, "that if Kent had the fetish with him when the shadoweyes attacked, he was somehow protected by it."

"It makes a hell of a lot of sense to me," he admitted. "And," he continued, "it means that whoever goes after the creatures should have the fetish. It's an amulet against evil. That evil."

Not whoever.

There was just one candidate. Had always been, but he'd been too stupid to see. He looked up to see Sunny watching him, her eyes were filled with sympathy. And realized something in that moment.

"It's me they've wanted all along," he whispered. "Me."

Laura's voice held cynical amusement. "And why you, Chato? Why would these creatures select you, of all the people in the world? Isn't that fairly egotistical of you? And what do they want you for anyway?"

"Do you have a better explanation for what he's gone through?" Sunny demanded. She stared at the other woman until Laura dropped her eyes. "I believe him—he knows more about all of this than we do. Why can't you just listen to him?"

"Tenorio tried to warn me, but I wouldn't listen. Then they killed him—had him killed rather—and he still came back, still tried to help, and I was so goddamned thick-headed, so filled with modern ideas, so—"

"Why you?" Laura shouted. "Why, why, why?" She was standing now, her face flushed, her chest rising and falling rapidly.

He looked up at her, his face pleading. "Because I'd planned on being a shaman. Because I didn't become one, and because my faith wasn't as strong as it should be—and because I had a power—a gift, if you will—that I refused to recognize. Josanie said I should use it, but the burden was too great. God, I was only fifteen, sixteen." He was up, pacing agitatedly, running his hands through his hair. Sunny watched him, said nothing. "Because my faith was so weak, because I'd turned my back on it, and because I had this gift after all, they could seduce me more easily than someone who'd found his faith, his ways."

"No," Laura said, shaking her head adamantly. "It's just a bunch of crap. Old Indian crap. I won't listen to this."

"You're going to have to," he said quietly, "because I expect you to help me."

She laughed—a shrill, ugly sound that grated. "I'm not going to help some dumb bastard kill himself. No way, Chato. You found another white woman. You go ahead and use *her*."

Before he could respond, Laura moved swiftly across the living room, grabbed her purse and left the apartment, slamming the door so hard that one of the pictures fell off the wall.

He stared at the door, at the cracked glass, at Sunny's concerned face. "It's going to be soon. So soon. I have to do something. But I don't know what to do. I really don't."

Sunny's arms went around him. "Don't worry," she said, her breath warm by his ear, "we'll work something out."

And oddly he was comforted.

He took a deep breath. "We have to find Kent. Where he is, we'll find the fetish. I have to get that first, before we do anything else. But where?"

"Does she have an address book?" Sunny asked, nodding toward the office.

"Probably." He went into the office, and they both began searching, taking little care to keep stacks of paper neat. He was angry at Laura, although perhaps he shouldn't be. He couldn't expect her to believe in what he had himself just come to accept. And yet, nagged one part of him, Sunny accepted.

Sunny's different, he told himself, and knew he was

260

lucky she was with him. Knew that it had been the right thing to rescue her the day before. They had known each for only a day, and yet it seemed longer, as if they had been together for always.

"Got it!" she said triumphantly, holding up a small maroon book.

They grabbed sandwiches, hopped into the truck and pulled away from the apartment complex. She thumbed through the book until she came to the K's, brushed the crumbs away she'd dropped on the pages.

"Here it is. His address—local, that is—is given as Ranchos de Vista. There's a P.O. box. Its address is San Tomas."

"I know where that is," he said quietly. "On the other side of the mountains, on the road to Santa Fe. He must live out in one of those fancy developments."

"How quickly can we get there?"

"In about thirty minutes. I've got to get to the freeway now."

As they stopped at a light, just before they turned right onto Wyoming, a blue car slid to a stop beside him. The driver glanced at him, then away.

Chato saw the fear reflected on the man's face. The fear that kept many people off the streets today, even though it was Saturday morning and there should have been a lot of traffic. But there were only a few cars out, his and the blue car and a handful of others. Fear of the murders, of the tragedy that had happened last night, and a sense of unease that something terrible threatened the city. He hadn't seen any balloon gondolas in the backs of pickups. The Fiesta had probably been cancelled, after last night's disaster.

They rode in silence, Chato concentrating on his driving and feeling the urgency beating at him inside. Twisting and squeezing, taking his breath away, and he had to do something *now*. But he couldn't—not until he found Kent, not until he found the fetish.

"Wait a minute," Sunny said as they were approaching the freeway entrance. "Would Kent go to his house—where all the reporters would be sure to follow?"

"Probably not," he said slowly. He hit the steering wheel with the heel of his hand. "Jesus. We'll never find him now. Goddammit."

"Oh yes we will, Chato." She smiled at him, the expression broadening at his apparent confusion. "Go and get on the freeway. Okay. Now, where else could Kent have gone?"

"I don't know," he replied, his voice sounding as defeated as he was feeling. There were so many places Kent could have holed up in. He could have left the city, the state, be far away by now, and they'd never find him. Never in all the time left to them.

And the voices chuckled.

"Where could he go that would be discreet, where he could come and go at his own will, where he could be protected, where there is some connection with him?" she asked softly.

"I don't know—"

"Oh, but you do." She smiled, and he thought—inanely, so out of place now—how pretty she was. "I was there."

"Jesus. The monastery."

CHAPTER TWENTY-NINE

They passed four city cop cars on the freeway as they headed for Tijeras Canyon, so Chato let up on the accelerator.

"Looking for Kent, probably," he said to Sunny, when she glanced his way. "I don't want to attract attention. They may not remember me—but they might, and we can't have any delay now."

She nodded, and the rest of the ride was made in silence. As they drove down the dirt road to the monastery, he wondered how she felt returning to what had been her prison. He glanced over at her, and she responded by giving him a jaunty smile.

He parked; they got out, and he took a deep breath. Kent had to be here, and if he weren't—what then? No, he wouldn't think about that. At least not yet.

"We aren't armed," she said, as they headed for the main building.

"I didn't think we'd need to be, but now that I'm here,

I don't know," he replied truthfully. "I don't think the monks are armed. God, I hope not."

"The Church Militant?" she said, and he laughed. "Look, Chato." She pointed to the far end of the parking lot.

A black Buick sat there.

"I thought I saw a priest driving it. A priest from here, I wonder?" he asked thoughtfully. They paused before the front doors. "They probably know we're here. I mean, we didn't exactly sneak up." She nodded, didn't speak. "Okay then, let's go."

He tried the door, found it locked. He kicked at it. Once, twice, three times, and on the fifth kick there was a sharp splintering of wood and the door fell open. They pushed in past it and looked around. They were in a sort of reception area. A few plastic-covered couches sat among some potted plants. There was a gift shop off to one side and a piano along another wall, and beyond it another doorway. And no sign of a single monk.

"Through that door," he said, pointing. She nodded and they started for it.

"You can't come in here," said a monk, stepping through the doorway. They stopped abruptly.

"We're looking for Senator Kent."

"I know why you're here," the monk said. "This is God's house. Leave at once."

"Not before we see Kent." Chato started through the doorway, but the man blocked him. "I'm sorry, Brother." Before the monk could respond, Chato grabbed him by the shoulders, shook him so vigorously that his tonsured head snapped back and forth. "Where is he?" Chato gritted. "Where's the Senator?"

"I-In the chapel," the monk said, pointing to the outside.

Chato flung the man away from him; he crashed into the piano, slumped to the ground.

"Come on."

They ran down the breezeway to the double door of the chapel, and paused. Then Chato resolutely pushed through the doors, and halted until his eyes adjusted to the gloom of the church. What light came in was filtered through stain-glass windows high above their heads on the sides. It was furnished with rows of simple wooden pews. The Twelve Stations of the Cross were crudely painted plaster-of-Paris statues, and a tortured and bloodied Christ, carved of dark brown wood, hung on a wooden cross behind the free-standing altar. Two pewter candlesticks stood atop a plain altar cloth.

In the front pew, just before the communion railing, sat a man who was facing the altar. At the sound of the doors closing, he stood and turned to the back of the church.

"I'm been waiting for you to find me," Kent said evenly, studying them as they walked up the aisle. "I'm surprised it was this quickly, though."

"We've had previous experience with the monastery," Chato said slowly.

"So you're the blanket Indian I've heard so much about," Kent said with a slight smile. Chato ignored the slight, didn't respond. "Where's your reporter friend? Or didn't she make it?"

"Oh, she made it all right. In fact, it was through her that we found you."

Kent's smile faded a little. Now that he stood close to the man, Chato thought he didn't look well. Deep dark circles lay under his eyes, and his eyes were never still— they moved constantly, as if he feared something were creeping up on him. After what had happened at the fire, Chato wasn't surprised.

"What now, Del-Klinne?"

"We want the fetish."

"It won't do you any good," the Senator said, somewhat smugly.

"I don't know about that. It helped you survive, didn't it?"

"Yes," the man whispered. "What do you want it for then?"

"I want to survive, too. Those creatures must be destroyed."

"Those creatures," Kent repeated hollowly. He turned away for a moment, shuddered, looked back at them. "Creatures of hell."

"Yes. And the fetish is the only thing that will protect me when I go against them."

"You?" the senator asked skeptically. "How can you destroy them?"

Chato glanced at Sunny, who smiled encouragingly. "I don't know. I just know I'm the one who has to do it. They've been calling me, those voices, and I have to do something."

"Voices? What voices?" Kent asked sharply.

"The ones I hear, from the shadoweyes. Look, we're just wasting time. Hand over the fetish."

"No, it's mine."

"You stole it."

"Originally. But it's been mine all these years. My key to power. I'll be President yet. I'll make it."

"Even though your friends are dead?" Chato asked. Kent nodded, didn't speak. Out of the corner of his eye Chato could see that Sunny was moving slowly, inch by inch, away from the two men, and stopping from time to time so that she wouldn't attract attention.

"The fetish will give me all that I want."

"Maybe you don't know how to use it properly," Chato said easily. Kent shook his head. "Why don't you tell me more about it? About how you found it?"

"I took it from the archeologist at the University. He never connected its disappearance with my visit. Stupid academic bastard."

"How do you know the fetish will do all that you think it will?" Chato asked. Sunny had reached the communion railing and paused.

"Because of the papers."

"What papers?" Chato asked with interest, the woman's progress momentarily forgotten.

"I thought it was a typical fetish, nothing special, at first. Although when I dropped it, and nothing happened, I knew it was something remarkable. I could *feel* that it was different. When I got it back to my apartment, I took a hammer to it and battered it, and it was unscathed. I knew then we had something . . . magical. Richard scoffed a little. Of course, he would, because he was a young priest in those days. He didn't believe in the strength of Indian religions. Doug didn't want to believe in it, but I did. I was no fool; I knew power when I saw it, and it didn't matter to me if it came from a Christian religion or a long-dead Indian one. It was still power."

"The papers," Chato urged.

"The professor had made some notes on the fetish. I took them, too. I never told the others." He paused, licked his lips. His eyes were almost feverish. "I read them all that evening, and I knew then how strong the religion was. He had talked with old Indians, had found out a legend of a powerful fetish that could be controlled by only one person. It was black and hideous, and I knew my fetish was the one from the legends.''

Sunny had reached the altar now; Chato forced himself to turn his complete attention to the Senator. ''Did you test it?''

''Of course. I was a good lawyer, not a brilliant one, and with the help of the fetish I began to win case after case. My career began to advance. But I didn't want anything to happen to the fetish, and when I wasn't using it, Richard had it, where it would be safe.''

''What did he think of all of this? I mean, with him being a good Catholic and all?''

''His career began to advance, too. He became a little more favorably disposed toward the fetish. Now Doug . . . .'' He shook his head ruefully. ''He was always uncomfortable with it, loathe to use it, and his career advanced the least of the three.''

''But you waited . . . you wanted the Presidency.''

''I knew I would have unlimited power.''

''The notes?''

''I burned them. Page after page.''

''The professor never accused you of taking the fetish? Never suspected?'' Sunny was grasping a candlestick in her hand now, and was heading carefully back toward the communion railing.

''He may have suspected, but he never came after me. Good God, I was a powerful attorney. Why should I have stolen it? Then he died, and there was no one left who knew about it. Except—'' His expression darkened.

''Except?'' Chato pursued.

''This half-breed went to Richard's church about half a year later and was asking about a fetish. Richard sent him packing. He was an unpleasant old guy, and he said the fetish belonged to him.''

''Did you ever see him again?'' Chato knew who the old man had been.

''Yes. He kept coming back. He was convinced that we had the fetish, and he was determined to get it, but we were too damned clever and kept him away from it.''

''Yeah, I guess you were clever.'' She was close now, so very close, and was raising her arm.

Without warning Kent whirled, saw Sunny's arm raised, the heavy candlestick poised to hit him, and he charged down the pew, away from her. Chato flung himself over the back of the pews and grabbed the Senator around the middle. Together they crashed to the floor.

Sunny ran around to the end of the pew. She raised the candlestick again, watched as first Chato, then Kent was on top. Kent kicked out, caught Chato in the stomach. In that moment Kent started to crawl off. Chato seized his foot, pulled himself up a few inches and launched himself at the other man. Once more they were knocked to the ground, but this time with Chato on top. He drew back his fist, followed through with a punch to Kent's chin. The man's head jerked back, and just as it did, Sunny brought the candlestick down on his forehead. There was a sickening thud, and he went limp. The candlestick left a shallow depression, red and black in color. She swallowed quickly and dropped the candlestick, turned to the door.

''I hear voices outside.''

''The monks.''

He managed to squat, ignoring his outraged abdominal muscles, and searched Kent's pockets. Inside the dead man's coat he found a wrapped box about the size of his fist. He rattled it, and knew the fetish was in it. He didn't have time to check; they had to get out before the monks stopped them. Just to be sure, though, he rummaged through the senator's other pockets, found nothing beyond the usual contents.

So the fetish had to be in the box. He slipped it in his own pocket and stood. "Come on."

He grabbed her hand, ran toward the front doors, burst through them just as a handful of monks run toward them on the breezeway. He released her hand, got out his keys, and raced for the truck, realizing this was the second time he and Sunny had left the monastery in such a way. Getting to be a habit, he thought wryly.

They jumped in and he started the engine. He backed up wildly, not caring this time if he knocked monks down. Two tried to climb into the truck's bed, but he backed up abruptly and they fell off the bumper. Then they were speeding away, away from the monastery, and down the dirt road.

They didn't talk until they reached town, and then Chato lifted his foot from the accelerator and brought the pickup down to the speed limit. He glanced over at her, remembered again the first time. "Thanks."

She nodded. "You saved mine. It was the least I could do for you."

"I've got to see the fetish. I can't wait any longer, so I'm going to get off on the Wyoming exit. There's a library a few blocks off the street and a park. No one will notice us."

Once they got to the park, he took the box out of his pocket and ripped the paper off, removed the lid, plucked away the cotton padding.

They stared, both unable to speak.

The fetish. Nightblack and a little smaller than his fist,

it was carved from obsidian. Volcanic glass. Smooth and shiny and cool and hard under his touch.

A shadow.

A shadoweyes.

Complete to the fangs, talons and eyes.

A shadoweyes.

Do you fight fire with fire? He smiled bleakly to himself, feeling the surge of terror inside.

A shadoweyes.

Touched.

Tag! You're it!

But I don't—

And his fingers trembled as he wrapped the fetish once more.

CHAPTER THIRTY

"I've got to do it right away," he said, after the box had been tucked into a pocket. "I can't wait."

"I know."

He ran a hand through his hair and breathed deeply, feeling the pain of fear constrict his chest. Even though he had this gift that Josanie and Tenorio had said he had—what if he still didn't know what to do. But he did. He knew all right.

Feather, and stone, and seed.

Today he would test his learning, his teacher's confidence in him, his life.

"I've got errands to run. If you want, I'll drop you off at Laura's."

"I'd rather come with you, Chato," she said quietly. He nodded, grateful. "What do you need?"

He frowned for a moment in thought. "Some crystals, petrified wood, eagle feathers, rattlesnake rattles. Pollen. Silly stuff." It was strange speaking aloud, strange to be telling this woman what he needed in his preparation. Did she think he was ridiculous, that he was playing with toys?

"There's a rock shop .on South Eubank, almost by Central. I remember seeing it last week. You can probably get the minerals there."

"Okay." She hadn't laughed. He breathed with relief, not wanting to think how Laura would have reacted.

He stopped for gas for the truck, filled both tanks, and then found the shop with little difficulty. He found a buckskin pouch there, too, with a long cord. The medicine bag, Josanie and Tenorio had mentioned. Most potent. It would hold what he needed to take into the mountains. He also purchased a second buckskin pouch—for the black fetish.

Back in the truck he'd stared wordlessly at his purchases. "He probably thought I was crazy," he said slowly.

"I doubt it. For all he knows, you could be an artist who needs unusual material for his work."

"True," he admitted. He glanced over at her. "You must think I'm nuts. We've only known each other for a few days, and yet all I've done is drag you all over the place, and now we're looking for stuff to put in a medicine bag, for God's sake. I'm surprised you haven't had me committed to Nazareth yet!"

She smiled. "You're not ready for the sanitorium, Chato. Not yet. Don't worry, though. I'll let you know when it's time."

He smiled and patted her hand, reassured once again by her presence. Then, suddenly self-conscious, he pulled his hand away and started the truck.

"God, where am I going to get the feathers?"

"Hatbands. For cowboy hats. They're usually made of

274

feathers, and there's bound to be some eagle feathers there. As long as you can recognize them.''

''Sure can.'' He grinned at her, and wished he could make love to her just one more time. Just once, that was all he asked. But he couldn't. He didn't have time, and after that—he didn't want to think about what might—or might not—come afterward.

They found a western apparel store down on Central and he searched through the racks of hatbands until he found what he needed. It took twenty bands, but he finally had enough feathers.

She frowned a little, her eyes darkening. ''What about lightning-struck twigs. You say it has to be that? They have more power?''

''Right. At least that's what my teacher claimed. And there's no need to worry about that. I know a place where we can get them.''

In the mountains, not far from where he'd been chased by the unnatural lightning, he found what he wanted. Then he stopped off at the motel and threw a few articles in a bag before they returned to Laura's apartment. She wasn't back yet.

While Sunny fixed them lunch, he studied the various items. Suddenly he felt foolish. It was like being a little kid again and collecting pretty rocks and unusual shells. Only this time it wasn't a game.

The front door slammed; he looked up, caught Sunny's eye on him from across the kitchen counter.

''When do you get the sandbox?''

Laura stood there, hands on hips, and she wasn't smiling. Sunny had come out of the kitchen and was standing well away from the other woman. But she was there for support, he thought, if he needed it.

"What?"

"You're going through with it." She hadn't asked a question.

"Someone has to."

"I can't believe this!" Laura laughed harshly. "It's so stupid. You don't have to do it. No one appointed you savior of the human race. Maybe those things will go away and never bother us again."

"And maybe they won't," Sunny said softly. "Maybe they'll decide to come down out of the mountains and kill everyone here." Laura looked at her, hatred and jealousy in her eyes, but didn't speak.

He said nothing, continued sorting his purchases.

"Please let someone else do it. You'll just get hurt—or worse."

"I told you, Laura," he said with a calmness he did not totally feel, *"I* have to do it. I was the one who was *touched* by the shadoweyes. It's my responsibility. It was my responsibility a long time ago, but I put it off. I tried to pretend it wasn't important. But it is, and only I can do it." He finished putting the shells and twigs into the pouch. He closed the opening tightly, set it down on the table. He took out the fetish and carefully slipped it into the other pouch. "Excuse me." He got up and headed toward the bathroom to change. Laura laughed again, just once, a high sound, and turned away, but he thought he saw tears in her eyes.

"You talked him into it," Laura accused, staring at Sunny. The blonde woman shook her head, remained silent. "You're just a scheming Texan bitch, who—"

"Laura!" He stood outside the bathroom. "That's enough."

She turned away, walked to the balcony, the balcony

from which he'd seen the shadoweyes that night they'd made love.

He finished changing and came out. Laura was still on the back porch. Sunny was waiting for him.

"I'll drive you," she said.

He nodded his thanks, slowly gathered together all his stuff, then paused by the sliding glass doors.

"Laura—"

"Go away. Go up there and get killed." Her voice was muffled and she wouldn't face him.

"I—"

"Get out."

He gathered up the pouches and walked out of the apartment without looking back. They said nothing as they drove away from the complex. When they reached Juan Tabo, Sunny reached out and her fingers stroked his, giving him some comfort, and yet the fear balled coldly in the pit of his stomach and his mouth tasted bitter.

I am going to die.

No. I can't be pessimistic.

I'm not. I'm being realistic.

I'm going to die; I'm not going to be able to defeat the shadows, and they'll take over, and—

No, no, no.

His head ached, and the beckoning voices grew stronger the closer they came to the mountains. Overhead dark clouds formed as they approached the Sandias, collected above the mountain slopes, and rain was now an awesome threat. Some clouds had settled, mantle-like, onto the uppermost regions of the high peaks, and he hoped he would not have to climb that far, not into the midst of the storm clouds. Jagged lightning arched through the clouds, and he heard a faint rumble. He shivered as a cool, gusting breeze hit his shoulders.

Yet, though it looked as if it would rain any moment, the air was hot and thick and still, and his tongue seemed swollen in his mouth. He needed a drink, but wanted to save the water he'd brought for later.

They drove past the Piñon Flats picnic grounds, or rather what remained of them. The entire area, still cordoned off, lay blackened from the ravages of the fire. They stared at it silently, remembering Laura's account of that night, and then Sunny was taking an unpaved road eastward to the mountains. Behind them, far away now, were all the houses of the city, all the artificial signs of man, and as they rumbled down the rough track, farther and farther into the wilderness, he stared morosely out the window of the truck. A jack rabbit bounded past them, then was gone with a white flash of its tail.

They took a right, heading into the Sandia Game Management Area, far away from the road, back where the campgrounds were located. They drove past scrub oak and sage, tamarisk and chimasa, and stopped at a sign. She glanced at it, then drove onward for a few winding miles. She stopped at the junction of two dirt roads, both of them restricted to vehicles.

Looking around and seeing no one, she proceeded along the dirt road, and the truck jounced with each dip and bump. Finally she came to a flat area, parked, set the handbrake and turned to him.

"This is very close to the spot where we were camping that night," she said. He nodded. "Don't forget this," she said with a faint smile, and handed him the flashlight. "I know it's not traditional, but—"

He accepted it gratefully. "Thanks."

They both got out. He wore jogging shorts, Adidas running shoes, and a knife in a sheath at his side. He'd placed the black fetish in the small pouch and slipped it around his neck. He had braided his hair, not wanting it to get in the way, then had put a sweatband around his forehead. The larger buckskin pouch hung at his side.

Not quite the way his scout forebears had dressed, he thought with sudden humor, but just as effective. Or so he hoped.

He stretched slowly, massaged a bicep, looked around as he did so.

"Over there," she said, pointing to a large group of piñon trees. "I think that's the spot. And Montoya was talking about the hidden place being straight behind where we were."

He nodded. She laughed a little, sadly, and her eyes were darker than normal. "I'll see you later."

He tried to smile, failed, and kissed her, long, her lips opening under the pressure of his. He breathed deeply of her fragrance, then pulled away.

"Later."

She walked back to the truck—a graceful, swaying walk he'd never noticed before—slid under the wheel, and drove slowly down the road that was more washed-out arroyo than anything else.

He waved, once, but wasn't sure she saw. He watched as she drove away, dust rising behind, and then he could no longer hear the truck.

CHAPTER THIRTY-ONE

Keenly aware of the silence now, he faced the mountain. No birds sang in the nearby trees, and even the normally whispering wind was silent as it brushed the boughs.

He was alone. And he felt it.

Sweat trickled down his back already, although he hadn't yet moved. A wisp of wind caressed his cheek, and his fingers went to the soft pouch, grasped it. It hung level with his sternum. It would work, would keep him safe. It had to.

Thunder again rumbled, and he smelled the faint odor of ozone.

From where he stood he could look out over the flat reaches of the reservation land of Sandia Pueblo miles away to the west, close to the river, and he could see straight down to the river and to the cluster of houses and trees along it. Distantly on the highway, heading west to Grants and to Arizona beyond, he saw the glint of cars.

Lightning twisted overhead; closeby he heard the crack

of thunder. The wind shifted, colder now than a moment before, and he wished he'd worn a shirt. Still, activity would keep him warm, and with that he decided he'd stalled long enough.

He breathed deeply once, scanned the oblique face of the mountain and wondered if anything watched him, then began walking toward the area Sunny had indicated. When he reached it, he found a ring of rocks, the inner sides blackened by fire. A broken Jim Beam bottle lay next to it. A compact lay half-buried in the dirt.

Still no sound, no sight of birds in the trees. He walked past the small campground, aware now that he was cut off from the vista to the west.

His running shoes made little noise as he climbed steadily upward, seeking paths in the forest through the trees and shrubs. Here, at the higher elevation, most of the trees had shed their leaves, giving them wintery, skeletal appearances. The leaves formed a grey-brown carpet underfoot and it was hard not to make noise because of the dry leaves.

How had his ancestors slipped through the woods so quietly? It had to take long years of practice. Something a University-trained geologist didn't have. His mother and father had worked at the Inn of the Mountain Gods in Mescalero, where he'd grown up. Before that they'd owned a small store. They'd never worked outdoors. What did they know of tracking, of slipping silently through a forest? He had missed so much, he knew now. So very much. So much . . . like the old ways.

He didn't know what he was looking for. The entrance to the pueblo—and that had to be where he would find the shadoweyes—might be no more than a slit in the face of the mountain. Easily overlooked.

Something blurred in the corner of his eye, and as he whirled, he reached for the pouch. But when he looked, he saw nothing. Whatever it was had gone—or was hiding from him. He started walking again. He walked for what he thought was miles, and knew that it was heading toward late afternoon as the light was growing dimmer.

It was still silent, the air motionless. As if everything waited.

He licked his lips and looked around slowly. A soft whisper touched his mind, then was gone. Sweat sprang out on his forehead. His heartbeat accelerated, and he could barely breathe.

Fear. It was going to kill him unless he got under control.

The pouch radiated warmth on his skin, as if the black stone inside glowed red-hot. For a moment he almost took the pouch off to check, then stopped, the thong halfway over his head. It was a trick. With the pouch no longer around his neck, he could be tricked somehow—made to drop it, lose it so it could no longer protect him. And then they would come. No. He slipped the pouch back against his chest. Instantly it seemed cooler.

A few minutes later the whispers returned, the coaxing voices calling to him. He had trouble keeping his eyes open, and he yawned. He wanted to sleep, wanted to curl up at the foot of one of these big trees, pull a pile of warm leaves over him and just doze. Doze for as long as he wanted. Doze and not worry about a thing. Doze. . . .

His head jerked up. He had almost fallen face first to the ground. He stopped, wiped the sweat from the back of his neck, drank from the canteen he was carrying. The water was tepid, but at least it was wet and helped his dry lips.

Another trick.

He sat on a flat rock then. The trees crowded together here; he felt far more closed in than where he'd entered the forest. He was above the piñon-juniper line now, up into the Ponderosa pines, almost at eight thousand feet above sea level. The bark blurred into a brown-grey, some with streaks of black as though they'd been charred by flames, and again he heard the deep-voiced thunder, only it was closer than it had been before.

He would never find them. He would look for hours . . . days . . . go right by them, and they would laugh in their whispery ways, and the only way he'd find them was if they wanted him to . . . when they called him to them . . . when they called . . . .

Something rustled in the bushes, and he squinted into the gloom.

A flash of darkness. That was all. But it was enough. Instantly he was on his feet. He ran after the shadow, oblivious to the noise made in his pursuit, and felt the slap of leather against his side, against his chest. He could still see the shadow, could see it race away from him, drop back to become tantalizingly close, then draw farther and farther away.

He had to keep track of it, had to find where it would go.

The sky changed, fading to a yellow-white color as lightning charge followed lightning charge, ripping through the atmosphere. A tree to his right exploded as it was struck. Wood hurled outward, pieces of bark striking him, stinging his skin.

He had lost track of the creature. Damnit. He brought his fist down on his thigh in frustration, ground his teeth. He was close, very close now, to the face of the mountain. Piles of boulders, fallen long ago from higher slopes, lay heaped at the bottom. The vegetation was sparser, more stunted than in the actual forest.

He still did not hear any birds singing. Had the shadows driven them all away? And where the hell was the pueblo? He would be running out of light in a few hours, and then he would have to work by moonlight. He didn't want that, not when the night gave them powers, gave them more strength.

He fingered the pouch again, unable to keep his hands away for very long, and wondered if the stone could help him find the pueblo. The bag was cooler than before. He started up again, winding his way along the base of the mountain slope. He passed giant boulder after giant boulder, paused at times to push at them to see if they would move. They wouldn't. Again he touched the pouch. The cold shocked his fingers. He frowned. It was downright icy now. He climbed up past outcroppings of rock, slipped once and scraped his hand along a rock, left a smear of blood on the gritty surface.

He licked the blood off and stared up and saw it. A slight cleft against the face of the cliff. He peered at it, wondering if it were a shadow, some trick of the shifting clouds. From this distance he couldn't tell. It was too far above him. He would have to climb up there. What appeared to be handholds formed a rough path up the sheer cliff.

His hand went to the pouch, but stopped inches before it reached the leather. A pulsating coldness radiated from the pouch, spread across his fingers, frosting them with white ice crystals. He tried to move them, forced them to bend, felt the crystals breaking, shattering like fragile icicles. He cried out with pain as hot pokers jabbed up into his arm, as fire spread through his veins. With his other hand he grabbed his right one, jerked it away. A faint blue tinged his fingers, darkened his fingernails, but otherwise the hand was all right. Against his chest the bag was warm, not cold. He frowned, took a drink from his canteen, wiped and flexed his hands.

He reached up, grabbed the first hollow, slowly eased himself up. It was time-consuming, inching his way up the vertical face of the rock. He would place his foot carefully in a hollow, extend an arm to the next notch and pull up, one hollow at a time. Slow and tiring, and he wanted nothing more than to rest and take a long, slow drink of water. His hands grew slick with sweat, and from time to time he had to pause to wipe them, one at a time, on his shorts.

He looked down, then wished he hadn't. He had come well over a hundred feet up from the base. One slip of his hand, one fumble with a foot, and he would crash within seconds to the ground, smashing his body on the sharp rocks below.

He closed his eyes, feeling the vertigo sweep through him, nauseating him. His body swayed, bulged away from the rock, and the toe of one shoe found only loose gravel in the handhold. The foot slipped, missed the hollow, and his body slammed against the rock. He opened his eyes, stared into the grainy surface of the cliff, sought desperately to heave himself upward. Finally his foot found the hollow again, and he kicked away the gravel. Bouncing wildly, it clattered like hail down the cliff. Secure once more, he rested for a moment, waiting for his heart to stop its erratic pounding, for his breath, so harsh in his ears, to quiet. Sweat poured down his body, mingled with the dust that coated his skin. When he had calmed down, he once more began his ascent.

The crack widened as he climbed upward, and now he could see it was a true break in the cliff face and not a mere fracture in the granite. He reached it, then heaved himself upward, his back foot dislodging a cluster of rocks that threatened to throw him off balance. The fissure extended only a few feet above his head, and he had to turn sideways to slip into it. Overhead the rock met to form a solid chunk once more, and he could feel the solid weight of the mountain pressing downward toward him. The avenue inside stretched into blackness; the two sides of the rock pushed inward, coming toward him, grinding together, crushing him, pounding his body into a bloody pulp of sinews and bone.

He took a deep breath, shut his eyes momentarily. It was all an illusion. Nothing more. The rock wouldn't crush him; it had stood stationary for countless centuries, and it wasn't about to shift now.

He opened his eyes, stepped forward. As he walked slowly, one hand trailing against a wall, he found the roof of the fissure dropping, forcing him to move on his hands and knees. Underneath, sand scraped, stinging his palms and knees.

He lost track of all time in the blackness. Thought once that he saw twin yellow lights ahead, and stopped, squinting into the darkness until his eyes watered. He listened for noise, but all he heard was the harsh rise and fall of his breath echoing in his ears. He knew his breath pounded into the rock, cracking it, splitting the granite into minute lines. He caught his breath, held it for a moment, then slowly expelled it. The act served to calm him.

He knew now why men and women panicked underground. Why they lost all sense of time and direction. He didn't know how long he'd been there, didn't know how far he'd come. It might have been a few feet; it might have been a mile or more.

He squatted on his haunches, his head brushing the roof, uncapped his canteen and drank deeply. Then rubbed the bag on his chest. It was warm, and the touch somehow reassured him. He could go on now.

He crawled on through the tunnel, farther and farther away from the outside. Farther and farther away from safety. Finally a soft tendril of air brushed against his face. Ahead light glimmered, and he could once more walk upright. The light increased, forcing him to squint until his eyes adjusted. Finally he was out of the fissure, standing on a ledge jutting out of the rock.

He looked around. Stared at what he saw.

CHAPTER THIRTY-TWO

It was the pueblo.

The sun had already set behind the steep walls, surrendering the canyon to shadow. Cliff faces, devoid of handholds, thrust upward on either side of him for hundreds of feet. It was like being in the bottom of a stone well. Far up in the grey sky a solitary star gleamed.

He stepped forward on the ledge, looked around. To one side broken rubble trailed downward. He half-walked, half-slid until he stood on the bottom of the canyon and the pueblo was right above him.

There the cliff face yawned, like the great mouth of some granite monster. There, in the low-ceilinged cave, the nameless Indians of thousands of years ago had built their home. He thought with admiration of the back-breaking labor that had gone into the construction of the pueblo. Each adobe brick had been mixed and individually formed on the floor of the canyon; there it had dried, over a long period of time, for there weren't many hours of sunlight here; and when there were sufficient numbers, the bricks had been set carefully into baskets woven of yucca fiber and hauled up to the workers laboring in the cave. The rooms were all small, about eight by ten feet, with ceilings from four to eight feet high; there were no windows, only narrow, low doors with high sills. Long, heavy poles laid over the walls made the roof, and that was thatched with sticks and twigs, then covered with a thick mud plaster. Inside he knew he'd find a smooth floor of hard clay washed with animal blood. Burnt gypsum was used to polish the walls.

In the vanishing light the mud of the adobe had darkened, turned almost black. Even blacker were the openings of the doorways to the adobe rooms that stared at him like mournful eyes.

Nothing stirred along the bottom of the canyon; no birds sang; nothing grew. The ground was bleak, barren, almost as if it had once been scorched and had never recovered.

He scanned the cliff, searching for a pathway leading to the pueblo, wondering when he found none of the yucca fiber ladders used by the early Indians.

Rubble was strewn at the base of the cliff. Apparently the pueblo dwellers had thrown down their broken crockery, and he walked through pottery shards ankle-deep. There were also the crumbling remains of sandals made of yucca fiber and some scraps of dried leather that once must have been rawhide.

He proceeded with care, from time to time scuffing some of the shards aside with the toe of his shoe. Finally, behind an angular boulder stained with grey lichen, he found a rough ladder of piñon branches strapped together with leather thongs. It was long; but he thought it would reach. He set it against the rock, began to climb.

The rough bark scratched at his palms, and from time to time he had to stop and rub his hands, again one at a time, on his shorts.

The wind whistled through the cleft in the cliff where he'd entered the canyon, but that was the only sound. He did not even hear the distant hum of insects.

He stopped, looked up and cursed. He'd misjudged. And it was a hell of a distance, too—the ladder ended a full seven feet below the lip of the cave.

Damn. He stared up. What next? He had come too far to turn back. And he couldn't. He had to find the creatures, had to so that he could be free.

He reached up with one hand, groped along the rock until he found a handhold just inches above the top rung of the ladder. He eased up, reached for another depression. Found it. He carefully searched for hand- and footholds, and finding them, he began inching himself upward until his feet no longer touched the ladder. When he had almost reached the top of the cliff, there was a scraping noise below him. He looked down, saw the ladder fall sideways, hit the ground with a resounding thud.

He licked his dry lips. There would be no turning back for him now. He was trapped.

He looked back up the cliff, groped for the next handhold and hauled himself up level with the floor of the cave. He managed to crawl into the cave, then sat, trying to catch his breath.

He found he couldn't straighten completely. He had to hunch his shoulders and bend forward slightly, for otherwise his head would scrape along the top of the cave. As his eyes adjusted to the further darkness, he looked around. All he saw were the walls of the adobe houses.

His breathing grew sharper as he looked around. The

shadoweyes were here. He knew they had to be. He caressed the pouch at his chest, fingered the outline of the black stone. What did it look like now? Did it glow with a dark light? Or did it look the same as when he'd first taken it from the protective paper at the park?

The park, and Sunny. How long ago that had been; yet it had only been earlier in the day. No, had been a lifetime ago. Centuries before. He wiped the back of his hand across his mouth, sucked in a deep breath.

He had to find the creatures, would have to search until . . . until he found them.

The fear was growing inside him, trying to escape, trying to take over, trying to make him fail. But he wouldn't. Some calmness came over him, and when he thought he was okay, he moved again.

He walked forward, hesitated before entering the first adobe room. Wisps and tendrils of something insubstantial seemed to drift through the air toward him. He pushed a strand aside with his hand, and a voice whispered. He jerked his fingers back, took a deep breath and entered. Here it was even darker than in the cave, and he could barely see. He took out the flashlight, pulled a feather from it, stuck that back in the pouch. He switched it on, flashed the light around. The room was empty; here there were no shadoweyes. Only the bleached remnants of ghosts of a long-dead people. Something crunched underfoot. He stooped to pick it up and examined it. A bone. Slender. Like that from a finger. He dropped it, dusted his fingers on his shorts.

His uneasiness increased. He wasn't happy being in a place filled with the spirits of dead people. A dead people who were not his, either. He licked his lips, felt a chill cross his shoulders.

Better get going. Time was passing, and he still hadn't found a damned thing.

He entered each room, searched it carefully. The fetish belonged here. Somewhere. In a kiva. He would have to find the round underground chamber built for religious and ceremonial uses. But as yet he hadn't seen anything remotely resembling one. The cone of light flickered; he shook the flashlight; the cone wavered, strengthened, faded, went out.

Goddamn it.

Angrily he threw the now-useless flashlight as far away as he could. It landed against an adobe wall with a metallic clack that was very much out of place in this dead pueblo. The sound echoed throughout the cave.

Smart, Chato, real smart. If they didn't know you were here before, they do now.

Past the last adobe house the path veered sharply, digging deeper into the mountain. As he followed the path, the light from outside faded, faltered, was gone. Yet he was able to see. The walls glowed with a faint phosphorescence, and when he reached out, the stone felt slightly moist. He held his fingers to his nose, wrinkled it at the sour odor. He didn't know what gave the light, but it certainly didn't smell pleasant.

Finger-like veins of glittering minerals radiated in all directions in the walls. He stopped to admire one design. Then he stepped forward, feeling too late the stickiness that clung to his face, chest and upper arms. Panicked, swallowing the scream that wanted out, he stumbled backward, batting at the tenacious substance.

A spider's web.

They call the strands of the web sunbeams, he thought,

and say that if you damage them, the sun will make a web inside you and kill you.

If it wasn't the shadoweyes, it would be the sun. Great. He tried to grin, and failed, his facial muscles as stiff as though they had been frozen. He brushed away the last of the silken strands, started forward, stopped, the back of his neck prickling.

He was being watched. He could feel the force of their eyes staring at him, but when he looked, he could see nothing.

They were watching and waiting. For him. For the *touched* one.

His mouth was completely dry. Each footstep became harder, and he made an effort to move forward again.

Doom, he thought, he was going to his doom, and he thought he heard laughter echoing in his mind.

The pathway delved deeper into the rock of the mountain, leading downward until he thought he surely must have reached the lowest region of hell. At one point, slightly out of breath, he paused and listened, thinking he heard the sound of rushing water far away. It had to be his imagination, and yet, when the path twisted abruptly to the right, he stepped without warning into icy water that bit at his ankles.

Startled, he jumped back. The underground stream was dark and turbulent and he did not like its look. There was a flicker of white, gone in an instant. He squinted. An albino fish, blind because there was no light where it lived. He wrinkled his nose in disgust.

He didn't want to have to wade the stream or swim through it, but he wasn't sure he had any other alternative. He stooped, found a stone the size of his palm and picked it up. He hefted it, then dropped the stone into the water.

It sank without a sound. And he still could not discern the depth of the water. He wished for something to plumb the water, but there was nothing he could use. He stared at the stream, calculating its width, and at length decided he would risk jumping it.

He backed up, looked, decided to move back even more. He rubbed the sweat and dirt off his cheek, puffed slightly, then took off. He ran, and jumped, his arms held back, and landed on the other side, just bare inches from the edge of the water.

He breathed deeply with relief and started walking again. He didn't have much farther to go, for the path ended abruptly in a cavern filled with stalagmites and stalactites. He knew they were natural formations of limestone, but now they suggested nothing more than the fangs of some creature.

Straight ahead of him an oblong rock towered into the air. He stepped closer, frowned, brushed his fingers over the rough surface. On one side the semblance of a shadoweyes had been carved. He stepped back, flinching at the realism.

Still no kiva. There had to be one. This had been a pueblo culture, and at the center of all pueblo civilizations was the ceremonial kiva.

He paced the perimeter of the cavern, ran his hands along the smooth walls, seeking crevices he could enter, and when his foot hit air and he stumbled and almost pitched forward face-first, he knew he'd found it. The kiva.

He stared at the black hole.

He would have to enter it, descend into the greater darkness.

And he knew the shadoweyes waited for him there.

In hell.

His hands were shaking, and he rubbed them down his thigh, cringed at the clamminess of his touch. God, he had to go down in there. He didn't know what was there. It might be nothing, but— He shuddered. Things unknown lurked there. Things that might reach out for him, might touch him, grab him; things that—

Calm down, he told himself, taking deep breaths in gulps. He pushed back the hairs that had come loose, looked around, breathed rapidly.

Sunny. He thought of her, of how short a time he'd known her. He remembered telling his mother there wasn't a woman around who could interest him. She had cried, and he'd laughed. He had hurt her; why had he hurt her so, he asked himself, why, and now he didn't have a chance to tell her he was wrong, couldn't tell her that he had found a woman, couldn't—

The darkness beckoned seductively.

It was closing in on him, squeezing the breath from him; he had to take a leak; he had to do something; he had to get away from that darkness below, from that pit that he had to enter.

He could leave, turn around now. Leave town quickly, quietly, and no one would know. Sunny would go with him, and they'd wander from state to state.

He would know, though. And it would follow him wherever he went. He couldn't do that. Couldn't let Sunny down.

So he would have to descend. Go into a place he could not see into, go down into a darkness that was tangible, that could reach out and touch him, that could kill him.

He trembled again, clasped his hands together and tried

to pray, but no words came. His religion failed him, and he knew then that he would not come out alive.

He sucked in a breath, coughed explosively, and he knelt. His fingers groped, found the ladder. He started down.

CHAPTER THIRTY-THREE

He slowly descended into the kiva. Inside, the air was heavy, oily with some unknown substance, and he heard a rasping sound, as if someone were breathing heavily. The air pressed down on him, against him, was gagging him, choking him—

He touched the pouch, and the darkness cringed, and he breathed easier.

Cautiously he walked forward, brushing something with his knee, and a light suddenly flickered a few feet away. A torch burst into flame, and he stared at the object he had touched in the darkness.

It was a basket woven of natural fibers, and it was filled to the top with raw flesh. He had little doubt as to the origin of the flesh. Dozens of baskets, all containing the glistening pulp, littered the hard-packed dirt floor. Recoiling in horror, he stepped away, and something soft caressed his shoulders. He whirled and stared into the flat eyes of the creature. It hissed at him.

He leaped back then, knocking the first basket over. He slipped on the flesh, almost fell, managed to regain his balance. He kept retreating as the shadoweyes advanced. They were all around him, shades everywhere, the shadoweyes crowded into the chamber. When his spine was pressed flat against the kiva wall, he reached up to the pouch at his neck. The shadoweyes stopped.

And a high-pitched cackling filled the kiva.

He frowned. He'd heard that sound before. But—

Another torch flared.

And he saw the chair. Its arms and legs, back and sides were made of white bones, bones bleached by the sun, bones gnawed clean. A shadow swept across the grisly chair, a shadow larger than the others he'd seen, darker, and its yellow eyes were immense. At its side crouched Junior Montoya. The old half-breed cackled again.

"You are a very clever boy," Montoya said.

He said nothing. He was breathing rapidly from his earlier fright, and he was also evaluating his position. Ahead of him were the shadoweyes and Montoya. The other creatures were arranged in a circle around him. He couldn't tell how many there were, but dozens and dozens of eyes glowed, picking up the light of the torches.

"They respect you," Montoya said.

"Good for them."

"They think you're almost as clever as they. Almost. But it won't save you." He chortled, the choking sound eerily echoing in the kiva.

"It got me this far."

"Do you think you would have made it if they hadn't wanted it, hadn't allowed you to come this far?"

"Maybe, maybe not." He paused. "How long have you

served these things?'' He pointed to the baskets of flesh. "Are you responsible for those?''

The old man cocked his head, remembered. "I have been with them since I was a boy. I brought them campers. I brought them here. It was always good. Until a week ago.'' Montoya grinned, showing the stumps of his teeth. "But they are no longer content to stay here.''

While the old man had been talking, he had studied the round chamber. Faded line drawings in umber and ocher covered the walls, but the power of them had been lost long ago. They meant nothing now. Were useless. There was only one exit from the kiva, that now blocked by the shadoweyes crouching at the ladder. Pueblo Indians believed that the whole kiva was a powerful symbol. The interior gave way to the two worlds—the earth, the world above, and the netherworld below, from which man had come. That would be of little use to him now. He certainly wasn't about to enter the netherworld, not if he could help it.

He glanced around again. All he could see were the baskets with their grisly contents and the chair. Neither of which would help him. But something in the kiva had to be of help to him. Something here had to be able to stop the shadoweyes.

If the fetish had stopped the shadoweyes once, could it do it again?

He put his hand on the pouch.

How?

Again he looked around, wondering what he could do.

"What happened to the Indians here?''

"They went away. They left the shadoweyes to their home. They are older than the mountains.'' He cackled, scratched his cheek, flakes of skin peeling away. "Far older. Older than the idea of demons, as you have called them.''

Chato said nothing.

"Come join us, boy. Those others don't appreciate you or your ability. They don't know about your talents like we do. The whites . . . what use are they?'' He spat noisily. "Eh? It is not so very bad. No, not after a while. You might miss the girl at first, but there will be others, many others, more than you can count through all the years. Eh, come, boy, study with me. I will make you more powerful than any shaman. The darkness is better, far better.'' The old man laughed, the sound echoing.

He had to do something. And now. Before the creatures attacked him. They were restless; he could hear them rustling, shifting, waiting.

His back still against the wall, he scuffed a rough circle with the toe of his sneaker, stepped quickly into it. The creature on the throne hissed at him.

"What are you doing?'' Montoya demanded.

He did not answer. He must first protect himself. He closed his eyes, forcing himself to remember what he had heard long ago, what he had really not paid attention to, what he had forgotten after all the long years. Too late he understood the importance. Too late. He ground his teeth. He wouldn't give up. Not now.

Slowly words formed in his mind, words he thought he'd long ago forgotten.

He spat on the palm of his left hand, dipped the first finger of his right hand in it and made a cross on the left foot, thigh, forearm and cheek. As the crosses were made, he called out loudly upon the four thunders: Black Thunder, Blue Thunder, Yellow Thunder and White Thunder.

Then: "Black flint is over your body four times. Take your black weapon to the center of the sky. Let his weapons disappear from the earth."

Four times he repeated the prayer, changing only the colors. Then he rubbed the first finger of his right hand horizontally across his lips four times. He drew out his knife, held it against his chest, pointing first downward to the left, then upward to the right. At the same time he faced east and prayed. He then worked the weapon over the right shoulder, across the back, and down to the left hand. He ran the knife through his mouth, sucked some of the "juice" of the steel off. He spat that saliva into the palm of his left hand and began making the crosses once more. Again he repeated the prayer.

The crude circle glowed with a faint light.

The shadoweyes hissed, wavered in the torchlight, crept closer.

He opened the pouch at his side and began withdrawing its contents. Now, if only he would have the time to do something, to figure out *how* to do something.

Montoya watched with curiosity as Chato aligned the eagle feathers along the glowing lines of the circle. Outside the circle, abutting the feathers, he placed lightning-struck twigs. Inside the circle and over his shoes he dropped pebbles of red ocher, coral, jasper, turquoise, obsidian and agate.

"Stop it at once!" Montoya shouted. He stumbled to his feet, rushed toward him and tried to destroy the circle. He drew back a fist, slammed it into the old man's chest, and choking, Montoya fell back.

He heard the whispers. Rising and falling, calling him by name, asking him to come to them.

His hand trembling, he brought out the packet of pollen

and carefully opened it. The pollen of the piñon. He dipped his finger in it, slowly traced circles around his eyes, his mouth, and down to his chest, outlining his heart. The remaining pollen he put into his mouth and began to chew.

The hissing gained in volume, and outside the circle the torches had blown out. He could see the yellow of the eyes around him, on all sides steadily creeping toward him. The hissing filled the kiva, flooded his ears, permeated his body, ripped at his veins and muscles.

They summoned him, and he didn't know why he was trying to harm them. They had never hurt him. Never.

He sank to his knees and stared up into the kindly eyes. They whispered to him. Asked him to brush aside the twigs and feathers, so that they might help him to his feet. His hand twitched, then stopped as his fingers stroked the softness of a golden penna.

He had been *touched*.

He blinked his eyes and stared at the evil creatures. Even in the dark he could see their talons, their fangs. They waited for him.

Constantly they moved, making him look at them, keeping his attention from his work. With an effort he looked down, concentrated.

He piled fragrant piñon sticks, and the stiff, sharp-tipped leaves from the yucca in the middle of the ring, then stood and stepped back until his heels brushed the feathers.

The hissing almost drowned out his thoughts, making it difficult for him to think. He pulled the flint and steel out and struck it. A thin flame leaped up from his hands, and he saw the eyes, the eyes that stared, the eyes that devoured, the eyes, the eyes—

He dropped to his knees again, lit the pile of sticks and it ignited. From his pouch he pulled a handful of white clay and tossed it onto the fire. Instead of quenching the fire, the clay added fuel, causing the flames to dance taller, to turn blue and white and gold.

"Mountain People," he said aloud, his voice trembling with nervousness. He called upon the old gods of his people, the old gods he had turned his back upon for so many years. His voice strengthened. "I call upon you to strike down your enemies. Mountain People, come to the aid of your son. I ask you to strike down these unnatural creatures, these who are your enemies."

He heard laughter then, high, hissing, horrible, and saw the creatures reaching into the circle toward him with their talons. The hissing grew louder, hurting his ears, filling his head.

His voice faltered, stopped.

It wasn't working. All this time, effort, expectation. For nothing. It wouldn't work.

The laughter swelled, filled him, even as the hissing swept over him.

He stumbled backward, away from a downward-arching talon that sought his heart, and the pouch on his chest thumped hard against him. He had forgotten about it. Eagerly his hands tore at the thong, pried opened the leather, drew out the image.

Talons, colder than the icy stream, raked across his bare shoulders, down his thigh, bringing bloody welts. His fingers stroked the black fetish. And he stared at the fetish, feeling the panic rise in him.

Now that he had it out, he didn't know what to do with it. He didn't know how to use it to save himself. Didn't have the knowledge. Didn't know; hadn't learned. Had failed.

"Tenorio, help me!" His voice rattled in the kiva, cutting through the hideous hissing.

Shrill laughter, Junior's laughter, answered him.

The shades twisted, shifted in his eyesight, and the blackness moved to engulf him. From behind something clutched at him, and he cried out.

And dropped the black fetish.

It fell into the fire.

He stared, horrified, at the obsidian fetish, lying in the midst of the burning piñon and yucca. He reached for the stone, but white flames shot up, singeing the hairs on his arm.

Then the blue and yellow flames leaped beyond the circle of feathers and sticks, spread outward like a wave of water, stretching quickly throughout the kiva, igniting the dirt floor and walls. The white flame, still contained within the circle, towered toward the ceiling in an immense column of fire.

Outside the flames the shadoweyes danced, threw themselves toward the ring, were repelled. They screamed his name, and he could feel his mind, his will bending to them. Their power was too great. He was feeble. His beliefs were too weak.

He would give in, give in to them, succumb and at last rest.

Fire, blazing blue and golden, lapped at the throne of bones, scorched the shadoweyes, embraced him. He heard the hissing of the creatures, and he knew they had won. They were too strong for him, for any human.

His flesh was melting, oozing down his face, his chest, his legs. He was dying. His skin was burning away from him in great hunks, leaving raw muscle that would melt into greasy puddles, and soon, too soon, only his charred bones would remain.

The fire leaped to his eyes, to his hair, and he screamed in agony. He threw himself on the ground inside the circle, trying in vain to put out the flames. He rolled, shrieking, knowing it was too late, knowing that he couldn't stop the fire, and a great thundering blinding blackness swept down on him.

the adobe bricks in the wall, pulled out the loosened ones and stacked them until he could touch the frame of the doorway with his hands. Then, his muscles cramping from the effort, he pulled himself up and out.

He ran a hand through his hair, the brittle ends where the fire had burned his hair snapping off. He wiped his gritty face on his arm and started walking for the mouth of the cave. He coughed, choked, the greasy smoke still in his lungs.

He followed the path back the way he'd come. The large stone was gone, broken into hundreds and thousands of pebbles. The stream was gone, dried up, and he plodded toward the pueblo. Faint light came to him down the pathway, and as he walked out into the cave, he could see it was daylight out. He frowned. He'd entered in the late afternoon. Surely the light was gone now and it was night. He was puzzled, but could think no more about it because, even as he watched the pueblo, its mud walls began to crumple. Layer after layer of adobe brick collapsed, crumbling into fine golden powder.

The destruction thundered in his ears, deafening him, and dust in giant, throat-choking clouds billowed outward. He couldn't see, couldn't breathe. Under his feet the floor vibrated as tremor after tremor shot through it, and he knew that, somewhat belatedly, the Mountain People, the gods of his people, were answering him. Shaking off his languor, he staggered toward the lip of the cave. It was hard-going, with the floor shifting beneath his feet at each step, and with the obscuring dust swirling around him, he almost overstepped the rim. For a moment his arms windmilled as he balanced on the edge, and then he threw himself backward, away from the void. He lay on his back, cold sweat breaking out on his body, and thought how close he'd come to falling to his death.

Overhead, cracks appeared in the cave's ceiling, and chunks began falling. He leaped to his feet, almost fell, groped his way to the rim and stared down.

The ladder he'd originally used lay at the foot of the cliff. So what the hell was he supposed to do? A boulder whirled past him, and he hunkered down.

Jesus. The mountain was going to kill him. Whatever he was going to do, he'd best do quickly.

He stepped through the dusty fog, fingers feeling for something he could use. At last he found a single tree trunk with shallow gashes cut into it. He would have to use that, climb down it. There was no other way, no time for anything else.

He slid the trunk down the face of the cliff, watched and he saw it was short, too. Slowly he turned around, used the hand and footholds. It was difficult to hang on, with the cliff trembling, and he prayed that he could at least reach a low place where he could safely jump down. His feet found the primitive ladder, and he began descending that. He looked up in time to see the last of the pueblo disintegrate. The clouds surged out, and he choked, gasping for air. The cave shook, and he could feel the ladder waver. As quickly as possible he climbed down, slipping from time to time. As he reached the canyon floor, the cave collapsed, hurtling rocks hundreds of feet away. Slivers of stone shot outward. A rock thudded against his back, knocking him to the ground. He stood up unsteadily just as a rain of rocks poured down on him. He crouched down, covering his head with his arms, and felt the stones tearing at his skin.

Finally he staggered to his feet. Above, the canyon dust

swirled into a giant dust devil, sucked upward by the wind outside.

He had to get going. Ran for the crevice. It was shaking too, and he crawled as best he could through the narrow fissure. Above him the rock trembled, and a boulder, larger than his body, thudded downward, narrowly missing him, as he slipped from the crevice and began climbing down the face of the cliff.

So far to go. He wouldn't make it. He looked up, saw the rock cracking, splitting, disintegrating under his hands.

The granite crumbled into dust, and he fell. Was falling, falling, falling. Landed. The air knocked out of him, he lay there blinking upward, watched as rocks came pouring down. Rolled out of the way. Stood. Nearly fell. He hurt. All over. Bones and muscles and sinews. Even his hair.

He stumbled down the slope, staggered through the forest. Overhead, thunder hammered insanely, and wicked lightning, as yellow as the eyes of the shadows, sliced through the dark, boiling clouds, slammed into rock and trees, and beneath his feet the ground swayed, shaking him so hard he fell to his knees. He cried out at the added pain.

And then he was past the trees, out of the forest, still running, his heart pounding until he knew it would burst. Then he looked up and saw it, the most welcome sight of all.

Sunny and the truck.

Her arms folded against her breast, she leaned against the front end, and when she saw him, she waved frantically, happily. He tried to wave, couldn't, and she ran toward him. He stopped, unable to go on for the moment.

"Oh my God," she said when she reached him and saw him up close. He looked down at his body. Soot mingled with blisters; piñon pollen still clung to his face; blood seeped down his chest, arms and thighs.

312

She opened her arms and he went into them. He could hear her heart beating, and its steady beat was the most reassuring sound he'd heard in a long time. Calmness enveloped him. Slowly his pulse steadied, his breath returned.

"Are they—" she began.

"I think so." Weakly he raised his head, looked back as the western wall of the mountain collapsed, burying forever the entrance of the secret canyon. "I think so." He breathed deeply, listened to the birds sing overhead, and tried to smile, without success, at her. Her gentle fingers caressed his cheek. "Day," he gasped.

"Sunday," she said quietly, knowing what he meant. "You were gone all night, Chato."

All night he had been there, but he had survived his time in the underworld with its demons. Sunday.

He stared back at the mountain where he'd been such a short time ago. He felt . . . empty. Devoid of anything, of pleasure at his triumph, of fear, of surprise at being alive.

They had sucked him dry, those evil creatures; they had taken away his emotions, his humanness. He would have cried, but couldn't.

And who was this Chato? he wondered. Newly risen from the flames. No, he was no phoenix. No phoenix. But. But it had worked. The Old Ways. Those ways had triumphed over the shadoweyes, over the creatures in the kiva. Triumphed. He had his faith, his gift, his knowledge. Knew that his way was best.

God, he was so cold.

He drew in a ragged breath. "Let's go home now, Sunny."

She put her arm around him and helped him down to the truck parked only a few feet away. He eased into the cab, leaned his head back against the seat as she climbed in. She released the handbrake and they pulled away.

He did not look back, could not.

When they were once again in the city, he shifted positions and felt something hard in the pocket of his shorts. He frowned. He'd left everything behind in the kiva. Brought nothing out with him. Nothing but his life, thank God.

The frown increased as he thrust a hand into the pocket. He withdrew his hand, opened it. And stared at what lay on his palm.

Black and carved with eyes that bored into him.

The fetish.

It had returned to him.

From the shadows of the branches it watched, its eyes bright in the darkness. In its bulging belly the embryonic life it had been given stirred. And it watched as the humans left.

Beside the shadow the blackened heap of rags stirred, lifted its ruined head and stared through rheumy eyes toward the departing truck and its occupants. It laughed then, the demented sound cackling and echoing against the scarred mountainside. It rolled into silence, and when no birds remained to sing, the shadow slipped away.